Trust Me

CARLIE JEAN

Printed in the United States of America
First Printing, 2024
ISBN: 979-8-8678-4382-3
Kindle Direct Publishing

Line editor: Emily A. Lawrence
Developmental editor: Salma R.
Proofreader: Como La For
Cover Designer: Cat Imb at TRC Designs
Formatting: Qamber Designs
PR: Greys promotions

Content Warning

Explicit sexual content

Mention of death of a grandparent, and a panic attack

For the girls who love to be told how good they are at being bad, this is for you.

Playlist

Trust Me
Carlie Jean

"**Slow Dancing in a Burning Room**" - John Mayer

"**To You**" - SEVENTEEN

"**Un-thinkable (I'm Ready)**" - Alicia Keys

"**I Think He Knows**" - Taylor Swift

"**Planez**" - Jeremiah, J Cole

"**Hey Daddy (Daddy's Home)**" - Usher

"**Part 2 (On the Run)**" - Jay Z, Beyonce

"**Best Part (Feat. H.E.R)** " - Daniel Caesar, H.E.R.

"**You and I (Nobody in the World)**" - John Legend

"**Stan**" - 6LACK

"**Tuesdays**" - Jake Scott

"**Joy of My Life**" - Chris Stapleton

"**All I Need is You**" - Chris Janson

"**Unravel Me**" - Sabrina Claudio

"**One I Want (Feat. PARTYNEXTDOOR)**"
- Majid Jordan, PARTYNEXTDOOR

"**Secret Secret**" - Stray Kids

Prologue

I can't believe I have finally made it. I glance around my new room for the year, loving the way I can see myself reflected in it instead of my mother.

I am officially a college student and classes are starting next week. Aurora, who's my best friend and a year older than me, happened to need a roommate. And I was more than eager to accept her offer, not at all sad about skipping out on the dorms.

My phone vibrates with an incoming call, my father's cheerful face filling the screen. I swipe right and put the phone to my ear as I unpack more of my clothes.

"Hi, *Appa*, what's up?"

"I'm at the arena and wanted to see if you could swing by for a few. I wanted to catch up with you before all the joys of your freshman year take you away from your old man." He chuckles, the sound comforting.

I glance at the clock and see that I still have four hours before I need to get ready for the Greek row parties that are taking place tonight. "I'll be there in a few. See you then. Love you!"

He tells me he loves me too and then the line goes dead. It doesn't take long for me to hop in my car and drive over to the arena since our house is right off campus, close to the athletic facilities.

Rock Land University prides itself on its academic and athletic prowess, excelling in both areas at the highest levels. We're the home of the Coyotes. Our facilities are equipped with expensive training machines and modern locker rooms, along with a separate cafeteria from the normal school population that is tailored toward athletes.

Once inside the hockey arena, I make a left toward my father's office, a plaque titled "Head Coach" resting above the window on the door. It makes me beam with pride for my father for finally getting the position of his dreams younger than most do, after working his whole life in the hockey world.

I enter his office without knocking like always. When I lift my head up, I realize he's in a meeting, and another man is in the room with him.

"Sorry, I didn't mean to interrupt," I apologize.

My father waves me off. "Nonsense. I don't think you've met, but this is Elio Mazzo. I've been coaching him since he was seven, but now, he's in the NHL and plays for the Bears here in Denver," he explains, then points to me. "Elio, this is my daughter, Jasmine."

Elio stands and turns around to face me with a smile on his face. "Hi. It's nice to finally meet the girl I've heard about for years," he says, a slight Italian accent accompanying his words.

His dark green eyes are soft as he takes me in, the opposite of his sharp jaw and hollow cheeks under the darkness of his beard. He's tall, broad, and his body is perfectly sculpted. Although he's well-known, I get the feeling that he's not the arrogant asshole some athletes are.

It's the first time I've ever looked at a man with intrigue, which never really happens to me.

We both take each other in for a moment before putting our hands out to shake. My hand instantly tingles from the contact, and we both pull away quicker than normal.

A phone rings, drawing my attention away from Elio. "Oh shit, it's Paul. I have to take this, but I'll be right back," my father says before walking out of the room and shutting the door behind him. Paul is his best friend and the dean of our school. He also happens to be my best friend Aurora's father.

Our families have always been close growing up, having spent numerous vacations and holidays together.

Elio clears his throat, alerting me to the fact that we're now alone in my father's office.

He crosses his arms over his expansive chest and breaks the silence. "What are you studying?"

"Business," I answer, suddenly nervous that we're alone.

"That's what I took before I got drafted in my junior year. It was a breeze."

I chuckle half-heartedly. "I'm sure I'll have my work cut out for me."

"If you're half as smart as your dad says you are, I think you'll be fine." He smiles at me again. I know he's eight years older than me, but the smile he sends me nearly makes me blush.

What the hell is wrong with me?

"Thanks." I smile back at him. "How is it playing professionally?"

"It's a rush and I love the game," he says with an elated smile on his face, his eyes gleaming with passion. "You're an athlete too, right?"

"Yeah, volleyball, but I won't be going pro," I answer, not sure why I'm telling him anything about myself.

He grins, making my stomach flutter. "Don't sell yourself short. You can do anything you want in life. Remember that."

His words hit me deeper than he probably realizes because I feel like my life has always been the opposite, not doing what *I* want.

A small smile forms on my lips, but before I can reply, our time is cut off. My father reenters the room, his voice a tad cooler than before. "Elio, I got some of the team here to skate for an unofficial practice. You want to go show them a few things?"

He smirks, perking up at the idea. "Of course, it'll be fun."

My father then turns to me, an expectant look on his face. "Stick around for a bit? We can chat while the boys practice."

I agree, and a few minutes later, we're watching the guys on the ice with Elio. I can't help but admire how graceful he is. He's fast but sharp, every movement intentional and measured. Unlike the guys on our team, who are a bit rough around the edges at times.

"So, Aecha," my father starts, using my Korean name. It's how I know he's about to get serious with me. "How are you feeling about school starting?"

"Excited, but nervous about balancing my schedule," I say while watching the players. I'm on the volleyball team, and being a student-athlete isn't the easiest task in the world. Adding in the pressure from my parents to get straight A's doesn't help.

"You'll do great, as you always have." His words intend to be comforting, but they remind me that I have a standard to live up to.

Our conversation turns easy until my father brings up Elio. "He's quite the superstar, huh?"

"I don't watch his games, but he looks pretty good right now," I reply, unsure why he would mention Elio.

"He's one of the best hockey players I have ever seen," he boasts.

I turn to face my father head-on, sensing that this conversation has a purpose he's evading. "Where are you going with this?"

His face turns more serious now. "Because, Jasmine, I saw the way you were looking at him through the window of my office when I was on the phone and he's off-limits. He's too old and too much for you. Check online and you'll see what I mean. I like him as a student, but that doesn't mean I like him for you. Besides, you're not the type of girl he would be interested in."

My father's words are like a punch to the gut, and I swallow down the acid burning my throat. A girl like me—what the hell does that even mean? It's the first time I look at a man like that and of course someone has to ruin it.

But maybe it's for the best. It's not like I was going to pursue him anyway. He's a famous hockey player, and I have to start focusing on my future.

"I wasn't interested. You know me. Books over boys." I give him my fake smile, my eyes not moving with the motion of my lips, but he falls for it anyway.

"Good. You okay if I join the boys for a bit?"

"Yeah, of course."

Curiosity gets the best of me as my father joins them on the rink, causing me to pull out my phone. I do a quick search on Elio Mazzo and my screen is instantly flooded with pictures of him with various models and even some actresses on his arm.

Some articles simply highlight his skills as a hockey player, while others talk about his playboy ways, with a few comments on his arrogant attitude on and off the ice. He's even been rated the world's hottest player by *Starz* magazine.

Maybe my father is right. Maybe he's not the kind of guy for me because I don't want to be with someone like that. So I convince myself I don't like him because it's easier than admitting I can't have him.

Which only makes me want him that much more.

Chapter 1

Jasmine

*P*ride has a funny way of making people do things they think they never would and behave in ways that don't reflect their nature.

It's the reason why I've been struggling this past summer. I have too much pride to admit that I have nowhere to live this coming school year. My best friend Aurora made Team USA for volleyball and moved to California with her boyfriend, Cameron.

Leaving me roommate-less.

I've spent the entire summer at my parents' house on the outskirts of the city, hiding behind whispering trees and fancy façades. But come August 30, which happens to be *tomorrow*, I need to give my landlord an answer on whether or not I'm staying for the year.

I love that little house and all the memories Aurora and I have there, but I can't afford the rent on my own and I refuse to ask my parents for money, despite knowing they have plenty of it.

Growing up, I benefited from it, but once I turned eighteen, my mom insisted that I needed to figure it out on my own and that they wouldn't be supporting me financially anymore.

It might seem harsh to others, but I respect their values because they're the ones that have shaped me into the person I am now.

Responsible, smart, and hardworking.

At least those are the values I aspire to display, but deep down I know they don't fit me very well. Like when old T-shirts you insist on wearing because they're comfortable when you know damn well they need to go.

Having grown up in a partial Korean slash American family, I learned the value of familial relationships through my elders. Our extended family got together as often as we could, and we supported each other whenever it was needed. No questions asked.

My mother, on the other hand? Not so much. My father took on the role of peacemaker, often siding with my mother to avoid conflict. Or maybe it's because I never seemed opposed to any of her plans, so he thought nothing was wrong. And I think it's the familial values from our heritage that are ingrained in my father that saved our relationship, unlike my mother, who has more American-style ideals.

My mother, Madeline, is a renowned cardiac surgeon, and my father, Ned, is the head coach of the men's hockey team here at Rock Land University. My parents worked very hard to be in the roles they are today, and I'm happy for them.

But what I'm not so happy about is the constant pressure they put on me to be great like them, particularly my mother.

She has my whole life planned out already. Go to college, get a degree in a respectable field, get a good-paying job, then get married and have babies.

If I had it my way, I'd adjust the plan to go to college, get a degree, get a job I love, and be happy. I wouldn't be opposed to getting married and having kids one day, but if I don't, it's not a big deal to me.

I do fine on my own. I always have.

Thankfully, I was allowed to pick my degree, but I can only use it on what has been determined by her. I'm majoring in business, and she has made multiple comments about how I'd make a great accountant or financial analyst.

It's the complete opposite of what I want to do, but that's something I'll worry about later though, because my roommate situation needs fixing first.

It's been weighing on me all summer as I tried to find a new one. The girls on the volleyball team, my former teammates, all have their dorms or housing and are not up for moving their stuff again, which is understandable.

My other closest friend, Camille, who's doing a foreign exchange program from France, already has a roommate. And then, there are the random people who replied to my post around campus.

I tried to be hopeful, but I didn't connect with any of them. With me being a homebody, aside from attending parties occasionally, I need to like the person I'm living with since I spend the majority of my time at home.

I let out a dreadful sigh and exit my car in the hockey facility's parking lot at RLU. I know what I need to do, but I'm not happy about it. I either ask my father to help me with rent for a little while or sleep on someone's couch because I refuse to live with my mother any longer.

My phone vibrates in my shorts' pocket and I pull it out to see Camille's name on the screen. A smile tugs at my lips as I answer, "Hello?"

Her graceful voice pours through the speaker. "Morning, Jas, what are you up to?"

"About to make a fool of myself. You?"

She giggles lightly. "Wait, what's going on?"

Pushing the doors open, I make a left and head down the

hallway where my father's office is. "Well, you know I couldn't find a roommate this year, so I'm going to ask my father to help me with the rent for a little while. It's the only choice I have left."

"Aw, Jas, I wish I could help you out. Do you think he'll go for it?"

I stop outside his office to see that the blinds are closed, which means he's in a meeting, so I opt to pace the hallway while I wait. "Honestly, no clue. I'm his girl, but I know he wants me to learn the importance of making my own way."

"He's not going to let you sleep on the streets," she points out.

"No, he wouldn't, but he *would* suggest that I move back home. I won't do that. For one, it's too far," I whisper, realizing that anyone nearby could be listening.

My eyes snag on a picture on the bulletin board outside of my father's office.

It's a picture of my family when my father got hired as the head coach. My father is beaming, his arms wrapped around my mother and me. I inherited my mother's curly hair while looking more like my father. My father's Korean, and my mother is Black.

The photo reminds me of how much I truly do love them, despite our differing opinions.

"And for two?" she prompts.

"That's a story for another day, Cami."

I love my mother dearly, but our relationship is strained from years of her incessant pressure for me to be perfect.

It started when my parents found out they couldn't have any more kids. They began enrolling me in as many after-school programs as they could.

Growing up, I took ballet, piano, swimming, chess, horseback riding, golf, and eventually, volleyball because I begged my father, who is easier to sway than my mother.

Don't get me wrong, I'm thankful that I could engage in so

many different activities, to learn and expand my capabilities, and I still enjoy those things from time to time, but missing out on kid things?

Yeah, that hurt.

Since my schedule was always so busy, I missed birthday parties, shopping trips with my girlfriends, and sleepovers too.

Once I was in high school, they gave me a bit more freedom to stick with the activities I liked the most, chess and volleyball.

Then my grades became of utmost importance, and I still carry this stress with me to this day. It's the reason why my mom made a deal with me that once senior year came around, I'd quit volleyball and focus on my studies.

Even if it meant losing my scholarship and now having to pay my way through school. She said it would be a humbling experience and a life lesson I'd need.

Except I think the life lesson I need to undertake is the one on making choices for myself and not my mother.

I sense warmth behind me that wasn't there before, and when I turn around, my eyes land on a tall, strikingly beautiful man.

Elio Mazzo.

He's looking at me with interest as he casually leans against what I'm assuming is the door to his office, one leg crossed over the other, matching his arms across his chest.

"I have to go, but I'll talk to you later," I tell Cami before hanging up and sliding my phone back into my pocket.

"What do you want?" I ask gruffly, wanting to get this interaction over with already. He looks smug like he knows something I don't and I hate it because I'm used to being the smart one.

His eyes, a deep green, narrow slightly as he continues to stare at me. It's unnerving, but I'll never let him know that.

"A deal," he surmises, pushing off the wall and slanting his head toward his office.

"What the hell are you talking about?" I fold my arms over my chest, not moving an inch.

"Come inside my office and we'll talk," he suggests, sounding casual yet demanding.

I raise an eyebrow, a snarky chuckle falling from my lips. "Okay, Elio. Let's get a few things settled. Number one, I will never follow orders from you. Number two, it wouldn't go well for you and my father if you tried to make a move on me. And number three, I'm pretty sure it's grounds for termination for coaches to sleep with students."

Elio remains stoic, his face not revealing a single thing for a beat. Then a widespread grin forms on his lips. "To answer your second and third issue, I have no interest in you romantically. I would never betray your father. He's been a good friend and a mentor to me," he says, but I'm not shocked.

I knew he and my father were close. Still, it doesn't make the words sting less, reminding me of what my father told me three years ago.

"As for the first, I wouldn't expect you to follow my commands unless we were fucking. But as stated earlier, that won't ever pertain to you."

The way he casually talks about fucking makes me want to blush while also cringe at the same time, because I've never had a conversation about sex with a guy.

Besides, who the hell does he think he is?

Mr. You-would-follow-my-orders-if-we-were-in-bed.

Yeah, *okay*.

"Anyways," he continues, "I have a solution for your housing situation, but if you'd like to have the conversation right outside your dad's office, that's fine with me."

"What possible solution could you have for me?" I pose the question like a challenge, and that's my first mistake. If I remember anything my father told me about Elio is that he loves a challenge.

I call that the 'I'm a rich, entitled man who is never told no' syndrome.

"A mutually beneficial arrangement. I know about Minniebakes—"

"In," I cut him off, my head angling toward his office.

Elio smirks, putting his hand out for me to walk ahead of him. I do, only because I want to know how the hell he found my baking account.

It's my secret and greatest passion that no one knows about except for Aurora and Camille. I run a somewhat popular account where I post baking videos, and one day, I'd like to open my own store.

The videos are where I get my income for now, but it's not enough to pay all of the bills.

I squeeze past him into his office, taking it in. It's bleak, with stark white walls and walnut wood floors. A single boring white desk sits in the middle of the room with a desktop computer, papers, files, pens, and all the essential desk things on it.

Even his walls have no decorations or pictures. The only thing that gives the room any personality is the bookshelf behind his desk, which is full of books.

That's unexpected.

There's a multitude of textbooks that range from marketing strategies to psychology and history. It surprises me that he reads, let alone academic literature.

Elio shuts the door behind him, and that's when I remember how much taller he is than me. I know from his stats that he's six-foot-three, and just from looking at him right now, I can tell he's nothing but pure muscle underneath his clothes.

His chest is wide, his Dri-Fit long-sleeved shirt molding the muscles on his shoulders and arms.

A beard decorates his angular jaw, the dark scruff matching the locks on his head that are perfectly styled to the side, except for a singular piece falling onto the middle of his forehead.

It's only the second time I've really looked at a man quite this long, and both times involved him, but I don't dwell on that fact and focus on the problem here.

"How did you find it?" I ask, getting right to the point.

"Well, it is social media, Jasmine. Anyone could find it if they wanted to. I was scrolling through my feed and your account popped up. I know you never show your face, but I noticed the bracelet on your wrist. It was the same one you had on the day we met," he explains casually, shoving his hands in his pockets.

My fingers mindlessly move to brush against the dainty rose gold chain around my wrist, twisting the small heart that dangles from it. My *halmeoni* gave it to me a few years before she passed away.

"Please don't tell my father," I say, my voice softer this time. He has something over me and I can't have him tell anyone. "It's complicated."

Elio shakes his head. "I got a hint of that from your phone call I overheard, but I won't tell him. You have my word. That's where our deal comes in."

I don't say anything because as much as I hate to admit it, I'm intrigued.

"I'm offering you to move into my condo that's outside of campus. Before you protest, hear me out. Your videos are good, but you need a better backdrop for them and my kitchen is perfect for that. Besides, since marketing is my specialty, I can help you with that too. In return, I need you to watch my cats when I'm away for games and practices in general. We don't have to tell anyone, and you can tell your family that you moved in with Camille since she lives in the same building I do."

He must be joking.

Yet, why am I even considering it?

"Did you seriously just come up with this in the time you spent eavesdropping on my conversation? Also, I don't think I need the help of a hockey player with my business, but thanks anyway."

To Elio's credit, he doesn't flinch at my dig. Instead, he gives me a smirk. "I've been thinking about wanting to help you since I stumbled upon your videos, but the conversation you were having inspired an idea."

"Why do you want to help me?" I ask, perplexed by this man and his sudden generosity. I can usually read people with ease, but he's still a mystery to me.

"Because of everything your dad has done for me. I want to give back in any way I can," he answers honestly.

"And you don't want anything sexual out of this, right?" I clarify as I need to make sure nothing will happen between us.

Elio scoffs, looking annoyed. "I know you think I'm your typical jock and I don't care enough to convince you otherwise. I don't need to prove myself to anyone, but for your peace of mind, no, I don't. Your dad is like a father to me, so you're off-limits."

Before I can respond, he adds, "Do we have a deal or not? I'll be quite busy this semester with coaching and being a student, so we'll barely even see each other."

It's with the desperation I feel to keep my pride intact with my family that I square my shoulders and make a deal with the devil.

"It's a deal."

We quickly exchange numbers so that he can text me his address and I can come over to visit. Then I rush out of his office before my father could ever know I was here.

Chapter 2

Elio

I slam the front door to my condo closed, cursing under my breath.

What the fuck did I get myself into?

I've never let anyone into my home willingly before. I've never even brought a girl over in the nearly ten years that I've lived on my own.

And I invited one to live with me today.

I like my space, preferring quiet nights at home. My hockey era made me look like an entitled, rich, playboy asshole. But that couldn't be further from the truth. Except for the rich part because that's true.

Yes, I have fucked around quite a bit, but I wouldn't call myself a playboy. And I also worked my ass off to get to where I was in the league, but the media always liked to focus on the story they were spinning. The one Jasmine seems to buy into.

I meant it when I said I've been wanting to help her ever since I stumbled on her videos a few months ago, shortly after I came to RLU. There's potential in her content, but her account lacks good marketing.

I had no idea how to approach her because, from the first day we met, I found her intimidating. And that's never happened to me before.

Ever.

But there's something fiery about Jasmine underneath that perfect daughter persona she likes to put on for her family. Part of me wants to unravel her layers and discover who she really is underneath.

The other part of me wants to stay as far as I can be because I'm not sure what I'll do if I get to know her more.

She's beautiful beyond belief, and I already can't do a damn thing about it. I never will. Especially now that we're going to be roommates.

Why the hell did I think this was a good idea? Inviting temptation right to my door and giving it the opportunity to stay.

I'm twenty-nine and she's eight years younger than me. She's also the daughter of a man I look up to as a father figure and whom I consider as one of my closest friends, which makes her as far off-limits as someone can be.

Ned Park is my lifelong coach and friend, and he called me with a job offer months after I completely tore my ACL, taking me out of the NHL for good. I accepted, because I still enjoyed hockey and wanted to help those aspiring to make it to the league.

Although I was happy with the offer, I knew I'd need more to do with my time, so I decided to go back to school and finish my degree since I was drafted during my junior year and was never able to complete my degree.

I don't necessarily need to complete it, not with my money or intelligence, but I want it. To me, it means that I accomplished something, and I thrive on setting goals and reaching them.

For this school year, I want to get the team to the championship, have a ninety-nine average in my classes, and increase Jasmine's profits by at least seventy-five percent before the holiday break.

Oh, and to keep my damn hands off her.

Aside from those, I should also figure out what the hell I want to do with my life. Explore and see what else gets my blood pumping other than hockey. Before I can spiral down that thought train, an incoming call from my youngest sister, Bria, pulls me out of my thoughts.

"*Ciao*, Leoooo! How's it going?" she says as soon as I answer.

"*Ciao, bella*, I'm good. Just got home from practice. You?" I ask, instantly feeling better whenever I talk to one of my sisters.

"I'm at headquarters. I'm spending the night doing an observation with one of our satellites in orbit," she says, excitement clear in her voice.

Pride blooms in my chest. Bria is an astronomer and works for NASA at only twenty-four years old. "Sounds nerdy and fun for you," I tease, plopping onto my couch.

"What's wrong?" Bria inquires, knowing me better than anyone.

Since I don't like to hide things from her, I tell her the truth. "I asked Jasmine to move in with me."

The line is silent for a moment before her rich laughter filters through the phone. "What the hell have you gotten yourself into, Leo?"

"It's a win-win situation for both of us. She'll take care of the cats when I'm away, and I'll help her with her business."

"Sweet brother of mine, a genius from what the tests say, but oh so clueless at times. You? Living with someone else? You're a clean freak and an introvert who doesn't like to communicate with others unless you have to."

"Tell me something I don't already know, Bria. But it'll be

fine. She's coming over tomorrow to see the place," I say, unsure if I'm trying to convince her or myself.

"You know, this will be good for you. It'll be something new," she proposes.

I agree, and we continue our conversation, catching up on the newest things in our life. Bria's been working on a special project at work, which means she's too busy for men.

Thank goodness. The idea of anyone hurting my baby sister is like a knife twisting in my gut. I'm very protective of my family, and that'll never change.

"One last thing before I go. Are you listening?" Bria asks.

"Always."

"Repeat after me, okay? *I will not cross the line with Jasmine.*"

"Goodbye, Bria," I hang up on her and her boisterous laughter.

That stupid mantra has my mind circling back to Jasmine.

I consider her father a part of my family. Growing up, I had a special bond with him and we clicked instantly, understanding one another.

We had the ideal coach and player relationship.

Ned not only helped shape me into the amazing player I became, but the person I am today. And for that, I'll always respect and be grateful to him.

My gut churns with guilt because I just asked the man's daughter to move in with me.

I know how protective he is of her from the way he talks about her and I know he'd be livid if he found out.

The only thing keeping me from backing out of our deal is that I have this foreign incessant need to help her. She reminds me of myself and I understand where she's at with being at a crossroad.

Besides, I also need her help. There's no one else I'd trust to live with me.

I briefly wonder if Jasmine has a boyfriend. She is pretty adamant about nothing happening between us, so maybe she does. But then again, if she did, I doubt he'd be okay with her moving in with me.

I know I sure as fuck wouldn't.

If she were mine, it'd be known to everyone.

Chapter 3

Jasmine

I place my newest novel in the box I've labeled "girl stuff," just in case anyone tries to take a look at it. Because these novels aren't scholarly at all. They're full of smut. Learning about sex is still learning. I consider them educational literature.

Which is important when you've yet to have any experience in the matter.

I may not have had my first kiss or any kind of sexual experience with someone, but I'm very well acquainted with my fingers and my various toys.

It's empowering, knowing what I like and giving myself that release.

I don't know if I could trust someone else to do that. I've become so invested in my studies and extracurriculars that sex and romance became something I brushed to the side until someone could prove themselves to be worthy of that trust.

I've been on dates, but always eventually lost interest in every guy I met. None of them were able to stimulate me mentally, and that for me is huge.

I've always needed more than a simple physical attraction.

"Minnie!" Aurora chimes, reminding me that we're on FaceTime while I pack up what's left of our old house.

"Ro?"

She beams, her hazel eyes lit with excitement. "I got my schedule yesterday, and I'll be able to visit you the last weekend of October. I have a game in the city."

I grab my phone and sit up straighter. "Thank goodness. I miss your ass already and it's only been two months."

Aurora waggles her brows. "I know you miss my ass. It's pretty great huh?"

I roll my eyes and chuckle. "Yeah, yeah, but we all know my tits are superior."

"I'm sure that's the real reason why Elio asked you to move in," she teases, but I can tell she's wishful thinking.

"It better not be. I already told him no funny business."

"You told who what?" her boyfriend, Cameron, asks, appearing on the screen with his eyebrows narrowed.

"Elio, her new future roommate, remember?" Aurora says, her eyes lighting up as she looks at Cameron.

I never thought I'd see her settle down, but I'm glad she did. They couldn't be more perfect for each other if they tried. They're quite literally the definition of soulmates.

"Oh yeah, him. If he makes you uncomfortable in the slightest, call me and I'll be on the next flight out," he says, his overprotectiveness showing.

"Thanks, Cam. How was the hike this morning?" I ask, wanting to switch topics, because the more I think about moving in with Elio, the more nervous I get. It sounded great at first, easy even. But deep down, I can't believe I'm moving in with a fucking guy when I've never even touched one before.

"It wasn't too bad. The trail was pretty straightforward, but it was a bit steep near the top."

"The sex up there wasn't too bad either," Aurora pipes up, her boldness never easing up.

Cameron smiles, looking at her with so much love and desire. I look away because it feels like I'm intruding.

"All right, I'm going to finish packing before I head there to scope the place out. See you both in October."

"I'll see you tomorrow when we FaceTime again because I need to see your face at least once a day, got it?" Aurora reminds me.

"Of course, Ro. Love you both." I smile at the screen, two of my favorite smiles smiling back at me before saying their I love you's and goodbyes back.

With a deep sigh, I look around the room I've lived in for the past three years.

I spent so much of my energy working hard in school that my room became an outlet for me to let loose. It was my messy hideaway from the perfect image I was forced to live up to.

I liked that I could be myself here, let clothes hang off of chairs, and have books strewn around with plants and random knick knacks here and there.

And then there's the kitchen, where I started Minniebakes.

Baking is something I started to do for fun when I was tired of studying, even as a kid. I'd ask my *halmeoni*, who lived with us, if we could bake and she indulged me every time. We baked everything from traditional Korean desserts such as a Hotteok, to the latest trends.

My favorite desserts were always the ones that tasted like maple syrup.

Baking soothed me in a way no other activity in my life has. There was no pressure, only the joy of an afternoon spent with my grandmother, making things that tasted good.

It still feels that way to me, mindless and fun. Sure, there's the pressure to make sure it turns out well, but I still enjoy the process of it all.

When she passed before I started university, I created my account as a way to feel connected to her. I posted videos of myself baking, but never my face to avoid my parents finding it. Over the years, I've gained a pretty decent following and I love sharing recipes with them.

My hope one day is to open my own bakery, but I haven't worked up the courage to tell my parents that I want to use my business degree for that and not a boring desk job analyzing numbers all day.

To my mother, numbers are safe and predictable, but running your own business is not, which makes it to the bottom of the list for potential careers she sees as fit for me.

I push the thought out of my mind as I slip on my sandals and lock the door behind me. I get into my car to drive over to my...*new home.*

Great.

Chapter 4

Jasmine

*T*he drive over to Felix Avenue is short, which is not nearly enough time for me to talk myself out of doing this.

I had no idea Camille even lived here until Elio said something. It's something I need to remind myself to ask her about because I wonder how she's affording to live on this side of town.

Entering the digits Elio texted me yesterday along with his address, I pull into the designated lot to his condo and instantly feel out of place. There are luxurious cars in every spot, making my 2013 Corolla look ancient.

I may have grown up comfortably, but I didn't grow up in *this* kind of tax bracket.

After locking my car, I trudge myself through the glass revolving doors, the minimalist and sleek lobby catching my eye. It's clean, with white walls and marble floors, crystal chandeliers, and fresh flowers on every table.

I prefer my personal space to be more colorful and full of life, but I can't help but appreciate the beauty of things that scream elegance, and this entire building does that.

"Good morning, ma'am, how may I help you?" an older gentleman in a suit asks.

"Good morning. Uh, what's your name?" I ask because I was raised to always address people by their name. It's a sign of respect.

"Colin Patts. I'm the doorman here, and you are?"

"Nice to meet you, Colin. I'm Jasmine Park."

"Miss Park, welcome. What can I do for you?" His light blue eyes are welcoming, and I can tell he genuinely enjoys his job.

"Call me Jasmine, please. I'm here to meet with Elio Mazzo. He texted me the details if you need proof."

He waves me off. "There's no need, Miss Jasmine. If Mr. Mazzo has a visitor, I know it's because he's invited them. You can use the elevator right there and go up to the fourth floor."

I thank him and head off in the direction of the elevator, trying my best not to overthink what Colin told me. What did he mean by that?

In the elevator, I hit the fourth-floor button, waiting nervously for the cart to reach my destination. The doors ping open and I walk out into the hallway. It's lined with a sleek black carpet and art frames are strewn about on the white walls on each side.

Once at Elio's front door, I pat my mini black dress down. I opted for a simple skinny strap dress that hugs my breasts, the material flaring out at the waist. I paired it with sandals, wanting to look casual yet presentable.

With a calming breath, I knock on his door, 401, which I guess is soon to be *our* door. It instantly opens, as if Elio were waiting for me behind it.

He towers over me, his dark hair ruffled and not as perfectly kept as I've seen it before. I want to hate and find fault in it, but damn it, I think I like it. His black T-shirt accentuates his broad chest, the arms tight against his biceps, and I can see a hint of his defined abs underneath.

And to top it off, he's wearing gray sweatpants.

Asshole.

He knows girls are weak for that, and now I'm regretting getting so dressed up if he was going to look like he rolled out of bed.

"Are you done checking me out?" he teases, his tongue poking his cheek.

I roll my eyes, tempted to turn on my heel and get the hell out of here, but then I remember how much I need a place to stay and how much I want my business to grow so that I can eventually live on my own.

"I was wondering why you look so disheveled. It's not quite like your usual state of being," I remark, crossing my arms under my chest, unintentionally pressing my already-pressed cleavage together even more.

His forest-green eyes don't leave mine, but his jaw tightens.

"I don't usually get dressed up when my roommate is home, but if that's your thing, that's cool," he says, shrugging his shoulders casually as he steps back to let me in.

I ignore him and step past him and into the foyer. We silently walk down the short hallway, making a right into the living room.

My jaw wants to drop because the space is beautiful. Tones of navy blue, black, and white are perfectly balanced between the walls, floors, and furniture. Except it's a little too clean and organized for my liking, everything seeming to be in place. There's not a single cup on the counter, or a gym bag tossed to the side on the floor.

Elio remains quiet while I peruse his space, watching me as I do.

It surprises me to find his place so clean, yet it doesn't at the same time. Part of me thinks he's the type to get off on knowing he's in control and everything is the way it should be.

Stop making comments about him getting off, I scold myself internally. *He's your roommate and you don't like him.*

It's what I need to tell myself, condition my brain so that I don't see him the way I did the day I met him. I mentally shake my thoughts away, bringing myself back to the present.

The living room has a white leather L-shaped couch sitting across a large TV and a black brick stone fireplace. But what piques my interest is the chessboard on the table in the corner, facing the floor-to-ceiling windows that overlook this part of town.

My stomach flutters with joy at the sight, having loved playing chess growing up. It's one of the extracurriculars my parents made me do that I ended up loving and keeping up with.

"You play?" I ask and instantly regret it, because duh? Why else would he have a chessboard that looks like it costs a hefty amount since the pieces and the board are made of glass?

"I told you I wasn't some dumb jock," is all he says in response.

I get the sense that there's more to him, but I can't quite put my finger on it yet.

My eyes eventually shift to the gigantic kitchen that is nearly as big as the living room, and I hate the sound that leaves my lips at the sight of it. A half squeal, half whimper escapes me before I can stop it, and instead of apologizing for it, I make a beeline for the kitchen.

It's stunning, not the perfect kitchen setup that I have in my dreams, but it's close enough. The cabinets are glossy black, with black subway tiles for the backsplash and the countertops are made of white quartz. It has two ovens, two sinks, and one big-ass fridge. The island has another sink and farther down is a set of bar chairs.

I hate to admit he's right, but I know all of it will look

beautiful as the backdrop for my videos, guaranteeing more traffic for my channel.

"How did you do this?" I ask, knowing damn well that as nice as this building is, there is no way the kitchen came like this.

"I like to cook, so it was a deal I worked out with the landlord. He let me hire someone to renovate it in exchange for free season tickets to the Bears games," he explains, walking into the kitchen and sitting on one of the bar stools.

The Bears are our state's professional hockey team, the best in the league and the team he used to play for.

I look down on the island where he's sitting and notice the paper and the two black pens that sit perfectly straight beside it. "Seems like you like to make a lot of deals Elio," I point out, still marveling at the beauty that is this kitchen.

Inspiration hits me in a wave, a bunch of ideas weaving themselves into my brain. I'm tempted to pull out my notes app to remember them, but then I recall that we have some rules to lay out first.

"Deals are how everything in life is done if you think about it," he retorts.

I slide into the chair across from him, my feet dangling in the air because I'm not very tall.

There's a reason why my closest friends call me Minnie.

"Then let's get to the bottom of ours. I need a start and end date, and rules." I snap my fingers.

He smirks at that. "Right down to business, I see." Then he picks up the pen, but before writing anything, he adds, "My advice? You should move in before classes start so that you feel prepared for your classes without the stress of moving after they've begun. When you move out is up to you. I personally would prefer if you stayed at least until hockey season is over because that's when I'll be the busiest and gone the most."

"You do know that the season runs from October to April, right? Which is pretty much the entire school year?" I point out.

"That okay with you?" he asks, his pen hovering over the paper.

Living with him for the entire school year sounds like torture, but I guess this is what my mom meant when she lectured me about sacrifices for the greater good.

I press my lips together, my gaze never wavering from his. "That's fine, but I want it written that it's conditional. I have the freedom to leave whenever I want, whether hockey season is still going on or not."

"Done," he says, writing down the first term of our deal.

"I'm paying you rent. Add that," I tell him.

This time when his head snaps up to mine, he looks annoyed, brows pinching inward. "Like hell you are."

"Elio, spare me the whole song and dance. I want to pay you like I would any normal roommate." I can't be a freeloader. It's not who I am and it's what I've been trying to avoid.

He gazes at me for a beat, eyes and jaw locked. "Fine, but I'm capping it at no more than five hundred dollars per month." His pen picks up again, adding it to the list.

I'm tempted to argue, but I know it's pointless and I've already got a win with him agreeing to let me pay.

"Clean up after yourself. I don't like messes. At least, not that kind," he says, writing it down before I've even agreed to it, but it's a fair request, one I can't refute.

"No going in my room unless I'm home and you ask me first," I add.

Elio's eyes light up at that. "Hiding something, are we?"

"Nope," I say casually. "I don't like strangers in my space. Do you?"

He doesn't say anything except for a shake of his head, indicating he agrees.

"If you're going to have people over or throw a party, it's cool with me, but tell me first so I'm not blindsided," I say. I love a good party now and then, but unexpected ones at my house? No, thanks.

"Understood." He pauses, shifts in his seat, then says, "And no hookups. I don't care what you do outside of this place, but you don't fuck anyone under my roof and neither will I."

"You can fuck whoever you want to. I have noise-canceling headphones." I shrug, seeming non-bothered when in reality the thought alone makes my skin crawl.

Elio's jaw ticks, the scruff of his beard prominent. "Yeah, well, I don't. No hookups here, got it?" he states, his tone cool.

I want to laugh because if he knew how innocent I am, he'd be embarrassed at himself right now. He has nothing to worry about.

"Got it. I will watch over your cats, and you'll help me do what exactly?"

He sits up straighter at that. "My goal is to increase your profits by seventy-five percent at least by the end of the semester. You'll use the kitchen to help with the aesthetic part and I'll help with the marketing logistics of your channel."

"Who knew you had so many talents," I joke lightheartedly.

"There is a lot you don't know about me, Jasmine," he drawls, and I hate the way my name sounds so good coming from his lips.

"Let's keep it that way." He flinches slightly at that, but I push how it makes me feel to the side. I don't need to get to know him. We're simply roommates who are helping one another out. We don't need to be friendly. "Is that all?" I ask, wanting this conversation to be over.

"Yes, this should do it. Anything else you want to add?" he asks, sounding sincere.

"I'm sure I'll find something to add in the future, but this is good for now."

I want to add that there will be no kissing, no touching, et cetera between us, but I think it's been implied enough times before when we were back in his office. I also know making it an official rule will only make it that much more tempting to break, at least for me.

"I wouldn't expect anything less." He grins slightly like he's in on some inside joke that I'm not aware of. He pens the top with the title 'Roommate Rules,' then signs the bottom and passes it to me to do the same.

I twirl the pen with my fingers as I take a moment to think everything over, but I don't have much of a choice. This option seems like the smartest one since it'll help my business and prevent me from having to ask my parents for help.

It's also in a safe, nice part of town. The best part is that Elio will barely be here once the season starts, but the only problem I'm facing is that I don't really like cats. I've never had one, so I'm honestly not sure how to care for them.

But I can figure it out.

I sign my name next to his, then push it back toward him.

Holy shit, I'm really doing this.

Before I can internally freak out, three cats jump onto the island.

"Perfect timing, girls," Elio coos at them. He picks up the white one with black spots. "This is Blossom," he says before pulling the ginger and gray ones into his arms. "And this is Buttercup. The gray one is Bubbles."

I'm not sure why I find it endearing to see a man as large and masculine as he is with three fluffy cats in his arms, but it is.

Snapping out of my momentary lapse of judgment, I gaze at him quizzically. "What's with the names?"

Elio's bottom lip drops, feigning offense. "You've never watched *The Powerpuff Girls?*"

"Uh, no. I didn't really watch much TV growing up, and I still don't," I reply, giving him more than I wanted to about myself.

"Interesting," is all he says. He stands from his chair, the three cats still in his arms. "When I'm gone, be sure to fill their food bowls twice a day. Once in the morning and once at night. Keep fresh water in their bowls, and the litter box cleans itself, but the tray will need to be replaced once a week. The girls have their own room filled with beds, scratching posts, and toys as well."

The fact that he has a freaking room dedicated to his cats whom he calls his girls is chipping at the coolness of my heart because no matter how much I try not to like him, I can't pretend that this isn't cute as hell.

"Okay, sounds easy enough," I answer, willing myself to sound more confident because truthfully, I've never taken care of anything besides plants.

As if they can sense my fear, all three cats pounce out of his arms and back onto the table, sauntering over to me. Bubbles is the first one to sniff my hand, then give it a lick once she decides that she likes me. A loud purr fills the air as she rubs her body against my arm. Blossom and Buttercup follow suit, mimicking her.

Dammit, they're cute.

"They're not usually a fan of women," Elio comments.

"Well, I guess it's a good thing you can't bring your hookups home anymore," I say, my tone icy.

The prick just laughs, shaking his head. "I meant my little sisters. I have never brought a girl here."

I want to ask where he brings them then. It's on the tip

of my tongue because if anything, I'm nosy. Instead, I bite my tongue. "That must have been fun growing up."

He cocks his head slightly, looking at me intently. "Yeah, your dad mentioned that you were his one and only."

I scoff at that, pushing the stool back so that I can stand because this conversation is turning friendly, and I don't need that.

"I'll be back in two days to move my stuff in. I'm going to have Camille wait outside so that my parents think I'm living with her, so don't be around, got it?" I tell him, walking back toward the living room.

"I'll wait up here so I can help you carry your boxes."

I look at him over my shoulder. "No need. There's really not much. I can handle it."

Suddenly, his large, warm hand is tugging at my wrist, halting my movement. I still, turning to face him.

Forest-green eyes bore into mine, a furrow between his brows. "Let's get one thing straight, *dolcezza*. If I want to help you, I'm going to help you, get me?"

I have no idea what *dolcezza* means, but I'm assuming it's probably something that's going to make me want to punch him in the face.

I smirk up at him, noting once again how he towers over me. I shrug out of his grip while taking a step toward him because I'm not intimidated by him in the slightest. "And I hope you get this. I may be little, but I don't *need* your help. I can carry some damn boxes myself."

His eyes soften a bit, his body retreating from mine. "Sorry, you're right."

I'm surprised by his ability to communicate rather than spar with me because he easily could've. It throws me off, and I'm left blinking at him as I try to comprehend why I was even putting up a fight over it.

"It's okay. Just don't try to be all macho man with me, okay? I can handle myself. I've done it for twenty-one years now."

His jaw clamps down, hiding the words he really wants to say. "I'll try, but no promises."

"That's all I can ask for." I turn and head toward the door.

"You don't want to see your room before you go?" he calls out.

I wave him off with my hand. "No. Whatever it is will be fine with me."

I'm truly grateful to have a space of my own, because I didn't think that would happen this year, so whatever he has will do.

I'm about to leave when his voice reaches out to me once more. "Thanks for doing this, Jasmine. I appreciate it. There's no one else I'd trust to be here and take care of my girls."

I so badly wish I could roll my eyes at that, but deep down warmth begins to spread from my tummy to my chest. I want to ask what he means by that, but think better of it. "And thank you for letting me stay here and wanting to help me with my business."

He nods, his lips tugging up to the side.

I take that as my cue to leave and shut the door softly behind me. I instantly sag against the door, tilting my neck back and resting my head against it.

Why do I feel like I took my first real breath in the last half hour?

Chapter 5

Elio

*O*nce the door closes behind her, I let out a deep breath. My brain is already a mess from having to see her in my space, from her being the first woman in here besides my family.

Granted, I only started living here last December, but still. A woman has never been in any of the spaces I've owned. I've always told myself that if I didn't want her in more than my bed, they weren't going to see it to begin with.

Whenever I needed my needs taken care of, I'd rent a room in the nearest hotel. It may sound sleazy, but it's what has worked for me.

I'm slightly stressed about the place becoming a mess, but that's a gamble I'm willing to take. What I'm more worried about is seeing her in intimate ways that don't involve our bodies melding under my sheets.

Seeing her fresh-faced in the morning or her wet hair and smelling her fresh, peachy scent after she showers. Watching her bake in my kitchen, or even lounge on the couch with my girls.

There are so many goddamn scenarios of ways I can unravel

the person she really is, that would give me a closer look into who's behind the façade I know she puts on.

But I can't let myself think of her that way.

I partially lied to her that day in my office when she asked if I wanted anything sexually out of this. Obviously, I'm not expecting anything to happen, and I'll do my fucking hardest to make sure it never does. But she's easily the most beautiful person I've ever laid my eyes on. And that's on her physical traits alone, which is why I'm afraid to get to know her on a deeper level.

The good news is that we won't be spending too much time together apart from working on her business, since I'll be gone a lot for hockey. Being an assistant coach to a university's hockey team wasn't on my list of things to do after I retired, but here I am.

RLU students and staff were informed ahead of time about my arrival as a coach and student, and it was stated that if anyone harassed me, they would be expelled. It was a stipulation I made during my negotiations with the school because I value my privacy and want to attend school like any other normal student.

I have no clue what I want to do once I get my degree, but the idea of figuring it out excites me. I've always loved challenges, new opportunities, and unknowns. I embrace them. It's how my parents raised us, having started with nothing when they first moved here as a young couple.

And my first challenge? Not crossing the line with Jasmine.

Hours later, I've changed into black slacks and a black blazer to meet my best friend, Brooks. We're meeting at an upscale bar called The Lot, which requires verification of your status in order to enter.

There are a few around the country, and while it sounds

pretentious, it's a safe haven for people in the media who want to relax at a bar without having fans to worry about. I never really liked going out. When I was in the NHL, on the rare occasions I did, it was for media appearances.

In reality, I've always preferred to stay home with my cats with a good gin and tonic, and a game of chess.

But Brooks insisted on coming here, telling me that we needed to catch up in person since the Bears were gearing up for their season.

The entire loft-style bar is sleek with black and dark wood details everywhere. Dim light fixtures hang from the ceiling along with TVs all around us with various different sports on from leagues around the world.

My eyes land on Brooks sitting at the bar by himself, his mid-length dark brown curls easy to find in a crowd, which he's famously known for. Brooks may be the best goalie in the league, but his hair is what both women and men are very fond of.

Brooks looks over his shoulder and spots me as I come up behind him. "Leo! My man, take a seat."

"How's it going, B?" I ask while signaling the bartender my way.

He turns his body to face mine. "I'm excited for the season, although it sucks that it's the second one without you. The team misses you."

"It was fun while it lasted, but I was going to retire soon anyways," I remind him because I've told him this already. "You guys are looking good according to the stats and predictions."

We talk about hockey for the next few minutes, and I'm not at all bothered that I can't play anymore. I could choose to sulk for the rest of my life about the fact that a cheap hit from another player ended my career earlier than I wanted, but I chose to accept it and move on.

"So what's new with you?" Brooks asks, ordering another whiskey neat while I ask the waiter for another gin and tonic.

I know he's not asking about school or coaching because he knows about that already. No, the nosy fucker wants to know about my romantic life.

"I still haven't slept with anyone since my ACL tear two years ago, if that's what you're getting at," I mutter, taking a sip of my drink.

It's not like the offers haven't been there. I don't like to randomly hook up as much as I used to. When I was a rookie in the league, it was thrilling. That's kind of how I earned the playboy image the media loved to talk about.

Since the tear, I told myself I was done with that shit. I wanted to rebrand myself completely, and that means no more hooking up unless I'm romantically involved with someone.

I'm twenty-nine, for fuck's sake. It's probably time I settle down soon and all that.

"Yikes," he huffs. "I couldn't imagine going that long. My hand would be exhausted."

I brush him off. "How does it feel that you'll become a husband soon?"

He's marrying his little sister's best friend, Stephanie. They grew up together, having gotten 'married' at ten years old. Their love never waned over the years, and they've only had eyes for each other ever since.

Brooks smiles at me, missing tooth and all. "I can't fucking wait to marry her," he says, beaming. "Did you find a date yet?"

"No, I told you I don't need a plus-one. Give it to someone else," I counter, hating that Jasmine popped up in my mind when he asked if I had found a date.

He eyes me, then shakes his head. "Nope, Stephanie insists

that we keep it open, just in case some lady happens to capture your attention."

I glance at my watch, seeing that it's September 10. "We have a little more than three months until the wedding. Don't hold your breath on me finding someone I can tolerate enough to fly to Bora Bora with and then spend the entire weekend with them on top of that. It's not likely."

"Yeah, I can't imagine why someone would want to spend time with you when you talk like that."

"What's that supposed to mean?" I ask, finishing off my second drink.

Brooks chuckles. "Nothing bad, but sometimes, you talk like you're better than everyone. Like no one could ever be good enough to be on your level or some shit. I get you're super smart and rich as fuck, but you might have to reevaluate your standards."

I jerk my head slightly. "Really? You think I should give that same advice to your future child?"

Brooks glares at me at the mention of his non-existent child. "This is different. I'm just saying, loosen up a bit, will you? You never know who you'll find when you do."

I want to tell him that I'm already loosening up a tad for a certain someone, but I leave that out. Because if anything, I need to tighten up and lock the fucking key anywhere she's concerned.

Chapter 6

Jasmine

"Wow, this place looks elegant," my mother comments as we pull into the parking lot of my new home for the year.

The leaves on the trees surrounding the property are slowly beginning to turn a mix of orange and red as we enter September, the chill in the air reminding us that fall is here.

"Yeah, Camille's parents are well-off," I lie. Truthfully, I don't know anything about her family. She keeps her personal life personal.

"And she's letting you stay here for free?" she scoffs in disbelief.

"No, Mother, I'm paying her rent, like any other roommate would."

"Good, that's only fair," she replies, getting out of the car along with my father.

"It looks safe. I like it here already for you," my father comments as we round to the trunk.

"And it seems quiet, a nice place for you to focus this year," my mother chimes in.

Camille comes around the corner, her long legs carrying her gracefully over to us. I swear Camille is the only person who can wear sweatpants and make them look cute. She paired them with a white crop top and white sneakers. Her almost champagne-blonde hair is tied into a ponytail, her hair swaying with each step.

She has this poise about her, something I can't quite put my finger on. My thoughts quickly dissipate when she introduces herself to my parents.

"Hello, Park family, it's nice to finally meet you. I'm Camille." She smiles widely and brings her hand forward.

That's exactly how I'd describe Camille if someone asked, always smiling. She is bubbly, adventurous, and so sweet.

"It's nice to meet you, Camille. Thanks for letting Jasmine stay with you," my father says, shaking her hand.

"The pleasure is all mine. We're going to have a blas—" she starts but stops once she sees my eyebrows meet my hairline. "A blast keeping each other motivated to study and focus this year since we're in the same classes." She adjusted her words almost too well.

"That's great to hear. Make sure you girls have some fun too. It's your last year, so enjoy it when you can," my father says, shocking me a bit.

I know he's the more relaxed one among my parents, but still.

My mother approaches her next, her finger dabbing her chin as she thinks. "You look very familiar. Where are you from, dear?"

Camille sobers at that, her bright smile dimming a bit. "I'm from France."

Sensing her discomfort, I cut the interaction short before my mother pesters her about elaborating exactly where in France. "It's pretty chilly. Mind if we unload the boxes so we can bring them up?"

There's two for my clothes, one for my books and *toys*, one for my school things, one for my skincare and hair products, and the last has my baking utensils and my favorite chessboard.

The boxes are piled onto a moving cart that Camille brought down so that my parents don't have to come upstairs and discover that I'm not actually rooming with Camille. No, instead I'm rooming with my father's protégé turned coworker and friend.

My mother hugs me first, squeezing me into her as she inhales deeply into my hair before pulling back to hold me at arm's length. "My daughter, you are so beautiful, smart, and driven. Keep your head in the books because this is it—the big year. Get good grades and companies will be begging you to work for them, not the other way around. You're a Park, and Parks don't fall short."

"Thanks, Mom," is all I say because her words don't pack the sentimental punch I think she was aiming for.

My father is next, gathering me into a hug, then swaying us back and forth. Pulling back, he smiles at me. "You know where to find me if you need something. Don't be afraid to call me, okay?"

I nod.

"Be safe, girls," is his final parting before both of my parents tell me they love me and pull out of the lot, leaving me and Camille on the sidewalk.

"*Bon.*" Camille claps her hands together. "Let's get this stuff upstairs. Maybe your new roomie can help us with the boxes."

I groan, rubbing at my temple with one hand while the other pushes the cart to the front of the building. "We're strong women. We don't need him."

"Agreed, but there's nothing wrong with a little help from a man." She winks at me as we enter through the doors.

"Good morning, Ms. Blanchette and Ms. Park," Colin says, tipping his hat as we push through the revolving doors.

"Oh, no, no, what did we say, Colin?" Camille admonishes him playfully. "Please call me Camille. I beg of you."

"What she said," I add, pointing my thumb out toward her.

"Forgive me, it's a habit of the job," he apologizes.

"Hmmm, I think I could be swayed by the sprinkle doughnuts that your wife loves to make." Camille beams, patting her stomach for the full effect.

"That can be arranged. Enjoy your day, girls." He tips his hat once more as we push the cart through the lobby and to the elevator.

"What floor are you on?" I ask Camille.

"Five, only one above you."

"Oh, that'll be fun. We can hang out and study together all the time." I realize, feeling better about the move already.

"Exactly, and have girls' nights too, with music, popcorn, and face masks," she adds, smiling.

The elevator dings, and once we've pushed the cart into the hallway, I stop. "Camille, can I ask you a few things?" I want to know why I never knew that she lived here, how she can afford it, and where she's really from and more.

She tilts her head in confusion. "What's up, Jas?"

"I—" I start, but my voice is cut off by the door swinging open a few feet away from us.

Elio peeks his head out, jutting his chin. "Need help?" he asks.

I want to tell him no, that it's literally only five boxes, but Camille beats me to it.

"We would love that, wouldn't we, Jas?" she says, looking at me expectantly.

Except, I don't go along with it. "No, I would love it if you went back inside and let us do it by ourselves, actually."

Camille's eyes widen a fraction, her gaze shifting from Elio to me. And then the little hell-raiser she is, smirks. "Actually, I'm not feeling too well, cramps and all that girl stuff. Text me later." She starts walking back to the elevator, then hits the button for it to open.

"I hate you," I mouth silently to her.

"I love you more," she mouths back.

I internally groan the loudest fucking groan and then turn back toward Elio, who's leaning against the door. He crosses his arms over his chest, watching me.

I square my shoulders and push the cart forward until I'm right in front of the door. I don't say anything. I grab the top box that is full of my clothes and suppress a grunt. These boxes may be few, but they're heavy.

I adjust my grip and then walk past him into the space when I realize I don't even know where my room is.

Damn it.

My arms are burning from carrying what has to be a sixty-pound box at least. I don't turn around to avoid taking more steps, and I shout over my shoulder. "Where's my room?" My voice sounded more strained than I'd like it to.

There's no response, but before I can wonder why, Elio's strutting past me with two of my boxes stacked on top of one another.

"Follow me," he orders and I do without arguing, only because my arms are about to give out. Thankfully, my room is the first one on the right.

I drop the box as soon as I enter the room, setting it on the white carpet. Standing, I glance around to see that the walls are gray, and there's a four-poster bed in the middle with a black headboard and a pale blue comforter. There's a matching black dresser on one wall, a bookshelf, and a mounted TV.

It doesn't feel like home, but I plan on changing that. I'll start by buying a brighter comforter, adding some plants, and filling up the space with my various knickknacks.

Once I'm done analyzing the room, I suddenly remember that Elio's in here too.

"I said I didn't need your help," I mutter, spinning on my heel to head back to the hallway for the last two boxes.

He falls into step with me, his smooth voice running over

my skin. "If you thought I was going to let you carry all of these boxes while I stood and watched, you are mistaken, *dolcezza*."

I hate the way that nickname makes the hairs on my body stand, how the velvety smoothness of his voice delivers it so perfectly.

"I can do it myself," I remind him as I swing the door open.

"I know you can, but you don't have to," he says, his tone unexpectedly soft.

I ignore the part of my brain that wants to overthink what he said and look toward the remaining two boxes—my school stuff box and my books/toys box that's labeled "*girl stuff*."

I quickly grab it, and in my rush to get it to my room, I run straight into Elio. The bottom of the box gives out from the impact, causing all of my spicy books and sex toys to fall to the ground.

Fuck.

We're both silent.

My eyes are stuck to the ground, staring at my assortment of vibrators. I fumble and sink to my knees, refolding the bottom of the box so that I can shove them back in there.

"That's quite the collection you got there," Elio finally speaks up, with no hint of teasing in his voice. It's genuine appreciation, which somehow makes all of this even worse.

"Just please stop talking," I groan while putting them back in the box. Well, it's more like chucking because I want them off his floor this instant. Warmth spreads across my cheeks from embarrassment.

"This one looks fun," he says, crouching down to pick up a clit stimulator.

My mind instantly conjures an image of me on the couch, legs spread as Elio fucks me while using the stimulator at the same time. He'd be telling me what a dirty girl I am and—wait, *no*.

I swat his hand away. "What the hell, Elio? Don't touch my stuff, especially not that."

He throws both of his hands up in defense and then that panty-dropping smirk erupts on his face. "I said no hookups, so you had to bring in the cavalry, huh?"

I glare at him as the last vibrator gets tossed back into the box. Then I do the same with my books. Elio helps me with those, and I allow it because the sooner this moment is over, the better.

"These seem educational," he murmurs as he appraises them, picking one up and flipping through the pages of a spicy romance book between a girl and her brother's best friend.

I snatch it from his hands, the word *cock* catching my eyes multiple times on the page.

Fuck. Me.

This is so embarrassing.

I toss it back into the box with the rest, and then I practically run with the box to my room, not sparing him a glance. I drop it in the en suite bathroom because I'm going to clean all of those vibrators before I shove them in my nightstand.

As I exit the bathroom, Elio enters the room and plops the last box down on the floor next to the others. "I'll let you get settled in. Let me know if you need anything."

I'm surprised at his ability to let the last two minutes go. "I won't, but thanks."

"If you need any batteries for your friends, they're in the drawer beside the sink," he calls out as he leaves my room, tapping the doorframe on his way.

I take it back. This is exactly what I expected.

"Fuck off," I shout back, and all I hear is his laughter rumbling off the walls as he retreats.

Home sweet home.

Chapter 7

Elio

I officially had the worst sleep of my life last night.

I tossed and turned all night, and it all had to do with my roommate.

I'm not uncomfortable with her being here, but now knowing the spicy books she likes to read, I feel fucked. It makes me want to read them so that I can learn what she likes.

And to top it off? Seeing all her goddamn vibrators made it hard not to imagine her using them under my roof.

I could picture it perfectly in my mind. Jasmine's curls fanned on her pillow, her soft skin glistening with sweat as her fingers and toy worked between her thighs. I imagined she'd pinch her nipple every so often and that I could hear the sweetest moans coming from her lips.

It's not like I could hear anything happening from my room, but if a box of vibrators falls to my feet, then it's obviously going to cross my mind.

The problem with that is that I couldn't get it off my mind. And usually, I'm good at centering myself, like I did before going on the ice. Not last night, though. It was fucking pointless trying to stop the thoughts.

It's just because she's off-limits, I tell myself. That must be it.

My alarm goes off at seven, announcing the first day of classes, but I've already been up for an hour. Since I'm not the kind of person to lie in bed all morning despite how tired I am, I get up and hop in the shower. A much-needed cold one.

Once I'm showered and dressed in jeans and a hoodie, I make my way to the kitchen for a quick meal before heading out to my 9:00 a.m. class. I'm thinking of making myself some over-easy eggs and toast when the sight in my kitchen halts me in my steps.

I wasn't prepared to wake up to Jasmine cooking in my kitchen.

She has sleep shorts on with an oversized T-shirt and white ankle socks. Her hair is in a messy bun atop her head, and her body is keeled over a drawer while she looks for what I'm assuming is a frying pan based on the uncooked French toast sticks on the plate next to her.

"It's in the drawer to your left," I speak up, clearing my throat while desperately trying not to stare at her perfect ass.

Jasmine doesn't flinch from my presence as she straightens up, seeming comfortable in the apartment already. "Thanks."

I slide up to the island, a waft of cinnamon and maple hitting me. "That smells good," I say, rubbing a hand over my stomach. "I'm going to make eggs. Do you want some?"

Jasmine turns, her eyes flicking to mine instantly. "Shit, I forgot to tell you that I'm allergic to eggs. You're fine to eat them and have them in the house, but I can't ingest them or I'll be on my way to the ER. I have a few EpiPens in my bedside drawer and one in my purse at all times, in case you ever need to use it. And it's blue to the sky, orange to the thigh."

That has the hair on my arms standing at the image of me ever having to use it. I pray that never happens.

"Got it. You'll never see eggs here again. Don't worry," I assure her.

"Elio," she begins to protest, propping her hip against the counter.

"Don't," I cut her off.

She surprises me, a shy smile forming on her lips. This is new. "You don't need to do that for me. I told you that you can eat them. It doesn't hurt me."

"Yeah, well, I'm not taking any chances where you're concerned." The words fall from my lips faster than I register them because I wouldn't have said that if I was thinking straight.

Get it together, man.

Wanting to switch the topic, I ask, "How did you make the French toast sticks then?"

After putting the pan on the stove and flicking the heat on, she places a dollop of butter on the warming pan, the sizzling sound of melting butter filling the air.

"I used the almond milk in your fridge, ground some flaxseed, then added cinnamon and maple syrup to the mix. It's a creation my *halmeoni* and I concocted. Maple is my favorite flavor. It's my shot of choice in my coffee too," she explains, her eyes lighting up more than I've ever seen. She really seems to love food with the way she's beaming talking about it.

"Is that your grandma?"

"Yeah, I miss her a lot. She passed away three years ago," she tells me, keeping her eyes on her food.

"I'm sorry, Jasmine."

Before I can say anything, she adds, "I hope that was okay, me using your food. I'm going to get my own groceries today after class. I'll pay you back for what I used."

"No, you're not," my voice slices through the air.

"I'll send you extra money each month, and don't fight me on it, please? I need to contribute."

I nod even though I don't agree.

Jasmine places a few sticks of coated bread on the pan, the sizzling intensifying before it settles. "Would you like me to make you breakfast?" She thankfully changes the subject.

"Please," I nearly beg, loving the way her lips twitch to fight a smile. She may say she doesn't like me, but I think I can change that.

"Well, I made only enough for me, so you're going to have to fend for yourself this morning. But maybe another time?"

"I'd like that. I enjoy cooking, so maybe I could cook dinners for us while you handle breakfast? That is when we're both home." I suggest.

"You like to cook?" she asks, flipping the sticks, revealing a perfectly toasted side.

"Yeah, it's a mindless task for me. Everything in my mind goes blank except for what I need to be doing with my hands. It's soothing," I respond, noting how natural it feels having her in my kitchen, cooking and chatting with me. It's something I've never experienced before and I can't say that I hate it.

"I'm in for the cooking schedule. When I lived with my best friend Aurora, I always cooked every meal since she loathed it. So it's kinda nice to share cooking duties."

I remember meeting Aurora briefly at the athletic gala last December. She was pretty and seemed nice. But that night, I couldn't take my eyes off Jasmine. Especially when she was dancing.

It's why I have no idea how the fuck I'll survive living with her and not giving into my temptation to see how she would feel beneath my lips.

"How is she doing? She made it to Team USA, right?" I inquire, watching as Jasmine plates four sticks of French toast on one plate with a hearty squeeze of maple syrup on the side.

Sliding her plate across the counter, she sits on the stool across from me. "She's great. She and her boyfriend, Cameron, have a house together, and she's loving working with the team. But what she's really excited about is starting her passion project."

"What's this passion project?"

"Oh"—she swallows a bite, holding her finger up to me—"she's opening a facility for kids with disabilities to learn how to play sports. They'll even have access to professional athletes and coaches."

"Wow, that's amazing. Do they need any help with funding? I'd love to support them."

"Uh, I think they're good, but I can find out," she says, tucking a black curl behind her ear.

I get the idea that she doesn't want me to think she wants me to dish out money to her friends, but this is different. Her friend's project sounds amazing and I'd love to help.

My stomach rumbles, wishing it were tasting the overly sweet French toast across from me. I'll wait until she leaves to make the eggs before getting rid of them. Then I'll buy a new pan.

"What time is your first class today?" I ask, getting up to grab a glass of water. I don't drink coffee, but she mentioned liking maple in hers, so I make a mental note to buy a machine for her to use.

"Nine a.m. It's Professor Tart's business leadership class, which I need to get going to before I end up being late," she says, standing and placing her empty plate along with the items she used to cook in the sink to rinse them off.

I debate telling her that I'm in the same class, but I think the look on her face when she sees me will be much more satisfying.

Once her dishes are clean, she places them in the dishwasher and proceeds to wipe the counter down. She's a good listener, having cleaned up after herself like I asked, and it makes me wonder if she'd be good at listening in other situations.

"I'm going to, uh, get ready," she mumbles while pointing in the direction of her room. She seems slightly nervous, and I'm not sure why, but I don't like it.

I want her to be comfortable with me more than I thought I did.

I smile softly at her, hoping it'll erase whatever is making her feel this way. "Have a good day. I'll see you around."

Turning her head slightly over her shoulder, her eyebrows narrow as she says, "God, I hope not."

Her response makes my smile broaden as I shake my head.

It's infuriating yet fascinating how she interacts with me because it's vastly different than what I'm used to. I'm used to girls falling at my feet, being agreeable and not giving me shit.

It's then that I tack on another item on my to-do list for the year. I'm going to get this girl to like me if it's the last damn thing I do.

I want to see if daddy's little girl is truly the perfect, obedient woman she pretends to be.

Chapter 8

Jasmine

It's my last first day of school, and I'm dreading it.

It means I'm that much closer to having to live out the plan my parents have for me. I thought three years would give me enough time to gain the courage to tell them how I actually want to use my degree and live my life, but I thought *very* wrong.

Three years flew by and I have no idea what the hell I'll do by the end of this year.

I usually love school and learning, but lately, I can't help feeling left out at times. A lot of my classmates are excited about the positions they're applying for post-grad, while I'm lost.

I know the positions my parents would like me to apply for, but all those options do is make my stomach churn.

The wind rustles against my arms, a chill shooting its way up my spine. I opted for a black T-shirt, ripped jeans, and my black sandals. Regretfully, I didn't bother bringing a jacket.

Outside of the business building, I spot Camille sitting on a bench, eyes glossy as she looks at her phone.

Standing in front of her now, I softly place my hand on her shoulder, giving it a shake. "Cami, what's wrong?"

She jumps and lets out a shriek, a hand going to her chest. "Oh, you scared me, Jasmine!"

I sit down next to her, taking in her shaken appearance. "I'm sorry. What's going on?"

She wipes away the tear that's escaped down her cheek while taking a quick, deep breath. "It's nothing."

"You're upset. It's clearly not nothing. Talk to me, let me help you," I plead, my eyes bouncing from one of her blue glassy eyes to the next.

"I will, but not right before class. Come over for a girls' night tonight and I'll tell you everything."

"I'll be there. I promise," I tell her, pulling her into a hug. Camille clutches onto me, and once she's ready, we pull apart and stand.

"All right." She beams, attempting to look more like herself. "Last first day of school ever. Let's do this!"

I chuckle, following her into the building and into our class—business leadership for fourth-year students. It's not as busy as a first-year class, but there are still about seventy-five people in the room already.

And of all the seventy-five people in the room, he just had to be one of them.

Elio.

Stifling a groan, I yank on Camille's arm, pulling her down to a seat in the back row with me. It's not where we usually sit, but for whatever reason, I don't want him to see me.

We literally live together, but I can't see him more than I already do.

He's at the front, talking to the professor and probably trying to weasel his way out of assignments because of hockey season. In the front row, a group of girls are perched in their seats, giggling and blushing as they unabashedly gawk at him.

My eyes roll into the back of my head. What do they see in him anyway?

"What's with the angry eyes?" Camille asks, nodding toward the front row as she takes her laptop out.

I snap out of it, realizing my face was indeed set in a scowl. "It's those girls. He's like any other person trying to get his degree. Why can't they be cool about it?" I ask before taking a sip from my water jug.

Camille half laughs, half scoffs. "It's because they are thinking *fuck the degree*, and about how can they fuck him instead. They want to be with the retired NHL player who was deemed the sexiest billionaire in America."

I nearly spit out my water. "A billionaire? How much money did they pay him?"

"The league would never pay him that much. Are you crazy? It's probably from his endorsements, investments, and other avenues he explored. He seems like a savvy businessman, which is why I can't figure out why he's even here in the first place," she ponders while opening her Word document.

I'm asking myself the same question, especially now, knowing that he's loaded.

Why is he here?

And why am I paying him rent? Oh, that would be because I'm an idiot with too much pride and self-respect.

I push the thought away and silence my phone, then pocket it in my bag to help me focus during class. Then I get my notebook, pens, and highlighters out. Unlike Camille, I prefer taking notes by hand and use a color-coded system I've used since I was a kid. It's the only thing that helps process information.

Eventually, I lose focus of the commotion at the front of the room and everything around me as I set myself up for class. Until I feel *him* beside me, his presence making itself known whether I want it to be or not.

"Funny seeing you here," he whispers just loud enough for me to hear as he plops down into the seat next to mine.

"Why are you here?" I whisper back while writing the date and title of the lecture.

"In this class, or sitting next to you?" he asks teasingly.

"In this class getting a degree when you don't need one, and that too. Why are you sitting next to me?" I huff, trying my best not to roll my eyes.

He adjusts in his seat, which looks too small for a man his size, and leans in closer. His expensive cologne hits me, a mix of smoked wood and spice. It's potent, making me want to nuzzle my nose into his neck and inhale it into every cell of my body.

Wait, what the fuck? Since when have I ever thought that about anybody?

Never.

"I'm finishing my degree because I don't like to leave things unfinished. It's an accomplishment and gives me the credentials I need to do whatever it is I want to do next," he explains quietly.

His breath hits my ear this time as he speaks, sending a chill down my spine. "And I'm sitting next to you, *dolcezza*, because there's no one else I'd rather sit with."

I finally spare a glance at him, my eyebrows tucked in. "The feeling isn't mutual. The front row seems more like your thing. Those girls will take all your notes and do whatever else you want. I'm sure." The words I said don't shock me. But what does is the jealousy I'm feeling.

Again, what the fuck?

A smile spreads on his lips, but he tucks it away before it blooms fully. "That's exactly why I'm sitting next to you, because I know you're not going to annoy me. You're not going to try to talk my ear off or touch me. And if you think those girls could hold a fraction of my interest, you're mistaken."

My eyes lock with his for a beat, my body forgetting where we are as I get lost in the different shades of green I can see this close.

The professor interrupts the moment, his voice coming through his microphone to signal the start of the class. That's when I notice Elio has no backpack. He only has his phone and a bottle of water on the tiny desk.

Before he begins, I quickly utter under my breath. "Don't bother me either then. I need to focus. Got it?"

I expect a snarky reply, but all he does is nod before fixing his gaze on the professor.

For the next hour, I take notes on the lecture because he's one of the only professors who actually teaches on the first day of class. My notebook is covered in annotations, highlights, and scrawls of my pen.

To my right, Camille's Word document is somewhat filled with short bullet points. To my left, the only thing Elio has done is finish his water. He hasn't taken any notes. Clearly, he doesn't care about his education as much as he says he does.

Occasionally, I feel him staring at me from time to time, each one making me blush, and pray to God that he doesn't see. I don't know why my body's doing this to me.

He's attractive, so what? I've sat next to plenty of attractive men before, so why is Elio any different?

Once class wraps up, I can't help but sarcastically point out to Elio, "You took a lot of notes for a guy who claims to care about his degree."

Elio smirks, glancing at my notes, then back at my face. "I don't need to take notes."

I stifle a groan of irritation because of course he doesn't. "Let me guess, you asked the professor to email you his notes?"

"Interesting that you care so much, *dolcezza*," he muses, but before I can tell him to stop calling me that, he says, "Ask me anything from the lecture."

I pin him with my gaze, not wanting to play this game of his.

Camille, however, does. "Give me a rundown of the main points."

I flip over my notebook so he can't cheat, which only makes him chuckle. Then he goes on to tell us every important detail from the lecture, along with some additional facts about the cases I didn't know about.

This makes me want to get my notebook out because how the hell did he catch that and I didn't?

"See, *sweetheart*, he pays attention," Camille defends Elio. *Sweetheart?*

I look at her quizzically, but Elio interrupts, this time looking directly at Camille. "*Quando dovete tornare ai vostri doveri reali, Vostra Altezza?*"

I don't understand a word of what he said, but it's clear that Camille does in the way her eyes widen. I had no idea Camille spoke Italian as well, but there seems to be quite a bit I don't know about her.

"*Come fai a saperlo?*" she whispers.

"*Io e vostro fratello Quentin siamo ottimi amici. Il vostro segreto è al sicuro con me. Lei lo sa?*" he says back.

I give up on trying to understand what's going on as I begin to shove my things back into my bag.

"*Grazie. Glielo dico stasera,*" she half smiles, giving him an appreciative look for whatever reason.

I stand, done listening to them have their secret conversation right in front of me. "This has been fun," I mutter. "But I have to go." I stand from my seat and move to leave.

"Jas, don't be mad. I'll tell you everything, soon" Camille pleads, standing as well, her silvery eyes intent on mine.

"Why does he know?"

Elio speaks up this time, "Because I know everything. Might as well get used to it."

"Not likely," I respond, not turning to address him directly.

"See you later, *roomie.*" He winks, then struts out of the lecture hall with the utmost confidence.

I want to shoot the finger at him, but I think better of it. He's the most aggravating person I know. One minute he's being sweet, and the next he's getting on my last nerve for a reason I can't explain.

Camille and I exit in the opposite direction, heading to our next class that's in twenty minutes. We may have made our schedules together so that we could study together and share notes.

Although we're in the same program, we have two different ideal outcomes. Camille loves sports and hopes to work within the social media department for a professional team. Whereas I'm hoping to use my degree to open my own café.

Once our business leadership class ends, we walk to the parking lot together toward my car since Camille and I are riding home together. We call Aurora on our way, all of us catching up and gossiping until we get to our building.

In the lobby, Camille claims she needs a nap, and I agree that I could rest because the first day of classes always tires me out. We make plans to meet up later around six to order pizza and talk.

But once I get in bed, I can't rest. Instead, I lie there, making a list of content ideas for the next three weeks, along with the groceries I'll need to complete them.

From time to time, I find myself wondering what Elio's doing and when he's going to start helping me. And more often than not, my mind circles back to what *he's* doing. I shake my head and tell myself that once this semester gets underway, I'll be able to get him out of my mind.

I need to keep busy. That's all.

Chapter 9

Elio

The boys from the team are off their game today, from what I'm assuming is the first day of school buzz. Many of them are goofing off, wasting ice time as they wait for practice to begin.

I used to hate those kinds of teammates, especially when I was in college, trying to get myself noticed and drafted. I pushed myself to be great, and since hockey is a team sport, I expected them to do the same so we could be great collectively. But that wasn't always the case.

It's even more frustrating being on the opposite end now because I can clearly see who's trying, who didn't practice at all over the summer break, and who needs specific skill drills.

Despite the frustrations of coaching, during the few practices we had over the last three weeks, I found myself enjoying the job. Being on the ice feels good. I can't move like I used to, but I can still skate well enough to show these guys why I retired a hockey legend.

"Coach Mazzo," Ned greets me as he skates across the ice toward me. "How was your first day of class after all these years?"

"It was okay, aside from our professor telling me things I already know." I smirk at him, crossing my arms over my chest.

Ned rolls his eyes with a grin on his face. "Always so damn arrogant. How are our boys looking so far?"

"Not great," I tell him honestly. "They need to get it together if we're going to make it to the playoffs, let alone the championship."

The last time RLU won was my junior year. I plan on winning again, this time as the assistant coach.

"Isaiah's looking good," Ned points out as he watches our junior power forward skate across the ice.

I remember him from my brief interaction with their table at the gala. He was the one who was overly curious about me. I'll keep that knowledge for another day because something tells me the kid is going to be invading the hell out of my privacy.

"He should be faster if he wants to make those goals on breakaways. I watched his tapes from last year, and he tends to struggle with that."

"Someone did their homework, I see," Ned says appreciatively.

When he called me with the job offer, he told me he knew I was the right one for the job for two reasons. One being that I was talented with on and off the ice knowledge. And two, there's a mutual respect between the two of us.

In some cases, coaches can butt heads in a fight for dominance over the team, but Ned knew that wasn't my style.

Unless it's in the bedroom. But that's a different story.

"How's my daughter doing? I know you two had the same class this morning, and don't ask how I know. Like you, I know everything." His words intend to come off as playful, but I don't miss the underlying threat there.

If anything were to happen between Jasmine and me, he'd somehow know.

"We sat next to each other, but we didn't talk. She was very focused, using her color-coded system and all."

Ned stares me down, then his hand lands on my shoulder, gripping me there. "That's good to hear. Keep an eye on her for me from time to time, will you?"

"Sure," is all that comes out because if he knew the view I had of her perfect ass in my kitchen this morning, his hand would be around my neck instead.

Ned skates off, giving instructions to our team. We run through drills for the next hour, and the guys are dripping in sweat. One of them even vomited in the trash can that I thankfully brought out with me.

A secretary at the facility interrupts us, letting us know that Ned is needed for a phone call. He skates off the ice, leaving me alone with the guys, who begin to chat amongst themselves for the allotted ten-minute break.

I skate by, collecting some pylons, when I hear something that stops me in my tracks.

"You guys know the coach's daughter?" McCoy pipes up.

"Jasmine?" Isaiah chimes in. "Yeah, why?"

"She's sexy as fuck. Have you seen the rack on her? They look like the perfect handful."

"Dude, you're lucky Coach isn't here right now. He'd kick you off the team without hesitation," Isaiah replies.

I see fucking red at the way McCoy is talking about her and it throws me off a bit because I haven't felt this enraged since my last hockey fight.

"She's a goody two-shoes anyways." McCoy waves Isaiah off.

"What do you mean?" another player, Peterson, asks.

"Jasmine is known to be RLU's good girl. She's never been kissed, never even fucked anyone. Which is funny because she hung out with Aurora Vallacourt, and that girl was a—"

I don't let the piece of shit finish his sentence. "McCoy, Thomas, and Peterson. I want fifty laps, *now.*"

"What the fuck for?" Dan McCoy questions stupidly.

I skate right into his space, my chest nearly brushing his head because of our height difference. "That's fifty-five for you now, McCoy. Let that set a precedent. Any of you talk about Jasmine or her friend like that again, and I'll kick you off this goddamn team. Understood?" I seethe, chest heaving up and down.

McCoy scoffs, skating over to the boards to begin his laps along with Peterson, who regrets joining the conversation. Technically, he didn't say anything wrong, but I don't give a fuck. I'm so pissed off about what McCoy said that I'm punishing anyone who was involved.

Isaiah skates over to me. "In my defense, I was telling him to stop talking about her. I'm just as pissed as you are."

"I know. You're doing them because you need endurance training. Go."

While they skate their laps, the rest of us watch as the guys take their break. I can't get over what he said about her. Has she really never been kissed? I was even more surprised to hear that she's a virgin as well, but it fits the image she portrays.

It makes me feel like a fucking idiot that I told her not to bring her hookups over because she's never even had any. McCoy could be lying, but if he's not, it only makes things that much worse for me.

Not only is Jasmine the daughter of my coach and friend, she's *innocent.* I absolutely cannot touch her now, or ever for that matter. Not with the kind of sex I'm into.

It would only scare her away.

But the second I think of some young fucker laying a hand on her, it makes me see red again. I know I can't have her, yet it makes it even more tempting. To be the one to teach her how to fuck? How to suck *my* cock or come on my tongue?

Yeah, I want that. *Badly.*

I want to claim all of her firsts, even though I have no right to. It's a physical pull, one I felt the day we met three years ago. And that's the problem, because it's purely lust, but I'm not going to fuck up my relationship with Ned or put a strain on her relationship with him all because I want her.

Fuck it.

If I can't have her, I'll make sure no one else does either.

Chapter 10

Jasmine

$\mathcal{E}$ lio hasn't come back home yet, and I know this morning he mentioned wanting to cook dinner for us tonight. I debate on texting him to let him know that I'll be at Camille's, but he's not my father.

He doesn't need to know when I'm coming and going.

So I leave the apartment and make my way to Camille's. I knock on her door and wonder if it'll be Camille or her roommate who I've never seen or heard of. I'm starting to think she doesn't have one, and it hurts, because why wouldn't she let me stay with her then?

Camille answers the door, dressed in a loose T-shirt and yoga shorts with slippers on her feet. "Pizza is here. Come on in."

I enter the space, noticing how different it looks from Elio's. Whereas his space is filled with dark tones, Camille's is bright. The walls are a cream color, and the couch is gray, but there's color everywhere else.

The throw pillows are pink and yellow, with a light blue blanket thrown over the chaise part of the couch. There's art on the walls, fresh flowers on the coffee table along with sports magazines.

It screams Camille.

After grabbing plates and a slice of the best pizza to exist, a classic pepperoni and cheese, we sit next to one another on her couch, a rock tune I don't recognize playing in the background.

After we finish our first slice, Camille sighs. "All right, what do you want to know first?"

I cross my legs, sitting up straighter so that I can face her properly. "For starters, where's your roommate?"

Camille's brows pinch, a wince on her face. "About that…I don't actually have one. I apologize, although I feel like I will be doing a lot of that throughout this conversation."

"Why did you lie? What's going on?" I prod. I hate being lied to, but if her reason is good enough, I'm willing to look past it.

Camille sets her plate on the coffee table, fiddling with her fingers in her lap as she takes a deep breath. "I'm going to start from the beginning and hope that it will make sense."

I nod in encouragement, taking one of her anxious hands in mine. She smiles at our hands then returns her gaze to mine. "I'm from Lorsica, a small island off the French coast of Marseille. The island is run by a royal family, and I'm its heir." She pauses before delivering another shocking news. "I'm the daughter of King Mylan Moulin and Queen Cecila Moulin."

I'm pretty sure I'm not breathing as I take in the fact that one of my best friends is an actual real-life fucking princess. I thought royal families were a thing of the past.

"You're a princess?" I whisper, still in shock.

Camille bites on her bottom lip, then nods. "*Oui*, my name is actually Princess Maribel Moulin. I have four older brothers, Antoine, Simon, Matheo, and Quentin."

My brain feels overloaded, unable to process what this all means. "Wait, so how are you here? Do you have a bodyguard?"

"No, I don't because I ran away. I'm secretly here in America, hiding from my family and what they're expecting of me. None of them know I'm here, except Quentin. He abdicated to come to America and play baseball professionally. He actually plays for the Detroit Panthers now. He's the one who helped me set everything up, from getting a new identification to providing me with the funds I need to live until I get a job post-graduation.

"So far, I haven't heard anything from my family. I don't know if they've stopped looking or caring, but I'm grateful they haven't found me. I'm finally living my life the way I want to."

I stay quiet, taking in all this information as I try to come to terms with everything she's saying. Not only is she a princess, but she's a princess on the run.

Wow.

I didn't see that one coming.

"What made you want to run away, if you don't mind me asking?" My voice is soft, not trying to sound invasive.

"I love my country and family, but I knew since I was a little girl that being a princess isn't for me. I wasn't your typical princess growing up. I loved playing rough with my brothers and watching all of their sporting events when I wasn't forced to attend my own duties, which were much less exciting. Since our island is so small, not many people outside of France even know who we are. In my own country, I'm about as famous as they come, but here, I can be myself. Although I did dye my hair blonde to cover my tracks."

"I'm glad you did what felt best for you. How long did it take to plan your escape? How did you even escape?" I word vomit, unable to stop asking questions.

"Not very long. It was after…an event that happened to me. I knew I needed to get out of there sooner than later, so I called Quentin from a burner phone and he set everything up for me. Two weeks later, he had a private jet ready for me. I told my maids I needed to run an errand and ditched them, heading for the airport instead. I was good at evading them. That part of the plan wasn't hard. The hardest part was leaving my nieces and nephews. I miss them dearly."

"What happened to you, Cami?" I fold my hand over hers, giving it a squeeze.

Clearing her throat and turning more serious now, her aqua eyes look strained as she adjusts in her spot. "During my last year of high school, we were having a celebration in the city, an all-night party in the streets with vendors and dancing under the stars. My bodyguards at the time got distracted by the events of the night, losing sight of me."

Camille exhales a shaky breath, her fingers fighting to fidget under my grasp. I squeeze her hand harder at her pained expression, letting her know I'm here for her. "I was hanging out with a crowd I probably shouldn't have. I liked to smoke weed from time to time, but I never should've gone with them," she croaks then clears her throat.

"One of the guys got handsy, feeling me up, and when I told him no, he gripped my ass. I slapped him and he didn't like that." She shivers. "He backhanded me across the cheek and threw me to the ground. I don't know how, but I got right back up and ran. And all three of those men chased after me. I was fucking terrified, Jasmine. I still get nightmares sometimes, and that's why I can't have anyone stay with me. It's not that I don't feel safe with you. I just value my personal space."

I pull her into my arms, letting her cry against my shoulder as she squeezes my body for dear life. "I'm so sorry that happened to you, Camille. It's not okay and I hope those fuckers got jail time."

"They did. They followed me and we happened to run into a group of police who were looking for me." Her words are nearly muffled by her tears, but I still hear them. "It's another reason I wanted to leave and come somewhere where no one knows who I am."

I rub her back soothingly, having a newfound appreciation for my best friend. She's so fucking strong. I don't know how she carries all that she does. "Thank you for trusting me and telling me. I appreciate it. I won't tell anyone either. Your secret life is safe with me."

Camille pulls back, wiping under her eyes. "Thank you. I swear I feel like Hannah Montana some days. So it feels good to let it out with someone else."

My head tilts at that. "Oh yeah. How did Elio know?"

"He's friends with Quentin, which means they must be really close if Quentin told him about us."

It all makes sense now.

"Why were you crying earlier?" I prod.

"I was looking at pictures online of my nieces and nephews, and I miss them so much."

"I'm so sorry, Cami. That's a lot you're dealing with." I grimace, grabbing her hand once more.

"Thank you, Jasmine. I'm glad I have someone to talk to about it now if I need it." She smiles softly, squeezing my hand.

Camille changes topics, sharing stories of growing up in a castle and her life as a princess. Her brothers seemed like fun to grow up with, making me ache for a sibling that I never had.

I often wonder what it would have been like had my parents had another child. Maybe then there wouldn't be so much pressure placed on me, and I could live the life I truly want.

It's a question I'll never know the answer to and one that will haunt me every day.

Chapter 11

Elio

*M*y apartment is quiet, the way I like it.

Except, I didn't *want* it to be quiet tonight. I was actually looking forward to seeing Jasmine, maybe lounging on the couch or studying, her absurd color-coded system to help her take notes while I cooked us dinner.

I made shrimp tacos, a favorite of mine, and it makes me wonder what her favorite food is. There's so much I don't know about this girl, and it makes me only want to learn more, even though I damn well know it should probably stay the way it is.

After cleaning the kitchen and storing the leftovers in the fridge for her, I decide to text her. I don't want to be an asshole, but I thought we had dinner plans. Not in the romantic sense, but when we made the schedule this morning, I assumed it meant that we were having dinner on the nights I was here.

Guess I forgot about the fact that she has her own life too, but part of me is worried. She didn't text me where she would be or when she would be back.

Maybe something happened to her?

My gut churns at the idea, my mind working quickly to

erase it. She's an adult and has been alone all her life. Like she said, she can handle herself.

But to be sure, I send her a text.

Me

Where are you? I made shrimp tacos and left them in the fridge for you.

I put my phone down, opting for an evening workout in order to burn off this restless energy I'm suddenly feeling. As I pull on my gym shorts and T-shirt, my phone pings.

Jasmine

If you must know, *Father*, I am a floor above you at Camille's. Thanks for the food, but we had pizza.

A rush of relief sweeps through my body knowing she's close and safe. Along with it is joy because her smart mouth is entertaining.

Me

I am older than you, but not old enough to be your father.

Jasmine

There's a discount on canes online, would you like me to order you one?

Me

Only if you have enough room in your cart. I heard there was a discount on vibrators too.

Jasmine

I'm blocking your number.

I smile down at my phone and think to myself that I can't remember the last time I did that. I don't reply and head to the gym instead where I run for thirty minutes, before doing an hour of weight-lifting. I don't train as a professional anymore, but I still enjoy working my body the best I can while being wary of my injury.

Leaving the gym sweaty as hell, I decide to take my shirt off during the short elevator ride back down to my apartment. I'm nearly on my floor when it stops at the one above mine.

The metal doors open, revealing Jasmine on the other side. Her mocha eyes widen, trailing a path over my bare chest and down to my abs where they linger. Then her gaze snaps back up to my face.

"Why are you shirtless?" she huffs, folding her arms across her chest.

I smirk, loving that she finds me attractive. She doesn't have to admit it, but I can read it in her body language and from the way her words came out all breathy.

The doors attempt to shut, but I put my arm out to stop them. "I was at the gym, and I'm about to go in the hot tub. Are you going to get in or not?"

Jasmine mulls it over for a second, her full lips pulling in. "You know, it's only one floor. I could use a good walk."

"Jasmine, get in the elevator," I groan, annoyed that she'd rather walk than be in here with me.

Her head snaps up at my tone. "I don't take orders from you, remember? See you at home, *roomie*."

She turns, walking in the direction of the stairs as the metal doors try to close once more. This time, I step out of the elevator, chasing after her.

Turning her head over her shoulder, she rolls her eyes at me. "Elio, what the hell are you doing?"

"Walking with you," I responded, falling into step with her. "You're right. I could use a good walk too."

"Didn't you just work out? I'm sure you don't need a walk."

"I have to make sure I stay in shape. It would be a shame to lose my physique."

It's quick, but I catch her eyes flick down to my abs again before she faces forward. "I don't think you need to worry about that." Before I have time to gloat in her subtle approval of my body, she adds, "We have a hot tub?"

I love the fact that she says 'we,' but I don't point that out to her. "Yeah, it's in my bathroom. Another perk of being persuasive and having money."

"Ugh, here I was excited to use it," she mutters as she attempts to open the door to the stairs. I put my hand on the glass, halting her movement.

"I got it," I say as I open the door, my voice lower than it was as I imagine her in my hot tub. Her in a bathing suit...*fuck*.

She shakes her head but walks through without a thank you.

Brat.

"You can use it too," I tell her, bringing up the hot tub situation once more.

"When you're not home, sure."

We reach the bottom of the staircase, where I once again open the door for her. "You can use it when I'm here too. I won't bite."

Jasmine whips around, facing me with determination in her eyes. "I'm not scared of you."

I step into her space, my bare, glistening chest mere inches from hers. I so badly want to close the space and feel what it would be like to have her body pressed against mine, but I stop myself.

"Then come in the hot tub with me tonight," I propose to her.

I'm playing with fire, but at the moment, I don't care enough to stop.

She turns around, walking away from me to our door, where she unlocks it with her key. I follow in right behind her, about to ask her if she heard me, knowing damn well she did.

I don't have to say anything though, because she turns around to face me once more, looking more confident than she did seconds ago. "I'll pass. It's late and I have an early class."

It shocks me that I feel disappointed in her response, because part of me was hoping she'd do it. Not that anything could happen, but I was curious to see it through. She's also the only woman to reject me, and I hate how much I like it.

"All right, *dolcezza*. Have a good night," I coo, leaving her as I head to my room where I strip and step into the hot tub.

Heat engulfs me, the jets soothing my exhausted muscles, but it does nothing to ease my mind. It's filled with thoughts of Jasmine, which is becoming my new normal and she's only been here one fucking day.

This is going to be a problem.

Chapter 13

Jasmine

*I*t's the first Friday of the semester, which means I'm exhausted and looking forward to a weekend spent doing nothing.

Except I can't sit here and do *nothing*.

I need to go over the notes from my classes this week, do the readings for next week, work on content for Minniebakes, and clean my room. It's only been four days and the space is already messy.

If Elio stepped foot in my room, I think he'd have a heart attack.

Speaking of Elio, we've fallen into a comfortable routine. I make breakfast, we have small talk where I usually roll my eyes at him and give him a smart-ass remark. He grins, and then we part ways for the day.

At night, he cooks us dinner and I eat with him at the table. Then I retreat to my room, where I've been hiding whenever he's home because of our interaction the other night.

Seeing Elio shirtless, his perfectly-chiseled body shining with sweat, I felt things only my vibrator can usually make me feel. It was bad, and that's why I've been slightly avoiding him.

I nearly accepted his offer the other night, until I remembered that we shouldn't. Besides, I'm not ready for that anyway.

When you have never been kissed, the event in itself becomes overhyped in your mind. I do want to get it over with, yet at the same time I get stressed thinking about it.

Kissing is one of the most intimate things in my mind, because it's a way to express so many different things. It's passion, love, desire, longing, and so much more. At least, that's what my books say.

So I don't want to experience that with just anyone.

Camille and I are currently on our way to the athletes' cafeteria to grab lunch. Even though I'm no longer on the volleyball team, it's still where I feel the most comfortable and they have the best food options on campus.

Once inside, we both head over to the panini press and make our own sandwiches at the DIY panini bar.

"Is this bread egg-free?" I ask the server, who retreats to confirm with someone else.

After the server confirms it, I pile my bread with hummus, spinach, tomatoes, and cucumbers, topping it with jalapeños and cheese. Camille pairs hers with avocado, lettuce, red onion, and falafel.

After pressing them, we make our way to a booth beside the windows that overlook the football field. We eat our lunch, discussing our latest assignment, when a familiar face comes into view.

"Jay Bay Bay!" Theo screams, literally, from across the cafeteria. All eyes turn to look at the person he's looking at, which is unfortunately me. I want to sink lower into my seat from the attention, but instead, I wave and smile at Aurora's friend, who's slowly becoming mine too.

Theo's a year younger than me, now the starting quarterback

for RLU. He's known for his witty antics and weird nicknames, making me like him that much more.

Once he approaches the table, I stand to give him a hug, but Theo doesn't do normal hugs. Instead, he spins me around and squeezes the life out of me in the process. When he sets me down, my head spins, so I use his forearm to steady myself.

"Jesus, Theo, why can't you hug like a normal person?" I chuckle.

"Oh, c'mon, what fun would that be?" he protests.

It's then that I feel a burning gaze on me. Glancing to the right, I see Elio talking with one of his players, his eyes darkening as he takes me in. I notice that my hand is still on Theo's arm, so I snatch it away, not because I think that's why he's mad, but because it's weird for us.

Theo and I don't like each other that way.

"How's it going with Marcela?" I ask while sitting back down in my seat, with Theo sliding in next to me. Marcela works as a waitress at Beers n Cheers, the on-campus sports bar that Aurora's brother, Nate, owns. Theo has been pining for her since last year, but nothing has happened yet. Or at least that I know of.

Theo's jaw works, irritation filling his features for the first time, a hand gripped tightly around the fidget cube he often has with him. I've never seen him look this way since I've known him. "She has a boyfriend. She finally told me the other night."

"What? How is that possible? I thought you guys were becoming friends?"

"We are, I think, but she told me they've been together since high school. And to top it off? Her boyfriend is none other than Hunter Johnson, the quarterback at the University of Aspen. Our fucking rival school."

"And he doesn't want her to be friends with you," Camille fills in.

He points at her. "Exactly. I can't blame the guy because I don't want to just be her friend. I want her to be mine."

"I'm sorry, Theo. I know how much you liked her," I apologize, knowing that must suck for him.

"I still like her and I won't stop trying to be her friend. Hunter is a fucking idiot, and he's going to mess up soon. I know it. Then I'll be there to swoop right in and take what's mine," he states, showing me a possessive side I never knew existed.

On one hand, I appreciate his devotion, but on the other, I wonder if he should let it go in case that doesn't happen.

"You got this. If you like her that much, don't give up hope yet," Camille encourages him.

Theo and Camille chat while I tune them out as my eyes scan the cafeteria, landing on Elio, who's still staring at me, looking as if he has no care for what the player is talking to him about.

I avert my gaze, my face flushing as I dig into my panini.

"Who has you blushing?" Theo teases, flicking his finger against my heated cheek.

I swat his hand away, making him chuckle. "It's warm in here, that's all."

It's a bullshit lie, but I can't tell him that the real reason I'm blushing is because my older, arrogant roommate is staring at me and I kind of like it, even though I shouldn't.

Camille glances over her shoulder, a sly smile on her face when she looks back at us. She attempts to open her mouth, but the glare I send her way has her lips closing just as quickly.

"How's football going?" I ask Theo, wanting to get my mind onto a different subject.

A smug expression takes over his face, his blue eyes shining. "Good, now that I'm starting QB. The team is strong, so I think we'll have a chance to win the championship this year."

Last year, they were in the championship game, but lost by a winning touchdown.

"All the teams are looking pretty good this year," Camille adds.

"You're still doing the sports section on the school paper, right?" Theo asks her.

"Yeah, I love it."

"That's amazing, Millie Moo. If you ever need any quotes, your boy is always good for media stuff." He winks at her, donning her with a Theo custom nickname that we're all victims of.

"I'll be sure to keep that in mind," she tells him, taking a bite of her panini.

We enjoy the rest of our lunch, laughing and catching up with what we did over the summer. Unlike my summer of staying home and avoiding my parents by 'studying' in my room, Camille traveled the country with her brother as he played baseball in different states, all while staying under the radar.

Theo, on the other hand, tells us he went back home to work around his family's farm for the summer.

We eventually part ways since Theo needs to head to a football meeting, and Camille has a meeting for the school paper.

I'm kind of happy I have no meetings to attend and that I can go home to read my book in peace.

The cherry on top for a perfect night for me? Elio has a pre-season game tonight here, which means he won't be home until later this evening. School is only going to get busier as the weeks go on, so I'm going to enjoy a night of rest.

Hell, I may even sneak into his hot tub for a bit.

Chapter 14

Elio

*T*onight was fucking awful.

The guys played their absolute worst, which is not the best way to start off our season. It may not count, since it's only a pre-season game, but to me? Every game matters.

The one thing I'm looking forward to is seeing Jasmine. I haven't seen much of her over the last few days as hockey season is gearing up soon and she's always in her room studying. I'm curious to see if she'll be home, to learn what she does on a Friday night after a long week of school.

Will she be studying? Reading? Baking, or watching a movie? Or maybe she's out at some frat party with boys who have no right to fucking look her way?

Pushing those thoughts away, I walk into my apartment and immediately notice Jasmine everywhere. Her orange throw blanket is on the couch, there are cookies on the counter, a pan on top of the stove, her highlighters and notebook on the island counter.

I can even smell her peachy floral scent all over the room.

I thought the sight would infuriate me, due to my need for things to be in order and clean. Instead, it makes me grin.

I like knowing that she lives here, that her things are under my roof.

Buttercup, Blossom, and Bubbles greet me at the door, purring as they take turns rubbing their bodies against my leg. Crouching, I rotate between their heads, giving them the scratches and love they're seeking.

So far, they seem to like her, which is good. Bubbles has taken an extra liking to her, as she's often missing from my bed where the three of them usually sleep. Jasmine confirmed this morning that Bubbles has been curling up with her instead.

Speaking of Jasmine, I'm about to call her name when I hear it. The sound of the jets from my hot tub.

My Adam's apple bobs as I swallow hard, trying to decide what I'll do. I could wait out here until she's done. That would be the respectable choice to make. As her dad's friend, I definitely should *not* be going anywhere near her in a bikini.

Especially not when I've been imagining this exact scenario with a less than innocent ending.

My curiosity takes over, along with the desire to see her. I want to know what she's doing there. Is she reading, scrolling on her phone, or drinking?

Besides, it's my house and my room, so I can do whatever and go wherever I please. At least, that's what I tell myself as I walk down the hall and toward my room.

The door to my bedroom is ajar, the soft melody of an instrumental pop song filtering in from my en suite bathroom. Regret begins to fill my body the closer I get, and I'm about to change my mind when I hear her suck in a breath.

Now concerned, I barrel into my bathroom, pushing on the slightly open door. My eyes instantly land on her body in my hot tub, her legs glistening and resting halfway out of the water on

82

the ledge. She has a book in her hands and a wine glass nearly empty on the ledge beside her head.

Her bikini is a terracotta hue, which I'm starting to learn is her favorite color, and it might be mine too. It complements her skin, and the strapless top exposes the swell of her breasts.

My cock hardens at the beautiful sight before me, and I'm thankful for the sweats I'm currently wearing. Not that it matters much because if I reach full mast, she'll be able to see.

It'd be impossible to miss.

Jasmine startles, throwing her legs back in the water, nearly dropping her book into the tub. She catches it, then narrows her eyes at me. "Elio, what the fuck? You scared me."

"Not expecting me home so soon?" I raise my brow at her, leaning against my sink, crossing one ankle over the other.

"I must have lost track of time. Sorry, I'll get out," she says, setting her book on the ledge.

I hold my hand up to her. "Don't be. I did say you could use it too. What are you reading?"

She holds my gaze for a moment, then decides to stay put, settling back into her seat.

"Nothing you'd be interested in." She sighs, closing her eyes and resting her head against the headrest.

"Based on the page I read in that one book, I actually think I'd be very interested," I say, my voice huskier than I'd like it to be.

She cracks one eye open to look at me, then closes it once more. "It's a marriage of convenience between a boss and his assistant."

I grin, folding my arms across my chest. "A bit taboo. I like it. How's the sex?"

Jasmine's eyes shoot open in shock. "Jesus, Elio. Do you have a filter? You can't ask me that."

"Why not?"

"Because I'm me, and you're you," she tries to explain.

"Meaning?" I prod, knowing exactly what she means.

She levels me with her stare. "You're a friend of my father's. You're older than me, and experienced at that. We definitely should not be talking about sex."

I push off the counter, walk to the edge of the hot tub, and rest my elbows on it, not caring that it's soaking through my long sleeves. "Tell me something. Is it because you've never been kissed and it makes you uncomfortable, or is it because you're daddy's perfect girl?"

Her mouth gapes open. "Who told you that?" she nearly whispers, looking less relaxed than she did before.

It makes me feel like an ass, but I'm too curious to stop. "Apparently, it's a known topic around campus, which pisses me the fuck off, by the way. But is it true?" I ask, my eyes bouncing between hers to try and get a read on her.

She does the same, a small sigh escaping her as her shoulders drop. "Yeah, it is."

"Do you mind me asking why?"

I don't think she's going to answer me after a full minute of being silent, but then she gives in. "Growing up, I was thrown into every extracurricular you could think of. My parents wanted me to have the opportunity to try and learn anything I possibly could, which is great and I'm thankful for it. On the downside, I didn't have time for many social interactions. So by the time I was in high school and started noticing and becoming interested in guys, it felt like I was too late. Everyone had their first kiss already. Some were even having sex. It also didn't help that all the guys at my school were idiots. So from there, I decided that I didn't want to kiss just *anyone*. I didn't want to kiss some guy only to get it over with, not when he'd probably laugh at how bad I was at it, or claim he stole it from me before another guy could. Now I still feel the same way. I want to kiss someone who stimulates my mind, not only my body. I need someone who *wants* to kiss me, not to claim what has yet to be taken."

It's the most she's ever said to me in one sitting, and I hang onto every word. It's fascinating to me to learn and uncover the person she truly is. One small detail she needs to learn, though? Someone can very much want to kiss her and claim her at the same time.

"Thank you for telling me that." My voice is silvery, much softer than it was minutes ago.

"You probably think I'm weird or whatever, but it's me. Like it or not, I don't care." She shrugs her shoulders, the movement creating a rippling effect in the water.

"I don't think that at all."

"What do you think then?" she asks, moving over to the seat closest to me and peering up at me with those damn eyes that intrigue the hell out of me.

It takes every ounce of my self-control not to look down at her cleavage. I swallow, forcing away the thoughts of yanking her top down and sucking her nipples.

A smile creeps up on my lips before I can stop it as I tell her exactly what I think. "I think you're a smart, beautiful, fascinating woman who likes to pretend she's this perfect person all the time. But underneath it all, you're messy, and there's more to you than what meets the eye. I'm a smart man, yet you evade me. It drives me wild," I breathe, the next words tumbling out of my mouth before I can stop them. "*You* drive me wild."

Her luscious lips part, sucking in an audible breath. Suddenly, she stands, and it's the worst fucking thing for the erection I've been trying to avoid having. Her bikini covers the areas I want to explore the most, exposing her lean stomach and slim legs while accentuating what I know are her perfect tits and her small, perky ass.

From this angle, with my elbows resting on the ledge and with her standing, she towers over me for once. I thought it would make me feel inferior, but I find myself liking it. I don't mind her having the power, not one bit.

In fact, it only adds to the blood rushing toward my cock.

"You know what I think?" she asks, sauntering over to the opposite end, grabs her glass of rosé and finishes it. Setting it back down, she turns to me. "I think you like to pretend that you're better than everyone so that you never get hurt. You can't get hurt if you don't trust anyone to let them get close enough, right?"

This I already knew, so it doesn't hit me the way she thinks it does. "Tell me something I don't already know, *dolcezza*."

The term of endearment started as a joke because she's not very sweet toward me, or at least, she wasn't. But now…I don't know how long it'll last in a teasing manner before it turns into something else.

"That your fly is undone," she fires back.

I shoot upright, looking down at my zipper, only to remember that I'm wearing sweatpants. Her laughter flows whimsically from her mouth, the one sound I want to keep hearing on repeat.

"You brat." I chuckle, backing up to grab her a towel from the cupboard. When I turn back around, she's out of the tub, shivering as she tries her best to cover her body.

I immediately rush over to her, concern pulsing through me. "What's wrong? Why are you shivering?"

"It's j-just me. I'm always cold, especially after getting out of the shower," she says through chattering teeth.

I wrap the towel around her shoulders, while being careful

not to touch her. I can't cross that line because I know that once I do, I'll be fucked.

The tension in my chest eases a bit as I see her wrap the towel tightly around her body, her shivering easing. I make a mental note to order her a towel heater for her bathroom. I can add it to the coffee machine order I still need to place as well.

"Thanks." She smiles softly at me. Grabbing her book, she pauses by my door. "Night, roomie."

"Good night, roomie." I wink at her playfully, making her eyes roll as she smiles and walks out of my room.

I may have told her good night, but I won't be sleeping. Not anytime soon with the pent-up sexual frustration I feel in my entire body. No, it's going to be a very long and hard night trying to clear my mind from the one girl it shouldn't have in it.

Chapter 15

Jasmine

I roll over for what feels like the hundredth time.

I came back to my room a while ago where I showered, then got ready for bed, changing into some sleep shorts and my favorite oversized T-shirt.

My problem? I can't stop thinking about Elio.

About our interaction in the hot tub, the intensity in his eyes, that green hue turning darker, nearly black as I stood from the water and held his gaze, standing above him. It felt good knowing that I had an effect on him, but it was also scary.

Which is why I turned away, trying to gather my wits before I lost it and did something stupid like inch closer to him.

With a groan, I sit up, blowing a curl out of my face. I've been tossing and turning for what feels like hours and I need to get out of this bed. I throw my comforter to the side, swinging my legs off my bed, startling Bubbles, who was curled up beside me.

"Sorry, Bubbles," I coo, petting her. She stretches out, then hops down from my bed and sashays out of the room.

I follow her, thinking a glass of water is what I need in

order to fall asleep. Sometimes I need to move my body for a bit, drink some water, and then try to sleep again.

Truthfully, I know I need to get off. It's been too long since I've had a release. The last time I did was the night before I moved in here because I've been too nervous to do it with Elio being home.

Which means the need to release some tension is high. Add in our moment in his bathroom, I think I could come in seconds if I put even the slightest pressure on my clit.

I tiptoe my way down the hallway, being careful not to wake Elio. His door is shut with the lights off when I peek that way, so I assume he's asleep. I come to a halt when I near the open space because boy was I fucking wrong.

Elio is on the couch, his bare, muscular thighs spread wide, his back against the pillow, head thrown back in ecstasy as he wraps his hand around his cock. It's the first time I've ever seen one in real life, and it startles me.

But the more I watch it, the more it turns me on. It's long and thick, a tuft of hair at the base. I don't understand how that would ever fit inside of me.

Not that I'm planning on trying, but still.

My mouth waters then drops, and I quickly hide behind the wall so that he can't see me, but I can still see him.

His moans ricochet lightly off the walls, not loud enough that I would've heard from my room, but loud enough that I can hear him from where I'm hiding.

"Fuck," he grunts, sliding his large hand over his massive cock rapidly, tugging harder at the tip. A spurt of cum spills from it, and he uses it to lubricate his cock, his hand gliding along it a bit smoother now. "Jasmine," my name is a cursed plea on his lips as he pleasures himself.

My eyes threaten to fall out of my head, my mouth hanging

open in shock at hearing him say my name. I throw my hand over my mouth to avoid making any sound.

My much older roommate, who has told me many times that I'm off-limits, is currently jacking off to thoughts of me on the couch.

Holy. Fucking. Shit.

It feels wrong to watch him, but I can't stop. I also can't stop my hand from falling from my mouth, trailing a path down my chin, over my neck, and my collarbone. I continue downward, fingers skimming my breasts, then pinching my nipple.

I use my other hand to clamp my mouth shut, knowing a sound was about to come out of my mouth. I keep trailing my hand down over my stomach, where I finally inch it under the waistband of my shorts.

A single digit runs down my slit, instantly coated in my arousal. I'm so wet, more than I've ever been before.

It feels wrong as I debate slipping a finger inside, but as soon as I do, I'm reminded how right it feels. I want to sigh in relief, but I hold it back. I insert another, then begin pumping them in time with Elio's thrusts, his hips moving in sync with his hand now.

I imagine that it's his long fingers inside of me instead, stretching and filling me.

Elio grunts, picking up his pace. I think he's close from the pained look on his face, his bottom lip a victim to his teeth. I match his efforts, hoping that the sound of his hand running over his cock is louder than my fingers sliding in and out of my wet pussy.

I marvel at the sight of him. How defined the muscles on his body are. Even the fucking veins on his hands that are gripping his cock are turning me on.

What the hell is wrong with me?

He's all man, and I've never been more attracted to one than I am at this moment.

Taking a risk, I remove the hand from my mouth and slide it under my shorts, using it to apply pressure to my clit. My knees buckle at the sensation, a rush of pleasure shooting through me.

It's not going to take long.

Elio's cock is slick with his arousal, shining in the dim lights of the living room, and the only thing I want more right now is for him to put it inside me—anywhere for that matter.

My fingers are soaked, moving rapidly in and out of me as I rub circles on my clit. It feels so wanton, watching him get off, but it's so fucking hot that I can't look away.

If my name didn't spill from his lips, I would've turned around, but after he said my name, I was done for. My thighs were coated in arousal from that alone.

A stifled growl punctuates the air, Elio's chest falling forward off the back of the couch as he finally comes, all while choking out my name over and over again. His breaths are heavy as his cum spills out of his cock, all over his abs and overflowing onto his hand.

The image sets me off along with the fact that it was my name on his tongue when he came. My own orgasm rips through me, nearly sending me to the floor from the impact.

My pussy clamps around my fingers, the pleasure so intense that I rip my other hand away from my clit, using it to cover my mouth as I ride out the aftershocks. I've given myself some good orgasms over the years, but nothing has ever compared to this.

Elio pants softly, lying back against the couch as he relaxes from his high. I relax against the cool wall, the chill welcome on my body that's overheated right now. Once I've come down from my own release, the panic sets in.

What in the absolute hell did I just do?

I tiptoe as quietly as I can back to my room, where I shut the door ever so softly to make sure he doesn't hear the click. Then I rush into my bed, where I throw myself under the covers like a five-year-old who thinks they saw a monster under their bed.

My breathing is erratic, my mind a jumbled mess as I think about what happened. Elio and I both got off thinking about each other, in the same damn room.

Except he doesn't know about it.

What's really freaking me out is that we are the last two people who should be attracted to one another. I'm off-limits. He's off-limits. It can't happen.

As I do my best to drift off to sleep, I repeat the mantra *"Nothing sexual will happen between my roommate and me,"* hoping that it will manifest into reality.

While slightly hoping it doesn't.

Chapter 16

Elio

$\mathcal{I}$t's Saturday morning, which means I'm currently lying on the couch, watching cartoons.

It's my guilty pleasure, and the only morning during the week that I allow myself to rest and have a slower start to the day. On most days, I opt for an early morning workout, reading a few chapters of a book, or cleaning up the apartment.

Mornings have always been my favorites, as I've always liked the idea of getting important tasks done before the day even started. It makes me feel accomplished and sets me up for the day.

I spoon a mouthful of Cinnamon Toast Crunch into my mouth, loving the sugar-filled cereal that I treat myself to once a week.

Another thing I've treated myself to recently? Stroking my cock last night with Jasmine's body invading my mind, her name a harsh breath off my lips.

It felt fucking wrong, but I couldn't help myself after seeing her perfect body last night when she stood up in my hot tub.

Coming to thoughts of her was the only thing that finally allowed me to sleep after days of restless sleep. She's been wreaking havoc in my head from the day she came here to sign the agreement in her little black sundress like the damn devil coming to torture me.

From the corner of my eye, I spot Jasmine walking right into the kitchen. She's wearing tiny shorts that barely cover her perky ass, showing off her short, yet toned legs. Her oversized shirt covers anything else I'd like to see, and I thank God for it.

Because seeing her like that is already making me adjust myself in my gym shorts.

"Morning, roomie," I call out, eyes fixed on the TV to tame my growing erection.

"Morning," she rasps.

"You sleep okay?" I ask, turning the volume down with the remote beside me.

Jasmine opens the fridge and pulls out yogurt and berries. "I slept fine," she says, but she's not convincing enough.

"I slept like crap too. Thanks for asking," I play along like she returned the kind gesture of asking how I slept last night.

She shoots me the finger while her other hand places blueberries into her bowl of yogurt.

A large smile dons my face. This fucking girl. No one else would ever dare do that to me.

She's feisty and I like it more than I know I should.

It's with a chuckle that she asks, "Do you want a yogurt parfait too?"

"Yes, please. See, those are manners and how one uses them."

"I have manners and know how to use them," she defends herself, making another bowl.

"Interesting because you haven't used them with me," I point out, sitting up on the couch.

"I do. I pay you rent when you don't need it, I help take care of the cats, I clean and cook breakfast for you," she points out, adding some granola to both bowls.

"It was you who insisted on paying me, remember?" I remind her because I never wanted her money. In fact, I planned on putting it in a separate account that I'll give back to her once she moves out.

As soon as the thought comes, a sour feeling churns in my gut at the idea of her moving out. It hasn't been long, but I've already grown accustomed to her being in my space.

Coming toward me on the couch, she passes me one of the bowls and I take it from her.

"That's because I indeed have manners. I was taught that I need to be responsible. So this is me being responsible," she says, sitting down a full seat away from me on the couch and crossing her legs underneath her.

She *was* raised very well. In the short time I've been around her, I've learned that she is responsible, smart, and a hard worker.

I dig into the yogurt, an appreciative moan getting stuck in my throat. "This is so good. Thank you. Is that maple syrup?"

"Yeah, I told you it's my favorite. I put it on pretty much anything, so that's why there's a drizzle of it on top," she explains, spooning some into her mouth.

My eyes are glued to the action, watching the way the silver slides between her full lips, her pink tongue poking out to lick the remaining yogurt off the spoon.

I cross my legs, knowing my erection is about to be on full display because my mind is now envisioning her doing that to something else.

Needing to divert my thoughts, I say, "Okay, so you do all those things for me, for the deal. But why aren't you warm toward me in moments like this?"

She folds her lips together, something I've noticed she does when she's hesitating to say something. "We can't be friends, okay?"

"Why the hell not?" I throw back, my face screwing up from confusion.

"We just can't," she mumbles, not at all believing her own words.

I want to pry, but seeing that it's a lost cause, I try something else. "Give me the day."

Her face scrunches up in confusion. "Huh?"

Setting my bowl on the coffee table, I look at her intently so she knows I'm serious. "Do something with me today. Let me prove that we can be friends and nothing bad will happen. We do have to live together for the year, so we may as well try to enjoy it if we can."

"And I should do this because?"

"Because you know that deep down you want to stop pretending like you hate me. It's probably exhausting. As much as I enjoy your fiery comebacks and don't want them to be gone entirely, let's do a trial today to see if we could get along. Make things less stressful for you?" I offer, knowing it's going to get to her. She already has so much going on, pretending to hate me is only adding to the weight on her shoulders.

Mocha eyes stare at mine for what feels like a lifetime, neither of us backing down. I love that she's not intimidated, never once breaking eye contact.

Finally, she sighs. "Fine. But I'm only doing this because if you're going to help me with my business, then I need to trust you."

"Let's get to know each other then," I propose, nodding toward the TV. "Do you like cartoons?"

She scrunches her lips to the side, shaking her head. "No, I don't like TV. I actually never watch it."

I put a hand over my heart, feigning offense. "Seriously? It's my guilty pleasure."

"I find it interesting that a grown man, who's a hockey legend and all that, enjoys watching cartoons made for kids."

A devilish smile curls on my lips. "So you think I'm a legend?"

She groans at that, putting a hand over her face. "No, I mean that's what it says online. But I've never seen you play."

I need to show her a highlight video one day, along with bringing her to the rink so she can see the skills I still possess.

"What would you expect me to watch?" I ask, rerouting back to her comment as I turn the TV off.

"You don't have to turn it off." There's an apology in her tone. "But I guess I expected sports networks, maybe some kind of mystery show?"

"I watch the sports network occasionally, but oftentimes, it aggravates me. So, it's mostly cartoons."

A half-smile dons her lips, and it makes me want to work harder to put a real smile on her face. I haven't seen one yet, except for the night I watched her dance at the gala. But I want it to be *me* who puts it there.

"Now tell me something about you. What do you like to do to relax on a weekend?" I ask, watching as she spoons the last bite of yogurt into her mouth.

"I like to read, obviously." Her cheeks turn pink as she fights off another smile. "I also like to play chess, bake, and do Pilates."

She likes chess too? I'm beginning to think God made this woman just for me.

"How long have you played chess for?" I ask, running a hand over my bearded jaw.

"Since I was ten," she answers, then stands and takes both of our empty bowls to the kitchen.

I follow right behind her, coming to her side at the sink and gently nudging her away. "Go sit down. You made breakfast. Let me clean."

Surprisingly, she doesn't argue with me, sliding out of the way. "Thanks," she grumbles, and it makes me laugh, knowing how damn hard it was for her to say thank you.

"Let's play once I'm done," I offer, jutting my chin in the direction of the chessboard.

"Not a chance." She crosses her arms over her chest.

"Why not?" I press, finishing off the dishes in the sink.

"Because since I quit doing competitions, it's something I like to do alone," she supplies.

I could accept her answer and move along, but I don't. "I think you're afraid I would destroy you, and that's your bullshit excuse."

Her mouth drops, her shoulders squaring as she attempts to stand up a little taller. "Fine, let me change and then we can play."

I want to tell her she looks fine, fucking fantastic if you ask me, but I don't say that. "If you're not back out here in five minutes, I'll conclude you're forfeiting, *dolcezza*."

"Yeah, okay," she mutters under her breath, turning to walk down the hallway to her room. I shamefully stare at her ass the entire time until Buttercup jumps onto the island.

"Hey, sweet girl," I coo, putting my hand out for her to nuzzle her head into. She does so, her soft orange fur rubbing into my palm. Blossom and Bubbles are chasing each other, zooming into the kitchen, making Buttercup jump down from the island to chase after her sisters.

I make my way to the chessboard set up on the table in front of the expansive floor-to-ceiling windows, sitting in one of the chairs.

Jasmine returns with her hair in a low ponytail, curls falling over her breasts that are covered by her white long-sleeved top, paired with gray tights. She looks fucking good, the tight fabric hugging her lean body while accentuating her curves.

She doesn't hesitate, sitting across from me with ease as she eyes up the board between us. "How long have you played for?" she asks, running a painted pink nail over the queen piece.

"Since college, actually. I was bored when everyone else was studying, and with the odd downtime from hockey, I wanted to challenge myself with something. I taught myself and found a club on campus to join."

"So what you're saying is that this is going to be like taking candy from a baby," she muses, a glint in her eyes.

"Not in the slightest." I smirk, loving that she's competitive. It fires me up, my brain ready to tackle and solve the challenges in front of me.

The chess game and her.

Hours later, we're still sitting at the chess table. We stopped once to use the washroom and have a quick lunch, which was leftover pasta from last night.

Our match has been back and forth, each of us eliminating key players off the board. Her queen and king are still intact, and one bishop. I only have my king left and two knights still in play.

I know the odds are in her favor to win as she has the queen in play, which in my opinion is the strongest piece on the board. Without it, the king is fucked.

We've mostly been quiet while we strategize our next moves, but we have been chatting here and there. We've shared stories from our childhoods, and Jasmine seemed to hang onto the stories I told about my sisters.

I know her dad mentioned that they never could have another child, and it seems like Jasmine shares that disappointment over not having a sibling. I cannot fathom my life without mine, so I could only imagine how hard it might have been to not have one at all.

I also learned that she doesn't like getting flowers. At one point, I teased her that if I win, I'd buy her some to soothe the pain of losing, but she informed me that while she admires their beauty, she doesn't like the idea of getting them because they end up dying.

She'd rather have a garden where she could tend and treat them properly.

It made my brain imagine things it did not need to imagine, like Jasmine kneeling, hands in the dirt as she planted flowers in *our* backyard.

But she's not mine. And neither is this game. She's destroying me.

With my two knights gone minutes later, it's now become a game of my king trying to avoid her queen. The similarities to our current situation make me stifle a laugh. The board reminds me of myself as I try my best to avoid the temptation of her, staying as far away from the queen as possible.

We move like that for a little while until I have nowhere to go, and she overtakes my king, ending the game.

"Yes!" she cheers, standing up from the chair and spinning happily while clapping her hands. It's fucking cute, and I hate that I love losing to her. I don't enjoy losing, ever. "Want to go again?" she asks, and I'm surprised by her wanting to spend more time with me.

I'd have taken her up on her offer, but we really should do

something other than sit at this table all day. "Rain check? My ego needs a break from that loss."

She twists her lips, looking unsatisfied with my response. "That's fine, I should get some content done today anyways."

"I've been meaning to get started on helping you with that, so it's perfect."

"Okay, let me get ready to film. It'll be about twenty minutes," she says, leaving the room.

As she walks away, all I can think is how much I've been enjoying today.

And how much I shouldn't be.

Chapter 17

Jasmine

*B*ack in my room, I pull out my notes app on my phone and filter through the list of ideas I have for content. I decide on cinnamon roll cookies, which are essentially sugar cookies made with cinnamon and topped with a cream cheese glaze.

I check my nails, ensuring my polish is perfect. Since viewers only see my hands in the videos, I like to make sure they look good. I take a few minutes to write down the steps on a sticky note, something I can follow and a list of the ingredients I will need.

While I do that, my mind can't help replaying this afternoon so far.

I couldn't tell Elio that the reason I don't want to get to know him is that I already am trying my best not to like him and suppress the attraction I've felt since the day we met. Getting to know him on a personal level will do nothing to help my efforts.

I caved and played chess with him because he had a good point. Part of me *was* tired of pretending that I didn't like him, and if he knew I was faking it, why bother anymore? I need to challenge myself by getting to know him while also controlling my feelings.

I can do that, right?

So far, he's not at all the man I tried to convince myself he was over the years. He's wickedly smart, attentive, funny, and easygoing. I've learned all of this from one day, so I'm partially afraid to see what's to come while also being partially excited to uncover more of the man behind what the tabloids say.

Entering the kitchen with my things, I nearly drop them to the floor as I take in the space in front of me. There's an expensive-looking camera propped up on a stand and some fancy lighting set up around the kitchen. There's even a new set of pastel orange baking utensils and bowls on the island counter.

"What is all of this?" I gesture to the kitchen with one hand.

Elio shrugs nonchalantly. "It's part of my end of the deal to help you with your business, no?"

"Yes, but I thought that was more internal business stuff, not buying new equipment and baking utensils." I marvel at the pastel orange mixer, not missing that it's one I've had my eyes on but could never afford.

"I'm going to need your social media passwords so that I can handle that stuff. For now, you need a new aesthetic if we're going to rebrand your page. That starts with a new and brighter space for one. The new camera will help with video quality, and the lights will help with clarity."

"What about the new baking tools?" I inquire, knowing this is exceeding what I can afford to pay him back.

"Also needed for your new branding. I got the hint that you liked the color orange, so I went and ordered this stuff last night. It arrived this morning, and I cleaned them and put everything away before you got up," he explains casually, as if the simple gesture isn't poking at my locked-up heart.

"Thank you. It'll take me a while to pay you back, so maybe we could set up a payment system."

"Absolutely not. You're not paying me anything for this." He scowls at me.

"But—" I try to protest, but he cuts me off.

"There's nothing to argue here. So I'll let you do your thing. Write your passwords down and I'll work on some stuff while you film," he instructs, passing me a sticky note and a pen.

I jot down the information for him, shyness creeping up my spine as I look back at him. "Could you, um, go in your room while I film? I don't usually let anyone watch me. I like to be alone when I work."

I know that's my excuse for a lot of things, that I like to do it alone, but it's all I've known.

I expect him to argue with me, but he doesn't. "Sure, I'll leave you to it." He raps his knuckles on the granite top, giving me a curt smile before heading down the hallway to his room.

I turn around and take in the kitchen, my eyes landing on a new coffee machine I haven't seen before. I was clearly half asleep this morning when I made breakfast because how did I not see it before?

Walking closer, I see that there's a mug that says '*book lover*' and a dispenser of maple syrup for my coffee. I let out a deep breath. I can't believe him. He easily spent thousands of dollars on all of this equipment and was observant enough to learn my favorite color to ensure it fit my personality when rebranding my channel.

To top it off, he bought me a coffee machine along with my favorite syrup flavor. The gestures are making me feel things I've never felt before. It's a fluttering in my stomach, warmth and excitement thrumming from my core to the rest of my body.

I send him a quick text before I begin.

Me

Thank you for everything, I really appreciate it. The coffee machine is too much, you didn't have to do that.

Elio

You like coffee and should be able to enjoy one in the morning at home. I can't return it, some lengthy return policy.

Me

Hmmm, I want to call bullshit, but I'm too happy to call you on it. Thanks again.

Elio

See, one day is all you needed and now you know your manners.

I groan, rolling my eyes at his message. He's such a smartass. And now I'm starting to see that he's much more than that.

Great.

I'm currently whipping the icing in a bowl, mixing the cream cheese, butter, heavy cream, and icing sugar, while the cookies cool. Once the consistency is where I want it to be, I let it sit while I pause the camera since there's nothing left to record until I top the cookies with the icing.

Bubbles patters into the kitchen, not stopping until she reaches me. She purrs while rubbing her body against my legs.

I bend down to pet her, feeling nothing but love for this cat. I never thought I would, but they are so damn cute and constantly curling up in my lap.

How could I not?

Elio clears his throat, making himself known. "The girls like you," he points out.

"I don't blame them." I tilt my head, looking at him with a playful smile.

The corners of Elio's lips tilt upward. I marvel at him, wondering what it would be like to press my lips against his, to feel his large, powerful body over mine...

I stand, abruptly ending the moment before my brain takes me to a place it should not go.

"Are you finished filming?" he questions, leaning his elbows on the island as he watches me wash my hands.

"Not yet. I need to put the icing on the cookies and then I'll be done."

Elio says nothing in response and sits on the bar stool while I bring the bowl full of icing over to the cookies that are cooling in front of him.

I turn the camera back on, not feeling as nervous to film in front of him as I was before. The hard work is done now, and it's not like I'm talking, so really, there's nothing to worry about.

I grab a spoon from the drawer and scoop up the icing. "Try it for me? I'm biased and think it's delicious, but I need another opinion."

Elio takes the spoon from me, careful not to let our hands brush. He brings the spoon to his lips, his tongue darting out to get the faintest taste. He hums deep in his chest before taking the spoon into his mouth, sucking and licking it clean.

Holy. Fuck.

Why did I think this was a good idea? Seeing Elio lick and suck on the spoon unlocked a new fantasy. Having Elio's mouth do *that* but on my body instead.

I feel something wetting my lips, so I quickly close them, realizing it's drool. I'm literally drooling over this man. This man is the last one I should be looking at like this.

I snap out of my lust-ridden haze, straightening as he hands me the spoon back.

"It's really good, Jasmine. You should be proud."

"Thanks." I smile shyly.

"And that drool was pretty impressive too."

It takes everything in me to keep my composure, holding on by a thread as I steel my features. If he caught me drooling, then I can give him a show too.

I take his spoon, not caring that my mouth will be on the same spot his tongue and lips were all over, and scoop up some of the icing. "I think I need another taste, to be sure," I tell him, ignoring his previous comment.

Putting the spoon upright, I lay my tongue flat and lick it from bottom to top, all while keeping eye contact with Elio. His eyes darken and zero in on my lips.

I slip the cool metal between my lips, the sugary icing hitting my tongue, making my eyes roll in pleasure. "Mmm," I hum, sucking the spoon clean before releasing it with a pop.

That causes Elio to look away, his eyes glued to the countertop instead of me. He takes a deep breath while I throw the spoon in the sink.

"*Dolcezza*, don't," he warns.

"Don't what?"

"Toy with me."

"Because you would never dare cross the line, right?" I remind him, even though it was me who brought this on.

Elio's gaze hardens, his jaw tight as he nods and pushes off his stool, walking away from me.

I'm left in the smoke of the fire between us as I return to my previous task. I top the cookies with the icing, but my previously happy mood is slightly soured. I only have myself to blame for the disappointment in my gut right now.

What did I think was going to happen? That I'd rile him up, like he did with me, and then what? He'd kiss me senseless?

We're newly friends. Roommates. That's it. And I'd do well to remember that, even if all I want is his lips on mine. It's only temporary, along with the flutters that he makes me feel every time he's around.

Temporary, that's it.

This situation. These feelings.

There's no point in ruining the important relationships in our lives over it when the resulting heartbreak and drama would be permanent.

Chapter 18

Jasmine

September came and went in a swoop of air, the summer wind leaving and the autumn chill entering early October. It's my favorite time of year, purely for all of the baking.

I've been busy with school, working on my channel with Elio (which is doing amazingly well), hanging out with Camille, and even with Elio at home, making the time fly by.

Hockey season starts this weekend, and Elio could not be more excited. We have a comfortable routine now. We make each other breakfast and dinner and hang out at night, either playing chess, a board game, or simply relaxing on the couch together.

We're finally friends, and it truly has lifted a weight off of my shoulders trying to avoid it.

There's a lightness between us now, an ease to be living in the same space. But there's also a palpable tension, at least that I feel on my end, since the icing incident.

It grows in the air every time we see each other looking somewhat indecent. Him with his shirt off or when my shorts are a little too short. When our gazes linger a little too long.

Our bodies have not once physically touched each other,

which only makes me that much more curious about what it would feel like if they did.

Would there be a spark like the day we shook hands? Would my skin warm and my heart flutter as they do in my books?

Those are the kind of thoughts I've been trying to ignore for the past few weeks. To do so, I've been trying to focus on the joy of the new season ahead.

Once I'm doing being sick that is.

I woke up early this morning with my head pounding, my body full of aches, and my stomach revolting against me. I dashed to my bathroom as soon as I woke up, where I threw up all the food I ate yesterday.

Elio had an early morning meeting today, and I thanked God he hasn't had to hear nor witness me in this state. I meant to text him that I wouldn't be in class today, but I fell back asleep before I could.

My phone ringing wakes me up hours later, the sound not helping with the pounding in my head. I blindly reach for my phone, cracking one eye open enough to answer the call.

"Hello?" I answer, my own voice groggy and unknown to myself.

"What's wrong? Where were you?" Elio's concerned voice pours through the speaker.

"In bed," I mumble, my mouth not wanting to open to talk. "I'm sick, so I didn't make it to class."

I already emailed my professor before I fell back asleep and have been internally stressing over it since. Camille hopefully took notes that I'll be able to borrow, but still. I hate missing the lecture.

He grumbles something under his breath that I can't decipher in this state of being, then he speaks more clearly. "Don't get out of bed. I'll be home soon."

I want to argue with him and ask how soon that is, but he hangs up before I can say anything else. I obey his order, only because I literally cannot get out of this bed.

I fall back asleep, only to be woken up by the warm touch of a hand on my forehead. I blink a couple of times, landing on dark green eyes I know all too well.

As I rub my eyes, Elio's face comes into view more clearly. His perfectly-tousled hair looks like he's been running his fingers through it, his jaw is locked tightly, eyes filled with worry.

It's the first time he's touched me, but it was so brief and I was half asleep for it.

Great.

"Hi," I whisper, my voice hoarse from sleep.

"Hi," he whispers back softly. "I know I'm not allowed in your room, but I needed to come check on you."

"I'm fine, don't worry about it," I say, willing more confidence into my voice. I sound and feel like shit. There's no use in hiding it.

He grimaces as if I slapped him. "Don't worry about it? You're my friend, and friends worry about each other."

Over the course of the last few weeks, I've really started to hate that word—friends. It's a constant reminder of all that we will ever be.

"How was class?" I ask, groggily sitting up.

He pulls out a stack of paper from behind him and places it in front of me. "See for yourself."

I take the papers, surprised to see that he actually took notes for me. He's never written anything down in the five weeks we've been at school. To top it off? He used my highlighter-coded system—green for new information, yellow for definitions, pink for random but possibly important things, and orange for items that go together.

I shake my head, utterly confused. "You never take notes."

"I did for you," his dark green eyes pierce mine with an unknown emotion glimmering in their depths.

My heart threatens to hammer out of my chest. It may not seem like your typical romantic gesture, but to a nerd like me? It's everything.

"Thank you for doing that," I tell him, doing my best to smile and have it reach my eyes, but it fails due to how awful I feel.

"What hurts?" he asks, his tone switching from soft to concerned.

"Everything," I huff. "My head is throbbing. My body aches all over. I feel warm and my stomach is upset."

His jaw tightens as his eyes run over my body, even though half of it is underneath my blanket. "Stay here, I'll make you some soup."

My instinct is to argue, to say that I can get myself better, but I find myself wanting someone to take care of me for once. "Okay," I say, lying back down and taking the comforter off because I'm sweating.

Elio's still seated on my bed, his eyes widening when they zero in on my lower half. I look down to see that I'm only in cheeky, satin panties. Fuck, I forgot.

I can barely focus on that because the motion sets off my stomach, causing me to bolt off the bed and stumble my way to the washroom. I fall to my knees, gripping the toilet rim as I throw up again.

Before I think about pulling my hair back, Elio's hands are there, holding it up for me while the other rubs my back soothingly. His touch makes my already warm body blaze even more.

Once I'm done, I lean back on my heels, putting my hands over my face in frustration and embarrassment. Elio lets go of my hair, the sink turning on moments after. He returns to me, prying my hand off my face, gently wiping my mouth and chin with a wet cloth.

I'm careful not to breathe with my mouth to avoid him smelling my sick breath. He stands, throws the cloth in the hamper, then crouches back down, his arms going under my shoulders, lifting me off the ground and into his arms like a baby.

"Elio, what are you doing?" I ask, murmuring against his chest and inhaling his spiced wood scent. I feel so small in his arms, loving the way I fit against him.

"Taking care of you. You nearly fell on your way in here. I'm not risking you falling on the way back," he explains, setting me down carefully on my bed.

"Take these and rest," he orders while placing two capsules in my hand and passing me a glass of water from my nightstand.

I swallow them, hoping they will get rid of everything that's wrong with me.

Elio leaves toward my bathroom once more, then comes back with a wet towel. He sits on my bedside again and gently places the cold towel on my sweaty forehead.

"I'm going to make you some soup. Call me if you need something. Don't get up."

"Thank you," is all I can muster because between the butterflies and my nausea, there's a probability that I'll throw up again.

He leaves my room, leaving my door slightly ajar. Bubbles, Buttercup, and Blossom saunter in, and jump up on the bed to cuddle up alongside my entire body. I hum in appreciation for their presence, stroking their furs as I slowly drift back to sleep.

I stir awake a few hours later. Rolling over, I check my phone and see that it's nearly four. I've been asleep since Elio got back from class, which was around eleven.

I check in with my body, noting that my fever seemed to have come down, the sweating replaced by chills. My head is no longer pounding, but my body still aches. My stomach is no longer nauseous, but rather ravenous now.

I push to sit up, throwing my legs over the side of my bed so that I can get up. I feel groggy, but I need to get up and move my body. I grab a throw blanket from my chair and wrap it around my body to warm me up. I then walk to my door and pull it open to see Elio sitting on the floor across from my door, his laptop on his lap.

His eyes flit up to mine, his jaw clenching when he takes me in. "I told you to call me if you need something." He stands up, snapping his laptop closed and putting it under his arm.

"I need to get up and move my body. I feel so lazy," I try to explain, rubbing at my tired eyes.

Those forest-green eyes soften as he frowns at me. "Resting when you're sick isn't lazy. You deserve rest, sick or not. Are you cold?"

"Y-yes," I chatter, wrapping the blanket even tighter around my body. "I came to get a bowl of the soup you made. I'm starving."

After putting his laptop on the floor, he steps toward me and picks me up into his arms once more. "I'll get you a bowl of soup while you lie back down."

I want to fight him on it so that he doesn't catch on to the fact that I like being in his arms, but I don't. I let him lay me back down gently, his fingers lingering on the sliver of bare skin showing on my shoulder.

I inhale sharply, and he notices, pulling his hand away immediately. He goes into my bathroom for whatever reason, then comes out with nothing in his hands seconds later. "I may have snuck in here to set up your towel heater. I put some towels on it now so that you can warm up."

Wait, what? Did he seriously buy me a towel heater?

"Why did you do that?" I ask, sounding puzzled.

"Because you were shivering that night you got out of the hot tub, and you mentioned that you're always cold. I don't want you to be cold," he explains, putting his hands in the pockets of his joggers.

My cheeks are warm despite my freezing body, a small smile on my lips at the fact that he remembered something like that and bought me a damn towel heater. He's more thoughtful than I ever could have imagined. It's messing with my head and heart.

"Stop being so nice. I've hit my quota of thanking you today," I tease.

He rolls his eyes at me while shaking his head. "Brat." He chuckles, then strolls out of my room.

He returns with a bowl of soup and crackers, along with a fresh glass of water. After placing them down on my nightstand, he sits at my bedside once again and passes me the bowl of soup.

"It's *pastina*, my nonna's recipe." He smiles at the mention of his grandma. "There's chicken, pasta, and vegetables in there."

I take a spoonful of it to my mouth, and the flavors burst on my tongue. "Mmm," I hum. "This is delicious."

Elio's eyes darken, his jaw ticking as he watches me. I don't shy away. Instead, I hold his gaze as I eat. Dipping a cracker every once in a while.

"Don't you have something better to do than watch me eat?"

"I want to make sure you don't get sick again," he states, making me regret being a smart-ass. Here he is being kind and thoughtful, and my brain is on autopilot, pushing him away.

I don't respond, finishing up the soup and crackers. I down

the glass of water too, feeling sated. "Thank you for making that. It was perfect."

"No problem. It was good to see you eat. Are you feeling any better?" he asks, a pinch between his brows.

"Yeah, a bit, but I think I need to sleep it off some more. My body still feels like crap," I huff, shifting so that I'm lying down once more.

"Sleep. I have practice tonight, but I'll text you to check in." He rises from my bed, taking my dirty dishes with him. He stares at me from my door, looking torn.

"I'll be fine, Elio. Go coach and kick ass or whatever it is that you even do." I try my best to muster up some enthusiasm.

He cracks a smile at that. "I'll try. Seriously, text me, okay?"

"I will. If you don't hear from me, it's probably because I'm sleeping."

He nods, then sets the dishes down on my side table and rushes to the bathroom. Coming out, he carries two towels with him, walking back over to me.

"Here, use these to warm up," he instructs, placing the warmed-up towels on me, one on my legs, the other on my upper half.

"Oh my God, this is amazing," I moan, loving how soft and warm the towels are.

"Good," he says all too quickly, taking the dishes and darting out of my room faster than he did before.

I start to wonder why, but sleep overtakes me once more, erasing it from my mind for the time being.

Chapter 19

Elio

"**McCoy**, are your skates dull or did you forget how to haul your ass?" I shout, taking out my frustration on him.

To his benefit, McCoy doesn't talk back, skating harder at the station he's in.

Why am I frustrated?

That would be because I'm stuck here while my roommate is at home, sick. I want to be there and take care of her, not here. It's driving me mad thinking about all the what-ifs.

Pulling out my phone, I send her a text, despite having left only an hour ago.

Me

How are you feeling?

Pocketing my phone, I try to focus on the practice in front of me instead of impatiently waiting for her response. I know she might be sleeping, but I still worry. It's unnerving how concerned I've been since I heard her weak voice over the phone.

It's as if a switch flipped inside of me, and I haven't been able to turn it off. Hell, I've gone as far as touching her, and it's been a testament to my control. Because now I know how soft her skin is, how good she feels in my arms.

Oh, and seeing her in her panties? Jesus. Christ.

My thoughts are cut short when Ned skates over to me. "What's going on, Mazzo? You seem agitated tonight," he observes, eyes focused on the guys doing their drills.

I release a breath, coming up with a bullshit excuse. "I have a lot of assignments and shit to do, that's all."

Ned levels me with a surprised look on his face. "You? Stressed about schoolwork? Since when?"

Shit, I should've known that would be a crap excuse. Ned knows how easy school is for me. "Yeah, I forgot what it's like to be in school. I'm still adjusting to coaching and being a student," I lie.

"If you ever need a break, let me know, kid." He claps me on the shoulder, making me chuckle. I'm far from a kid, but that's how he looks at me, like one of his own.

We have the boys skate a few more drills before calling it quits an hour later. I still haven't gotten a text from Jasmine, which makes my leg bounce nervously as I wait for Ned to finish up his speech in the locker room.

Once we dismiss them, I grab my bag from my office, then book it to my car. I race home, running a red light or two after checking that no one was coming the other way.

"Mr. Mazzo," Colin, my doorman, says, tipping his hat toward me.

"Have a good night, Colin," I say over my shoulder, not stopping in my trek to my apartment. I usually stop to talk to him about his wife and kids, but not now.

Minutes later, I'm barreling through my apartment door. I notice that everything looks the same, meaning she hasn't moved from her room, which is good, but also not, because it means she still feels like crap.

I head to her room and push her slightly open door wider. I see her curled on her side, her blanket wrapped tightly around her body. She's breathing peacefully, her curls covering parts of her face.

Even sick, she's the prettiest woman I've ever seen.

I ball my fist up at my side, fighting the urge to lean over and brush them out of her face. Just as I'm about to turn on my heel and leave, her sleepy voice fills the room.

"Elio?"

"Yeah?" I ask, swallowing harshly. I want so badly to lie in bed with her, feel her heartbeat against my own, ensuring that she's okay.

"What are you doing?" She yawns, propping up on her elbow. It's then that I notice she changed into a gray tank top, with no fucking bra on.

I do everything I can to keep my eyes on hers as I reply, "I was checking on you. Go back to sleep."

I'm about to leave when her raspy voice speaks up once more. "Wait."

I turn my head over my shoulder. "What do you need?"

She folds her lips together, her eyes bouncing between mine. "It's silly, but my dad would always lie with me when I was sick and read me a story. I've been alone all day and I..." she trails off.

"You want me to lie with you?" My words are clipped, afraid to show her how much I wish she meant them in a different way.

"Oh, God," she lies back, throwing her hands over her face. "Forget I said anything. This flu is making me delusional."

Seeing her so embarrassed has me moving before I can think it through, dipping onto the mattress.

She peeks at me through her hands at the feel of my weight on the bed. "You don't have to. I know it's probably weird for you."

It's not weird for me in the way she's thinking. It's weird because I want to touch and kiss her. To say to hell with that line we can't cross.

But I'm finding myself caring less about the line these days. After seeing her like this, and the urge I feel to take care of her, it's made me realize how deeply I long for this woman.

It goes beyond how any "friend" should feel.

I lie beside her, careful not to let our arms brush against one another. "Pass me your book. Let me read to you."

"Not a chance." She chuckles, the sound like a breath of fresh air after worrying about her all day. "Tell me about practice, and I'm sure I'll be able to fall asleep."

"Give me the book, Jasmine," I demand, motioning for her to give it to me.

She surprises me by rolling over to her nightstand and grabbing the book that is on top of it.

I take it from her and open it up to where the bookmark is. "Ready? You're tucked in and cozy?"

She rolls her eyes. "Just read the damn thing so I can fall back asleep."

I begin reading in a soft voice. The male character is a hockey player, and he's currently about to smash his girlfriend's ex into the boards for being an asshole to her.

I find myself interested in the plot, wanting to know more. I also find it interesting that she's reading a hockey romance novel, but I'm not going to tease her about it right now.

Jasmine's breathing eventually turns soft and shallow, so I stop. Turning to look at her, I see that she's fallen asleep. I want so badly to press my lips to her forehead, knowing damn well that I can't.

The feeling confuses me, as I've never wanted to care for a woman this way. Not until *her.*

Ignoring it, I get up and take the book with me to my room. I spend the rest of the night reading, memorizing her tabbed pages until the early morning, finishing it around 3:00 a.m.

I was intrigued by the spicy scenes in particular, wondering if that's the kind of thing Jasmine is into.

Obedient, rough, and dirty.

Because if so? She might be my perfect woman.

Chapter 20

Jasmine

I'm currently studying on the couch, the cats lounging around the living room with me. They miss Elio. That much is obvious. They've been less playful since he left yesterday morning for an away game the team has this weekend.

There's a knock at the door, so I get up to check who it is through the peephole. When I see Colin's familiar face, I swing the door open.

"Colin, what are you doing up here?" I ask, confused by his presence. "Can I get you a coffee or tea?"

"No, thank you, Jasmine, but it's sweet of you to offer. I was only dropping off a delivery for you." He smiles, handing me a manila package.

"Oh, I didn't order anything. It must be for Elio."

"It has your name on it." He raises his brow, smiling before tipping his hat and heading back to the elevator.

"Thank you. Have a good night," I call out to him, and he says the same.

Back in the apartment, I sit on the couch, tearing into the package. I pull out a book and realize it's the second one in the hockey series I've been reading, the one Elio read to me when I got sick two weeks ago.

There's a note between the pages, so I pull it out and read it.

You said you don't like receiving flowers, so I thought a book would be a good replacement to put a smile on your face

– Your roomie.

My hand goes over my chest, feeling my heart wanting to break free with the way it's pounding against it. I wish I didn't feel something over this gesture, like I did for all the other things he's done for me, but I can't stop it.

He listens to me and does things for me that no one else has. These are specific, curated, and special to *me*.

Before I can go down a rabbit hole of sorting out my feelings for him, Aurora's face lights up on my phone, right on time for her incoming daily call.

"Jasmine, I cannot wait to see your face! I miss you," Aurora whines through the screen, pouting at me.

"I know. I miss you more, Ro. Only two more weeks."

"I have a game to play and then I can crush you with the world's tightest hug."

I smile, feeling much better than I did a few days ago. "I can't wait to watch you play at that kind of level. I'm so proud of you!"

"Thank you." She blushes, a wide smile on her lips. "Then we're going to the Halloween party, right?"

"Yeah, it's at Beers n Cheers. I'm excited. My costume this year is going to be hilarious." I smirk devilishly.

"I bet. You always do something witty yet cute. Cam and I are being basic, but I'm keeping it a secret," she says, pretending to zip her lips and lock them.

"What are you two up to this weekend?" I ask.

"We're going to my aunt's house for dinner tonight, then

tomorrow we're having a beach day, just the two of us." She brightens like a girl in love, and it makes me happy to see it. I never thought Aurora would settle down this early in life, but she did. "How about you?"

"You guys are so cute, it's almost gross." I snicker. "I'm cat-sitting for the weekend since Elio is away for their first game, but Camille and I are going out tonight. We both need to dance some steam off from midterms."

Aurora waggles her brows at me suggestively. "Oh, Elio, I still can't believe he read to you and you didn't jump his bones."

"Listen, it's not like that. We're roommates who help each other out, okay?" I defend, doing my best to sound serious. I opt not to tell her about the book he sent me because I know it'll only weaken my argument.

"You could help each other out with a few orgasms," she quips.

"Oh, my God, Aurora! Not going to happen. He's older, experienced, and will not want to walk me through everything I need to be walked through."

"Minnie, you have more vibrators than the average person and have watched plenty of porn. I'm sure you don't need that much of a walkthrough. Plus, a lot of guys find teaching girls what they like hot. I know *I* thought it was hot when I taught Cam what I liked," she muses.

I mull it over, knowing she's right. "That may be true, but it doesn't change the fact that we're off-limits to each other. My dad told both of us to stay away."

"Is your father the one living your life?" she questions.

"My family is important to me. I can't let them down," I explain, knowing she's right, but so am I.

"Why is it okay to let yourself down, Minnie? If you really think he's not worth it, then fine, don't risk it. But from what you've told me about your chemistry, all the things you have in common, and the gestures he's made for you, I think it would be insanely stupid not to give it a try."

I nod in agreement, knowing every word she's said is true, ones I've already thought about. My voice squeaks with my next words, voicing my biggest fear. "I don't even know what to do. I have zero experience with guys. What if he doesn't want me, Ro?"

Aurora gives me an understanding look. "That must be scary, I will admit. But I will also ask you this. What do you want to remember at the end of your life? That you played it safe, or that you took chances and told fear to fuck off?"

I groan, flopping back on the couch. "I want to tell fear to fuck off."

"Damn right, you do," she agrees. "Elio is one hundred percent into you. I think he was from the day he invited you to live with him. He seems like a really private guy, so him letting you in his space is huge. Not to mention him being such a sweetheart when you were sick."

"He was being a nice human, that's all," I deflect, trying not to get wrapped up in the fantasy she's painting so well.

"Remember when I had those really bad cramps and Cam came to take care of me? I wondered the same thing, but it's different. Not just anyone will do what they did for us."

A knock comes at the door. Thank God. "I think Camille's here to bring me up to her place to get ready. I'll text you later. Love you, bye."

She tells me she loves me and to have fun, but be safe. Minutes later, I'm pulling open the door, and Camille bursts with joy as she squeals my name. "Jasmine! Let's go, time to get you ready."

"Yeah, yeah. Let me tell the girls bye and make sure their bowls are filled."

"Girls?" Camille questions, an eyebrow perched.

Oh God, I called them what Elio does. "It's what Elio calls them. It rubbed off on me, okay?"

"I'm sure they will miss their mom very much, but we have preparing to do."

I ignore her comment about calling me their mom because part of me likes it. They've grown on me. I don't even want to think about how much I'll miss them once I eventually move out. I might even miss their dad too.

Back up in Camille's apartment, there are outfits strung across the couch, makeup set up on the coffee table, and a mirror that was put in the living room for the occasion.

"What is all of this?" I ask, running my hand over a tulle pink dress.

"These are our outfit choices for tonight. I know you like to get dressed up, so that's why my wardrobe is all over my couch."

We blast old pop music, with a wine glass in our hands, while we get ready for the night. This is honestly the best part of going out, getting ready with your bestie.

I settle on dark skinny jeans, paired with a black corset-style bodysuit and black heels. I feel really good in them. From the way the jeans hug me perfectly, to the way the corset accentuates my cleavage, and the heels give me an extra boost of confidence.

I leave my face bare of makeup, minus some nude lipstick. My curls are loose and free, trailing above my breasts.

Camille has smokey eyes with a pink lip and her hair pin-straight. She's wearing a lilac cropped blazer, with a cropped white tube top underneath, paired with a matching lilac

miniskirt that molds her body and white boots that hit her knees.

She looks classy, a bit Parisian.

"Every guy in the club tonight is going to be looking at you," Camille purrs, dabbing some lip gloss on her lips.

"Next to you? Not a chance." I shake my head while she waves me off. "How about you? Are you going to dance with anyone?"

Camille pauses, looking at her fingernails, then back at me. "No. I want to dance and have fun. I sometimes freak out if a guy comes up behind me without telling me first."

The reminder of what happened to her makes my blood boil. I wish I could give those assholes a slap across the face or a knee to the balls for ever daring to hurt my friend.

"I'll be on the lookout too. Are you sure you want to go?" I ask, not wanting this night to go poorly for her.

"I need this outlet, and I can't let those men take away my present and future. Yes, I get shaken up easily, but I need to live. I can't hide from it," she explains, her voice sturdy and strong.

"You do know it's going to be packed, right?"

The club we're going to, Champagne Noir, is known to be the spot on Saturday nights. It's also athlete night, meaning you get a free drink if you have proof of being an athlete at RLU.

"I'll be okay. I want to have fun with my best friend." She squeezes my shoulders, and I follow her out the door and into the elevator. We bid Colin a good night before heading into her blacked-out SUV. It screams safety and privacy, both of which I am here for.

Minutes later, we're walking into the club, the neon lights flickering throughout the space.

Everything else is black and gold, hence the name of the

club. The bar is gold, with black stools, and gold table tops and black chairs fill the space. In the middle is the dance floor, which is made of black glass and gold glitter.

The music is flowing, a remix of popular songs that I love to dance to. We immediately go to the dance floor, joining the crowd that's already there as we move our bodies to the beat. We spend what feels like an hour dancing.

Eventually, I tell Camille I'll go and get us some water. While catching my breath, I order two glasses from the bar. I turn to watch Camille when I see it happen from afar.

A guy comes up from behind her and wraps his arms around her waist. Camille freezes, her eyes going wide, her body stilling. I try to push my way through the crowd, but I can't get there fast enough to prevent him from touching her at all.

As I get closer to her, I see that she's shoving him away.

"No, thank you," she tells him, but he doesn't seem to care.

He starts to move back in on her, but before he can get closer, a tattooed arm pulls him back forcefully. One I recognize from the gala last year.

Ryker.

"No means fucking no," Ryker grits out, shoving the guy back. "If I see you near her again, you better fucking run. 'Cause if I catch you, it won't be good." His chest heaves up and down, his tall stature, tattoos, and shoulder-length hair making him that much more intense.

The guy scurries away, and I take a step toward Camille.

"Camille, are you okay?" I whisper, noting the eyes on us.

She nods, but it's unconvincing.

"Let me take you home," I urge, but Ryker steps forward, crowding her body with his.

"I got her. You can go." The protective tone in his voice gives me chills.

I love moments like these in books, and to see it play out in real life has me rooting for them already.

Camille's lips part in what looks like shock, her eyes bouncing between Ryker and me.

"I'll be okay. I want to get some fresh air," she says.

"I'll go with you," Ryker states.

I look at Camille, who's staring at Ryker with curiosity.

"Okay," she breathes.

Ryker leans in toward Camille's ear, where he whispers something. She nods, and then he pulls her into his chest. The way he's cradling her makes it so that no one can touch her as he moves them toward the front door.

I know bits and pieces about Ryker from Aurora, so I know she'll be safe with him. Besides, that look in her eyes tells me there might be more there than I'm aware of.

I attempt to find an open chair to relax, when I hear my name being shouted over the beat of music.

"Jay Bay Bay!"

Theo.

I groan, muttering to myself how I'm going to hurt him for yelling that in the goddamn club. His large arms wrap me up in a hug, spinning me around once before setting me back on my feet.

"Who are you here with?" he asks over the music.

"Camille," I shout into his ear.

"Where is Millie Moo?"

"She's in the washroom," I lie. "Who are you here with?"

"Some guys from the team. Want to come sit and talk for a bit?" he asks, and when I nod in agreement, he walks us over to the booth where all of his friends are sitting.

He introduces me to everyone, and they're all kind.

Once we're sitting side by side, he pulls up his social media account and says, "Your dad's team won tonight. Isaiah posted a funny video of them. I need to show you."

When the video comes into view, I see that the entire team is at a bar. The focus of the video is on Isaiah and another player, who are up on stage doing karaoke, but my eyes latch on Elio in the background. He's leaning against the bar top, a bunch of girls surrounding him.

My stomach does somersaults, then abruptly falls to my ass.

What the hell is happening to me?

I've never had this feeling before, one where it's sinking into every crevice of my body, trying to inch its way out of my skin. I ask to watch it again, pretending that I thought it was funny when really I wanted to watch him again.

It hurts just as much the second time, watching him smile at the girls around him. Truthfully, I have no right to feel the way I am. We're roommates. He could have been sleeping around this entire time for all I know, but to see the possibility of it with my own eyes stings.

My throat clogs with emotion, but I tamp it down, remembering who I am and where I'm at. The only thing I want to do is forget what I saw and about the roommate I've been fantasizing about giving *all* of my firsts to.

You know what? I'm over that shit too. I think it's about time I get my first kiss over with. Why keep saving it when there's no one special to share it with anyways? I'll be waiting forever at this rate.

I need to find someone to go on a date with who will walk me to my door and kiss me. Plain and simple. Then it'll be over with.

Theo leaves the group to get some drinks, and as if the universe heard my internal dialogue, his friend Adam slides over to take his spot.

"How's it going?" He smiles, the action taking up his face. He's cute, a bit boyish-looking for my liking, but cute.

Filled with liquid courage, I ask him, "What's your number? I need to find my friend and leave, but I'd like to hang out with you sometime."

His mouth drops, his eyebrows rising. "Oh, uh, wow. I thought I'd have to beg for some of your attention, so this is great." He talks nervously, fiddling with his phone in his pocket.

The comment puts me off, but I ignore the feeling, wanting to push through and get this whole thing over with.

We exchange numbers, and then I stand. "Text me and we can plan something. It was nice to meet you." I force a smile, turning on my heel to search for Camille.

I don't have to look far because she enters the club again, but this time with no Ryker in sight. I thought he gave off protective vibes, but maybe I was wrong. I look at the window that showcases the downtown streets, and my previous assumption is proved wrong because there he is, his eyes pinned on her, a motorcycle helmet in his hand.

Camille stops in front of me, and I quickly turn my attention to her.

"You okay, Cami? We can go home."

"I'm good now, but yes, let's go," she agrees, looping her arm through mine.

We leave the club, stopping by Theo to say goodbye.

The ride home was quiet. Camille didn't want to talk about the incident again and said that Ryker helped her by taking her out of her head for a bit.

I smirk to myself, getting the same feeling about those two that I had for Aurora and Cameron.

Once I'm in bed, I pull out my phone, seeing that I have three texts from Elio.

Elio

What are you doing tonight?

Elio

How are the girls? The team won
tonight and your dad is forcing
me to go out to celebrate the
first win. Have I mentioned that
I hate going out?

That message makes me laugh spitefully because he looked like he was having fun.

Elio

Jasmine, is everything okay?

The last one came five minutes ago, and I debate replying. Knowing Elio, though, it's easier to text him back.

Me

The girls are good. I went
to the club with Camille.

Elio

Call me.

Me

I'm tired, I'll see you Monday.

I set my phone on the wireless charging pad, then roll over, attempting to sleep. It evades me all night, thoughts of Elio with those girls running laps in my mind.

I hate how jealous it makes me. More so, I hate how much it hurts me. Especially when I have no reason to be this upset. This is why I leave romance to books. Because in real life?

It fucking sucks.

Chapter 21

Elio

I don't know what the fuck happened tonight, but I don't like it. Jasmine's acting strangely and I don't know why.

The game was nearly impossible to focus on with her lingering at the back of my mind. I had texted her to see what she was doing, and no response.

Jasmine and I had finally gotten somewhere with our relationship, with her opening up a little and being nice to me, well, mostly. She still teases and taunts me, but I like that she does.

We're at the bar now and she still hasn't answered. I text her a third time and she finally replies, easing the tension in my chest. Until I read her message.

> Jasmine
>
> The girls are good. I went to the club with Camille.

What the fuck? She went to a club?

The possessiveness inside of me wants to know every detail I missed. I find myself not liking it one bit. The idea of her out, looking sexy as fuck with all those eyes on her and me not there to tell them to back the hell off.

Mine. My mind growls in protest, and this time I don't tell it to fuck off.

Because that's exactly what she feels like. She lives under my roof, takes care of my girls, we cook for each other, she sits next to me in class, and willingly spends her time at home with me now.

She feels like mine, even though I know she isn't.

I'm not sure when it happened, where the physical pull I felt toward her turned into something else.

I want all of her. She's on my mind more than I'd like. She's the first damn thing I think about in the morning and my last thought before I fall asleep. I've been worried about her since we left yesterday. I missed having breakfast with her this morning.

I like her, dammit. More than a roommate should. More than someone who works with her dad should.

She's fucking beautiful, selfless, and smart, with an even smarter mouth. How could I not like her?

She's everything.

I text her back to call me, telling Ned good night and leaving the bar. I don't know why I even came, but I felt pressured to by Ned. It was mostly okay. The players on the team who were old enough to drink were drunk, singing karaoke and having a good time, but I mostly sat there and watched, surrounded by annoying puck bunnies.

I used my best fake smile, the one I reserved for public settings with fans, signed some things, then sent them on their way. There was no chance in hell I'd be bringing them back to my hotel. Not when they weren't five-foot-four, with a smart mouth, a bold middle finger, and curls that I want to squeeze with my fist while I claim all of her firsts.

I don't know how we got to this point, but I'm not going to think twice about it. I'll feel guilty, especially because of my relationship with her father, but it's a price I'm willing to pay.

I receive another text telling me that she's going to bed and she'll see me Monday. I nearly throw my phone across the pavement in frustration. Why the hell is she pissed at me? I try to think of what happened but come up blank.

I'm not even there. What could I have done?

I don't text back. Instead, I call my pilot. I took it to get here, hating the idea of spending so many hours on a bus with the team.

My pilot answers on the first ring. "Mr. Mazzo, what can I do for you?"

"Get the plane ready. We're leaving as soon as possible," I tell him, nearly jogging down the street back to the hotel.

"On it, sir. See you shortly." He hangs up the call.

At the hotel, I quickly gather my things, then hail a cab to take me to the airport where my plane is waiting.

It's only Saturday. We're supposed to have another game here tomorrow night, a doubleheader, but I'm not waiting that long to see her. Not when I have no idea why she's so pissed at me. I need to get home and figure out what the hell happened.

Hockey used to be the most important thing to me, but now it's a hobby and a job. I'm not sure what it means for me that I'm leaving my job early to fly home and see her, but I'm sure it's something I'm not ready to face yet.

I text Ned a lie, telling him that there was a family emergency I needed to tend to. He quickly replies in understanding, sending me his best and to call him once I can.

We board the plane at ten and I make it back to our apartment around midnight. Pushing the front door open,

Buttercup and Blossom come dashing toward me. My knees bend, giving them a quick pet, noting that Bubbles is missing.

My footsteps carry me to Jasmine's room, but the door's shut. I'm tempted to open it and demand that she talk to me, but I fight the urge, knowing it'll only piss her off more. Frustrated, I go to my own room, but I leave the door open so that I can somewhat keep an eye on her.

Sleep evades me, my mind wandering and trying to figure out what happened. Around 6:00 a.m., I'm too restless to keep lying here, so I get up and shower. Then I go to the kitchen, deciding to make us breakfast for a change.

I start making oatmeal by putting the oats on the stovetop and grabbing fresh fruit from the fridge to chop. It's quiet, the only sound being the simmering of the oats. Until I hear Jasmine's door open.

My heart rate picks up, nervous as to what's going to happen. A first for me.

Jasmine peeks her head around the corner, fear etched on her face until she sees that it's me, then it changes to anger.

"Elio, what the hell are you doing here?" she breathes, letting out a sigh of relief.

"Did you think someone was in here? And you came out here with nothing in hand?" I question, jutting my chin toward her empty hands.

She ignores me, crossing her arms over her chest, her *braless* chest. "What are you doing here? I thought you didn't get back until tomorrow."

I take the oats off the stove and pour them into two bowls. "Yeah, well, I flew home early. You seemed mad at me, so I called my pilot and came home so we could talk."

Jasmine blinks at me once, twice.

"You have a private jet? And you used it to come home to talk to me?"

"Yeah, I did. Tell me why I pissed you off," I say to her while topping off our bowls with berries and a spoonful of peanut butter. Then I add a drizzle of maple syrup on hers.

"It's nothing. I'm stressed with school," she lies, taking the bowl I slide toward her. She furrows her brows at it, then begins to retreat without another word.

I'm hot on her heels, gently grabbing her free hand with mine, all too aware of how good it feels. "Don't lie to me. Midterms are over. What's really bugging you?"

She yanks her hand free. "Just leave me alone, please." Her voice is small, not the fiery girl I'm used to dealing with. It has me backing up, giving her the space she's asking for. It's fucking infuriating, knowing for certain that she's upset with me, but won't tell me why.

I take my bowl from the kitchen and head to the couch, where I sit and ponder what the fuck is going on. Not only about why she's mad at me, but why I no longer care about her being off-limits.

Why I'm about to say *fuck it* and take what's mine the first chance I get.

Chapter 22

Jasmine

*S*hutting my door behind me, I close my eyes, willing my stomach to stop fluttering.

Damn traitor.

So what if he flew home just to talk to me? It doesn't erase the fact that he was probably fucking some girl in the bathroom at the bar before that.

I sit on my bed, attempting to eat the oatmeal he made us, but my appetite is missing. Even if he did drizzle mine with maple syrup. If anything, it makes me feel even worse because why do that? Why be so damn thoughtful?

I wish he'd stop because the line we drew between us is starting to feel less clear than before.

My phone pings on my side table and I pick it up, seeing Adam's name on the screen. Oh, right. I was slightly tipsy and upset last night, nearly forgetting that I got Theo's friend's number to try and get all of this 'firsts' crap out of the way.

Adam

Hi, it's Adam from last night.
Would you like to get dinner
tonight at Riccardo's?

Me

Hi, Adam. Sure, what time?

Adam

I can pick you up at six,
send me your address.
Can't wait.

A pang of guilt hits me, feeling bad for using him to get over the hurt I felt last night.

People do it all the time, I tell myself. Plus, he really does seem nice, and he's cute. There's no harm in me going on a date, right? So I send him my address, telling him to wait for me in the lobby.

I stay holed up in my room all day, avoiding Elio. To his credit, he doesn't bang on my door or text me. He lets me be, except for the time he knocked and said lunch was on the other side of the door. I waited a few minutes, then opened the door, seeing a grilled cheese on a plate with a side salad.

I knew I was being childish, yet I couldn't help it. I'd never experienced this before, and I didn't know how to handle it. I hated the feeling of giving someone the power to hurt me, and it made me realize how close we've gotten and how bad that was.

We shouldn't have gotten to this point anyways. It's for the best if we take some time apart, so I can try to figure out how to get rid of these stupid feelings.

Around four, I start to get ready for my date, my feet dragging the entire time because the last thing I feel like doing is getting ready to go out for a second night in a row. It may also be the fact that I'm nervous, the way I always am for dates when I know in my gut it's not going to work out.

I pull my curls into a half-up, half-down style. I slip on a deep wine-colored dress that's tight-fitting, with a sweetheart neckline, skinny straps, and a slit that runs from the hemline at the knee to my upper thigh.

I pair it with black pumps that have a criss-cross strap around my ankle. I put on a matching red color for my lips, leaving the rest of my face bare. If he doesn't like my natural face, then that's too bad.

I'm nearly ready, throwing my things into a black clutch, when I get a text from Adam.

Adam

In the lobby, come down
whenever you're ready.

My entire body goes stiff, nausea in my gut. I really don't want to do this now that the time has come, but I can't cancel on him at the last second. It'll be fine. We can get to know each other, enjoy some good food, and then I'll get an Uber home.

Easy.

I open my door, squaring my shoulders while giving myself a mental pep talk as I walk down the hall.

In the living room, Elio's eyes are already on mine, like he was waiting. He must've heard my heels clacking on the floor. His inhale is sharp, his eyes roaming my body from head to toe as anguish begins to take over his face.

I look away, keeping my gaze toward the door. I'm nearly there when Elio speaks up, his voice cold yet laced with fury.

"Where are you going?"

"Out," is all I say, not looking directly at him as he stands from the couch, rounding it to come toward me.

He plants one hand on the door, the vein in his neck throbbing. "Not until you tell me where."

I scowl at him, finally meeting his gaze. "You don't own me. I'm not a prisoner. I'm your *roommate*, remember?"

His jaw works back and forth. "We're *friends*, remember? Tell me where, please. I'm going to worry all night if you don't," he admits, his anger on a tight leash.

I fold my lips together before standing taller in my heels. "I'm going on a date if you must know. Now move."

I take a step toward him, but he doesn't budge, making our bodies nearly touch. I can smell his cologne, the mix of spice and smoked wood. It threatens to crack my game face.

"With who? When did you even meet?" He throws his head back in disbelief, the motion giving me the motivation I need to go on this date.

"Is it that hard to believe that I was able to land one? God," I huff, a fake laugh tumbling after it. "We met last night. He's a friend of Theo's from the football team, and he's waiting in the lobby. Now, get out of the way, *please*." I bat my lashes at him, laying the sarcasm on thick.

His face screws up, his hand running through his hair in frustration. "No, that's not what I meant. I know how you feel about your firsts, so I'm surprised you're going out with someone you only met last night."

"Not that I need to explain it to you, but that's how you get to know people. You meet, go on a date, and then maybe he'll kiss me." I pause, noting the darkness in his eyes at what I said. "And maybe, just maybe I'll let him fuck me tonight. I'm feeling pretty bold. Who knows."

He pushes off the door, crowding me against the wall with his forearms resting above my head. "If you let him touch you, *dolcezza*, I promise he'll never play a game of football again. It'd be hard to do with broken bones."

"You won't touch him, like you're never going to touch me, right?" I challenge him, my voice shaky. I don't miss the way Elio always keeps his distance from me, careful not to brush or touch me since the day I moved in.

Except for when I was sick.

Our eyes meet in a fiery blaze, the intensity of it burning, making me want to tear my eyes away before we both get turned to smoke.

Elio sinks to his knees, keeping his eyes on me as he lifts my heel off the ground and onto his lap.

"What are you doing?" I breathe.

"Shh," he coos, looking down at my heel in his lap. His fingers lightly brush against my ankle, the contact making me shiver. Elio notices, smirking as he brings his fingers to the criss-cross straps, where one wasn't done up properly.

I watch him with bated breath, loving how he looks beneath me. I read about it all the time in my books, a man on his knees for a woman, and I have to agree.

The sight is powerful, equal to the lust that is coursing through my body.

He fixes the strap, then caresses my ankle. The motion sends a pulse right to my clit, and my lips part.

Elio's eyes flit back up to mine as his hand trails upward.

"You're the most beautiful thing to exist, you know that?" he tells me as his fingers dance across the smooth skin on my legs, trailing over my shin, behind my calf, then to my inner knee.

His words make me weak in the knees. They already wanted to buckle from the ache between my thighs, and the nerves in my belly are waiting to see what he does next.

But he doesn't do anything because my fucking phone rings

from inside my clutch. I tear my eyes away from his, putting my foot back on the floor. The trance has been broken.

I fish my phone out, seeing that it's Adam calling. I don't even spare Elio a second glance. I rush out the door, practically running to the elevator.

Once the doors shut, I release the biggest breath yet. I place a hand over my erratic heart, willing it to calm. That was the most intense thing I've experienced. I could feel the tension between us. It was a live, tangible thing.

I wanted to reach out and cut it by pressing my lips to his, but of course, I didn't do that. I'm still pissed off from last night. I could ask him what happened, but that would force me to admit that I care and I can't do that.

In the lobby, Adam perks up when he sees me. "Hi, Jasmine. Wow, you look beautiful." He beams.

"Thank you. You look pretty good yourself," I tell him honestly.

We walk toward the doors where I say good night to Colin, who eyes Adam a bit suspiciously before heading to the restaurant.

Our date is fine, not bad, but not great either. He's nice and very sweet. He talks about being an engineering major and a tight end on the football team. He also asks questions about me.

The conversation is light, but forced at times. We don't have great chemistry, despite how much he's trying to create it. To put it simply, there's no connection for me. No spark. No banter. I feel bad because he's a good guy, but he's not the one for me.

At the end of the night, he walks me to the front of my building, with his hands in his front pockets. "Thank you for letting me take you out. It was nice," he says, looking a bit shy.

"Thank you for dinner. It was really good." I smile at him because the food was pretty tasty.

"Can I kiss you? I know you haven't been kissed, so I feel

like I should ask," he babbles, talking faster than I can keep up with.

I'll admit, it's nice he asked me instead of leaning in, but I'm still not feeling it. My entire body shies away from his at the idea of his lips on mine.

"Adam, I'm really sorry. You're a great guy, but I think we should only be friends, okay?" I apologize to him, taking a step back for some distance.

"That's okay, Jasmine, really. Sometimes you don't get that vibe, and it's okay." He shrugs.

"I meant what I said. You're a really great guy. Please don't think it's you. Not to sound cliché, but it's me. I have so much going on that—"

"Jasmine, you don't need to explain yourself. I'm not offended because I get it. If I'm being honest, you're great too, but I didn't get that spark either. I wanted to kiss you to see if that would change things, that's all. So it's okay. Friends?" he says with a smile, opening his arms for a hug.

I step toward him, embrace him quickly, then step back. "Yeah, friends is good."

We say good night to one another, then I push my way through the lobby door, Colin's chipper face coming into view.

"Evening, Jasmine, where is the lad?" he asks, not afraid to be personal because in my time here, we've grown close.

"I sent him on his way," I tell him, my nerves beginning to ricochet in my body at the thought of what is going to happen upstairs once I see Elio. I left him in the heat of a moment to go on a date with another guy.

I'm sure he's not going to be exactly thrilled with me, but at the same time? Fuck him. He gets to go out with girls who he probably took back to his room, and I can't go on a respectable date?

"Ah, I see. Would that be why Mr. Mazzo was scowling when he came to get the food he ordered?" he ponders, one wrinkled finger going up to tap his chin.

Yeah, he's definitely mad. And you know what? *Good.* Let him be mad.

"It's none of my concern why he's upset," I say, trying my best to make my voice sound convincing.

Colin peers at me with his blue eyes, ages of wisdom in them. "Hmm. I hope you don't mind me saying this, but Mr. Mazzo has never looked as happy as he has until you moved in."

"Interesting," I whisper, not liking how his words are making my icy heart wonder things it shouldn't. "Have a good night, Colin."

"Have a good night, Jasmine." He tips his hat at me.

My ride up to the apartment is short, not long enough for me to overthink what to expect when I walk through the door.

Chapter 23

Jasmine

When I open the door, the lights are off, clouding the apartment in total darkness save for the light above the stove. Elio's sitting on the couch, an empty crystal glass in his hand on the armrest, facing the TV that's not on.

He doesn't look my way, his gruff voice breaking the silence. "How was it?"

"Fine. He was very nice, but we're going to be friends," I reply, already walking toward my room.

Before I get very far, his large hand wraps around my hip, halting my movement. His touch is searing, scorching my body through my dress. His fingers dig into my skin, the dress bunching as he does.

"Did he take what's mine?"

His words break me from my momentary lapse of awareness. I spin around to face him, our chests nearly touching. I look up at him, still shorter even in heels. "And what exactly would that be?"

He steps forward, causing me to take a few steps backward until my back hits the wall. He's like an animal stalking its prey.

I want to say the shiver running down my spine is from

the chill of the wall, but I think it has everything to do with Elio caging me in with his body, his scent surrounding me so much that I can barely think straight.

Elio brings his thumb up to my lips, making my heart cease to beat as he brushes the pad of his finger over them. "You. Your lips, your body, your mind, your heart." He trails a path down my chin and over my neck, causing a small gasp to escape my lips all while his eyes never leave mine. His thumb travels farther down to my collarbone and then lower, nearing the tops of my breasts.

"Is this okay?" he breathes.

"No." I surprise even myself with my answer, shoving at his chest.

He backs up instantly, a frown on his face. "What did I do, Jasmine?" He sounds defeated, and it's what makes me tell him the truth.

"I saw you in Isaiah's story, all those girls around you. It looked like you were enjoying yourself," I mutter, not liking how jealous I sound.

His eyes harden, his jaw set tightly as he leans back into me. "I was being nice. I signed some things and then they left. Next time, if something upsets you, talk to me, okay? That way we can figure it out together."

His solution sounds so simple, because it is. But in the heat of the moment when I was upset and confused, I wanted to push him away. I didn't want to admit I was hurt in the first place by seeming like a jealous girlfriend by confronting him about it.

"Okay. This is all so new and I shut down when I saw that. It triggered my insecurities," I admit, folding my lips together.

He takes a deep breath, closing his eyes. Releasing the breath, his eyes open, locking onto mine. "*Dolcezza*, no one else holds a fraction of my attention. Want to know why?"

"Why?" I breathe, my eyes trailing from his eyes to his lips, then back up.

He notices, his fists balling up at his sides for whatever reason. "Because you're all I see. It's infuriating. I'm usually so good at being in control of my mind, of every fucking thing in my life. But you? The way I want you so desperately, when I know I shouldn't? You haven't even fucking touched me and I'm done for because you've reached somewhere no one else has," he admits with a growl, his forehead dropping to mine as he points once to his heart and then to his forehead.

I suck in a breath at his proximity, at the knowledge that I could so easily tilt my head and press our lips together. But mostly, I can barely breathe because of his words, the way they're trying to wrap around my heart and take up residence there.

"How can I trust that you're not lying?"

He swallows, not moving his forehead away from mine. He takes my hand that's nearly shaking and places it over his heart. "Because I've never been this nervous yet desperate to taste someone's lips."

"You want them because no one else has had them," I argue, feeling his heart beat erratically under my palm.

"No, Jasmine. I want to kiss you because it's all I've thought about doing since you came to this apartment in that fucking dress. I want to kiss you because I admire your mind, your heart that's warming up to mine, and every fucking thing in between."

"What about my father?" I ask, trying to put up a wall between us.

His hands come up to the wall, one on either side of my head. "I'm willing to cross the line if you are."

My mouth gapes open, my pulse skittering at the prospect of doing exactly that.

"Do you trust me?" he rasps on a swallow.

I nod, knowing deep in my soul that I do. Maybe it's because of his gestures or our connection that's transcended the lust that was once there before.

"Words, *dolcezza*, I need words."

"Y-yes, I trust you," I stutter, nervous for what's about to come, yet eager.

"Good." He lifts his forehead off mine. Then, before I know what's happening, he's lifting me in the air, my legs instantly wrapping around his waist as he carries me to the couch. He sits down, with my legs straddling his thighs.

Holy shit, I'm straddling a man. And not any man, but Elio fucking Mazzo. I can feel his muscular thighs under mine, along with the rapid beating of my heart and the wet spot on my panties.

I rest my hands around his neck, feeling shy. "What are you doing?" I ask, wishing he would take the lead because I have no idea what to do.

"Letting you be in control." He stares at me intently, his forest-green eyes nearly black as his lips part. His hands are resting on my hips, squeezing me tighter to him.

"I don't know what to do," I murmur, tilting my head while my cheeks flush.

"What do you want to do?" he asks gently.

"I want to kiss you," I admit, my eyes on his lips.

"Then kiss me," he rasps.

I do as he says, leaning forward tentatively until our noses touch, our breaths mixing in the space between. My breath hitches in my throat and he swallows roughly.

I erase the last bit of distance between us, pressing my lips softly against his full ones. My entire body prickles at the contact, warmth flooding from my chest to my belly. He presses back, kissing me gently, letting me move my lips against his at my own pace.

Elio's hand comes up to cradle my jaw, titling my head, letting me deepen the kiss this way. A rush of pleasure courses throughout my body, making me moan into the kiss as I put one hand into his hair and tug, loving the way his hands are splayed around my back, his hands covering the span of it.

I have no idea if this is good for him, and the thought makes me pull back. "How was that for you? I have no idea what I'm doing," I pant, feeling embarrassed at the idea of being an awful kisser.

His hand comes up to cradle my face, and I lean into it. "How was it for me?" He chuckles, taking my hand from his neck and placing it on the hard length between his thighs.

I gasp at the feel of him hard beneath my touch, at knowing *I* did this to him. A wave of confidence pours through me at the fact.

"That's what happens when I get kissed by the prettiest fucking girl I've ever laid eyes on. That sum it up for you?"

I chuckle, realizing that I need to relax. "Kind of." I bite my lip, looking down at my hand on the thick, hard length under his sweats.

"What's wrong? Not what you expected?" he asks, a hint of defeat in his tone.

"No, it was more," I admit, blushing once more.

"Agreed. Did it feel like I *wanted* to kiss you?"

"Yes," I say without a doubt. I could feel how much he wanted me with his lips alone. I didn't think that was a thing, feeling people's intentions and emotions through their lips, but it is.

"Good, now I'm going to show you how it feels to be wanted and *claimed*." He crashes his lips to mine before I can respond, and I can instantly tell the difference.

His lips are rougher against mine, more demanding as he controls the pace. He kisses me like it's our last, our lips melding with an intensity that wasn't there moments ago. He nips at my bottom lip, then teases my lips with his tongue, seeking permission.

I give it to him, a moan trapped in my throat at the feel of his tongue on mine. He uses it expertly, not too much, not too sloppy. It's a craft, one he's well skilled at.

He has one hand in my hair and one on my hip, his fingers digging into my skin through my dress hard enough that I think there will be bruises tomorrow. I never understood why girls in books liked that, but I get it now. It's a sign that I was wanted, that I made someone come undone after testing their restraint.

I break the kiss, needing a moment to collect myself and the feelings that are hitting me for the first time. It all feels like too much, yet not enough. My body aches for more.

"Elio," I breathe shakily, resting my forehead against his.

"Do you get it now, *dolcezza*? How I wanted to kiss you and claim you at the same time? Because you're mine and always have been."

"I do," I half moan at his words, secretly loving this possessive side of him.

"Say it, tell me you're mine. I won't share you, Jasmine, not a fucking chance," he snaps, the words rough.

"I think you need to show me rather than tell me," I taunt him, needing more of him.

Desire blazes in his eyes, but he doesn't make a move. "I will, but not tonight. I want to take it slow with you."

"What if I don't want you to be gentle with me? Everyone else in my life is," I complain.

He leans forward and presses his lips to my forehead, letting them linger. The action makes the thread around my heart fray, threatening to loosen and open up to him.

"This isn't me denying you because I don't want to. Trust me, I want it more than anything. But today's been a lot and I want you to think about it before we do anything else, okay?"

I bring my hand up to his cheek and stroke his beard with my fingers. I don't know how he knew what I truly needed before I even came to the realization, but it only pulls that thread looser.

"Thank you," I whisper. Then I attempt to get off his lap, but he holds me firmly in place.

"Where do you think you're going?"

"To my room?"

"Just because we're not doing more doesn't mean I was done kissing you."

"Oh," I quip, a smile on my lips.

"Yeah, *oh*." He smiles back, the sight so beautiful it makes my chest ache.

I lean forward and press my lips to his once more, not nervous like I was at first, and not frantic like it was when he initiated it. Our kiss is slow this time, tender and sweet. His lips move against mine with precision, while I follow his lead, mimicking the way his lips move over mine.

He hasn't made me feel insecure about not knowing what I'm doing. He lets me be in control while guiding me the entire time. It makes me confident enough that I rock my hips against his.

A cry of pleasure crawls up my throat, but it's muffled by our lips on one another's. He groans into my mouth, the vibration thrumming right to my clit.

"I've thought about it, and I want you," I plead, while he kisses my neck, making me shiver. It's sensitive and the feeling of his scruff mixed with the softness of his lips there has my pulse ramping up.

"Let's make a deal," he muses, leaning back as his hand begins to trail up my thigh.

"What's that?" I rock against him, loving the feel of him hard beneath me, but loving the guttural groan he lets out when I do even more.

"If I slide my hand between your thighs and your cunt's dripping for me, I'll take care of it. If not, we go to bed."

I agree all too easily, knowing he'll be more than pleased when he makes his way there. "Sounds like an easy deal to take."

"We'll see," he gruffs, lifting my hips up off his lap where he grabs where the slit of my dress is, and tears it.

"Asshole, this was my favorite dress!" I slap my palm across his chest playfully.

"I'll buy you a hundred more if you want, but it's in my way," he grumbles, setting my back down on the couch, laying me out for him.

I suddenly get nervous, my knees knocking together.

"We can stop, *dolcezza*," he says softly as his body hovers over mine.

"I-I want you," I stutter. "But I'm nervous. This is all new."

His lips press against my cheek and then the other. "Let's go to bed, c'mon."

"I watched you," I speak up, catching him off guard, hoping it'll convince him to stay. He eyes me speculatively, so I continue. "That night out here when you were jacking off with my name on your lips."

"And?" he prompts, not a hint of embarrassment at being caught.

"I touched myself watching. I've never had an orgasm like

that before," I admit. "Your cock looked so big, it's kind of scary, to be honest."

He laughs at that, his eyes dark once again. "For one, I love that you touched yourself watching me. It's so fucking sexy. Makes me want to say to hell with my manners and treat you like the brat that you are."

My hips arch at his words, seeking friction. He notices and wraps one of my legs around his waist, allowing me to rock against his thigh.

"Two, I won't do anything you don't want me to do. When it's time, I'll prepare you properly, make sure you're dripping for me. I'll stretch you first with my fingers, and when I feel like there's enough room, I'll slowly push my cock into you."

I moan loudly, rocking my hips against his thigh in response.

"Not right now, though. Tonight, I want to get you off. If you're sure."

"I am. Touch me, please," I beg unashamedly.

Elio places his hand on the leg that's wrapped around his waist, skating his fingers down from my knee to my inner thigh. My breath catches when the tips of his fingers hit the string of my panties.

"You tell me to stop, and I will, okay?" he says, keeping his eyes on mine.

"Keep going," I urge him, needing to feel his hands on me.

Elio slips a single finger under the material, running it down my slit and inside my center, where I can feel him spread my wetness. I'm soaked.

A grunt erupts from his chest as he takes his finger out, then brings it up to his lips where he sucks it into his mouth. "Fucking delicious," he murmurs appreciatively.

Wow. I have no words for once. They all left my brain.

"Your cunt is soaked. Is that for me, *dolcezza?*" His voice is husky, unlike the smooth one I'm used to.

"I was on a date...maybe it was for him," I taunt him, loving the way his eyes flare with irritation. If there's one thing I enjoy doing, it's giving him a hard time.

"I'm trying to be a gentleman about this because that's what you deserve." He blows out a breath, closing his eyes. When they reopen, there's a fire in them. "But I think I might give you what you want."

I nod fervently, not wanting him to treat me like a porcelain doll, but rather like I'm his, willing to bend and form to his will. I didn't expect myself to crave that with him, but I do. I don't think I'd trust anyone else to do it.

He wraps an arm under my waist, hauling me up so he can place me ass-up over his lap as he sits on the couch. Elio tugs at the scraps of my dress, pushing them over my hips, leaving my ass exposed on his lap. I squirm on his lap, needing him to do something to ease the ache that's intensified between my thighs.

Before I can ask for something, anything, he delivers a smack to my ass, the sound echoing in the living room. I yelp at the sting, which then unfurls into pleasure.

What is wrong with me? Why do I like this?

He delivers another on the opposite cheek, his other hand yanking on my hair, lifting my head up so that he can whisper in my ear. "This is what happens when you're a brat. You'll get spanked until you learn your lesson. Got it?"

"And what's my lesson?" I ask, my breath shaking.

"To never mention another man's name when I'm the reason you're soaking wet," he says as his palm lands on my cheek once more, a whimper leaving my lips.

"Then take what's yours. Show me why I need you and not my vibrators."

He chuckles darkly. "Oh, we'll be using those in the future. They're allies, not enemies. But I'm going to show you how much you need me. Don't you worry."

He lets go of my hair and uses that hand to rip my panties off, then tosses them to the ground. Before I can yell at him for that, he slides a finger along my slit, making me buck against it.

He delivers another smack to my ass as he inserts his finger inside me, making me tense up around it. "Relax for me, *dolcezza*," he orders, pressing his lips to my ass where there are sure to be red marks.

I do, allowing him to put another finger inside, stretching me out more than I ever have with my small fingers. "Elio," I moan, not recognizing my voice.

He palms my ass while thrusting his fingers inside me, not leisurely. It's hard and deep, just like I need it. His ability to read my body and what I need amazes me. I convulse around his fingers, rocking my hips against them, my breasts rubbing against the couch, giving me the extra friction I need.

"Look at daddy's girl, getting punished for that smart mouth I can't wait to fuck one day," he growls, increasing his efforts.

Warmth begins to spread from my head to my toes, setting my body on fire. My core tightens when his fingers move back and forth instead of up and down, creating a friction I never knew I needed as I chase my orgasm.

I've had orgasms before. I know my telltale signs, but this feels different. More intense.

And it's all because of *him*.

He's attentive and precise, and the lust in his eyes tells me he's enjoying this as much as me. And that fact ramps up the tightening in my core. Elio Mazzo is fucking *me* with his fingers, and there's nothing hotter than that at this moment.

"You're close," he husks, landing another smack on my ass. "Be good and come all over my lap."

With a few more thrusts of his fingers and slaps on my ass, I do exactly that as I yell out his name over and over again. The release is unlike anything I've ever felt before, lasting longer than any previous orgasm I've had. The euphoria radiates throughout my entire body like fireworks, a feeling so intense I don't know how I'll ever accept anything less than this.

Once my orgasm subsides, I try to sit up, but all he does is flip me over onto my back. Before I can ask what he's doing, his head is between my thighs and what a sight it is.

Elio wastes no time, licking my slit from top to bottom, making a moan of approval as he wraps his arm around my hips, pulling me flush to him. My fingers find his hair, tightening when he flicks my clit.

"Suck on it," I mumble, surprising myself.

His head lifts up, my arousal on his beard. "What was that?"

"In my books, he usually sucks on her clit. But if you don't like it, you don't have to—"

"Like it? *Dolcezza*, I love it. You taste fucking phenomenal. Your cunt is perfect. Now let me take care of it because I enjoy it. Not because I feel obligated to, got it?" he clarifies. Once I nod, he adds, "And I was getting to that, but feel free to boss me around. I like it."

I laugh, feeling relieved that he can make me feel cherished, safe, and desired all at the same time. I didn't think I would be as comfortable as I am.

My laugh is cut short as he sucks on my clit, *hard*. My back arches, my hips rising, but he doesn't let up. He grips my waist harder, keeping me flush to him as he sucks my clit, then gives me long, languid strokes before teasing my entrance.

He lifts his mouth for a brief second, his nose inhaling deeply, nudging against my slit before replacing it with his tongue.

I didn't think I could feel the beginning of another orgasm, but I do. It's rapid, a warm churning in my gut that spreads to my entire body, making it feel as if it's on fire from his mouth.

His fingers enter me once more, and he fucks me with them rapidly as he traces my clit with his tongue. I yank on his hair, feeling a swirl of pleasure in my gut.

"Elio," I whimper, needing him to finish me off.

"You'll come when I'm done eating. Don't interrupt me," he snaps, returning to my pussy where he spends what feels like forever torturing me. He brings me close to the edge, only to pull back and ease up.

I'm dripping. I can feel a pool of wetness below my ass. In my books, I always assumed it was a fictional thing, where the guy loves going down on a woman.

Elio proved that theory wrong by the way his hands are tight on my body, making sure my pussy stays pressed up to his face, and the way he grunts and moans as he devours me with his tongue.

"It's yours," I whine, hoping this will grant me the orgasm I'm desperately seeking.

"Be more specific," he drawls, kissing my inner thighs.

"Me, my pussy. It's all yours to do with whatever you please. You've proven it."

"Damn right, it is," he growls, diving back into my pussy, sucking hard on my clit while his fingers pound into me in a brutal rhythm.

It sets me off, my orgasm ripping through my body violently as I scream his name over and over again. He doesn't let up, extending the bliss as he fucks me with his tongue.

Once my body relaxes, he sits up on his knees, staring at me with adoration. Reaching for my hands, he pulls me up and into his arms.

Kissing the side of my head, he whispers, "You did so good, *dolcezza*. Are you okay?"

"Never better," I tell him, kissing him on the lips, tasting myself and not minding one bit.

"I wasn't too rough?"

"I clearly enjoyed it, wouldn't you say?"

He smirks. "Yeah, you did."

I look down between us at the straining erection under his sweats. "Looks like you did too."

He picks me up, carrying me like a baby as he walks with me in his arms. "Another night. I already went too far with you."

"What do you mean?" I stroke his chest, his muscles twitching under my touch.

He walks into his room, where he sets me on his bed and then goes into the bathroom. He returns with a warm cloth, reminding me of how he did this a few weeks ago when I was sick, and now it's for a much different reason. He cleans me up gently, then tosses it in the hamper.

"I meant that I only planned to kiss you tonight. I don't want you to feel pressured. I know you wanted it, and that's why I gave in. But we need to stop here. I want to take my time with you. Show you that you can trust me to be the man you need, who understands your limits and respects them. If we do anything else, I think it'll overwhelm you tonight, right?"

I hate that he's right. "You're right. I need time to process it all before we...you know." I make a motion with my fists, bumping them together.

His laugh is deep, a rumble from his belly. "Yeah, that. There's no rush, *dolcezza*." Elio kisses my forehead, my heart pitter-pattering in my chest. "Stay with me tonight?" he asks, running his hand down my arm.

"Yeah, I'd like that." I smile shyly. "I need my clothes too."

He backs away from me, goes into his walk-in closet, and returns with one of his old hockey T-shirts. "Wear this."

I take it from him. "Okay, but I need my skincare stuff from my bathroom."

"I'll get it. Tell me what I'm looking for."

"That's silly. I can go grab it."

He glares at me. "Jasmine, tell me. Let me take care of you."

I glare back. "I have two feet and a heartbeat. I can get it." I stand and head toward the door.

His corded forearms wrap around my waist, bringing me against his chest. "So do I. You do everything for everyone else. Let me do things for you."

"Fine," I relent, telling him what I need before pushing out of his arms and walking into his bathroom instead to change. He knocks moments later with everything I need.

After doing my routine and brushing my teeth, I open the bathroom door and spot Elio on his bed, shirtless under the covers. I falter, feeling out of place. This is all new to me, navigating these feelings and how to be with him.

"Come here." His voice is low and commanding as he opens the comforter for me to slide under.

I crawl into bed beside him, wondering how in the hell I ended up in bed with my father's friend. Before I can think too much on that, he pulls me against him, my body resting halfway onto his, one leg and one arm on top of him.

I touch his bare chest tentatively, exploring the hard planes of his skin with curiosity. Elio sucks in a breath at my touch, his abs constricting. His arm wraps around my waist, keeping me close to him as he plants a kiss on my hair.

"Sleep," he murmurs.

I cease my exploration, letting my hand rest against his chest as I lift my head up to look at him. "One more kiss, please," I ask. The feeling of being kissed is so new and exciting, I never want to stop.

He cranes his neck, presses his lips against mine, and gives me one hell of a good night kiss. He breaks the kiss before it can turn heady. "Good night, *dolcezza*, sweet dreams."

"Night, roomie." I smile in the dark, knowing he's going to punish me for that later.

Chapter 24

Elio

*S*tirring awake from one of the most peaceful nights of rest I've had in a while, I inhale the scent of peaches and flowers, reminding me of who's in my bed.

Jasmine.

A contented sigh passes through my lips at the fact that she's in my bed, where she slept all night long with her body pressed tightly to mine.

I still can't believe last night happened. I was fucking livid when she went on a date with that kid who doesn't know a damn thing about her, who wouldn't be able to handle her the way I can.

And then that kiss we shared? I've never considered myself to be a man who enjoys kissing all that much, but with Jasmine, I couldn't stop.

Her lips are the sweetest thing I've ever tasted, their shape perfectly made for mine. We woke up once in the middle of the night, our mouths unable to stay apart for that long.

I went down on her again because those are another set of lips of hers that I can't seem to stay away from. It gives me a high like no other, knowing I'm the only man who's kissed her. Who's felt her smooth skin with my hands and tongue.

The only one who's touched her cunt and has given her an orgasm. It makes me feel like a caveman, far more possessive of her than I did before, which was already a lot.

My erection was nearing painful at that point because giving her three orgasms in one night turned me on like nothing else as I watched her come apart for me and me only.

Jasmine demanded that I take care of it, even though I wouldn't let her touch me yet. I jacked off while she watched, her eyes mesmerized with a tinge of apprehension in them. Most women I have had sex with before were shocked at the size, let alone Jasmine, who's never seen or touched one before.

It's why I need to go slow with her, despite my cock's wishes.

Jasmine shifts against me, her body half sprawled on top of me. I run my hand down her back soothingly, hoping she falls back asleep because we didn't sleep much last night.

"Mmm," her raspy voice croaks, rubbing her hand along the ridges of my abs.

I kiss her hair, smoothing it away from her face. "Go back to sleep."

Her movement on my stomach freezes, her body sitting up instantly. "Oh, God, that wasn't only a really good dream, was it?"

I sit up with my back against the headboard. "No, it's real."

Her cheeks pinken, her eyes moving to the comforter where she toys with it with her fingers. "Oh, God." She sighs, her tone not like the fiery girl I've come to know.

I reach for her hand, and she lets me pull her onto my lap, her thighs straddling mine. "What's wrong?" I ask, cupping her cheeks with both of my hands, my thumbs stroking the smooth skin there.

"It's just...I can't believe this happened. I'm happy it did, don't get me wrong. But what are we seriously going to do about my father? How does this play out? Are we messing around until I move out?"

Yeah, okay, as if I'm going to let her move out now.

"I'm happy too." I lean forward, taking her lips in a sweet, short kiss, feeling her body relax slightly against mine. "To be clear, this isn't a game for me, *dolcezza*. I was serious when I said I won't share you. Call it exclusive, dating—hell, you can call me your boyfriend. I don't care what the label is, so long as you're mine and mine only at the end of the day."

She mulls it over for a few seconds, her eyes studying mine closely. I stare back at her, letting her see how much I want her, not hiding it. "Of course I won't see anyone else, and I hope you won't either."

"Nobody else even exists to me. And to be clear, you're mine. Correct?" I prompt, needing to hear it, not only in the throes of passion, but in a moment like this one.

"You know I am." She tilts her head, looking at me incredulously. "What about my father?"

"What do you want to do? Because I'm all in. You want to tell your dad, I'll support it. You want to keep it on the down-low for now, I'll support it."

It may make things awkward at work for me, but it's a price I'm willing to pay to be with her. I'd do anything to keep her.

Jasmine wraps her arms around my neck, her hands playing with the tuft of hair at the back of it. "I know you will. That's not the issue. I don't want him to ruin this, you know? My whole life they've told me what to do—hell, my father told me explicitly to stay away from you and I finally want to do something for myself. Let's keep it between us for now. Is that okay?"

Ned did *what*? My stomach twists at the information, not because of the potential crap he said about me, but because of how it's made Jasmine feel.

"Wait, when did he say that? What did he say exactly?"

"It was the day we talked in his office three years ago. When you were skating with the team, he must've seen how I was looking at you, so he told me that you wouldn't be interested in me. Basically you're up here, and I'm way down here," she explains, bringing her hand up and down.

"What the fuck," I groan, my blood boiling.

Jasmine places a finger on my lips, shushing me. "Don't. It's not worth getting upset over. We ended up in this moment, right here. Let's focus on that."

I rub small circles along the small of her back, my hands always moving when they're on her. "You're right. And I want to make you comfortable as we explore this thing between us, so we can keep it a secret."

"Okay, good." She releases a breath, her eyes on my lips. She wets her lips with her tongue, her mocha eyes slowly making their way back to mine.

I give in to her before she even bothers asking, kissing her like I know she needs to be.

I break apart from her, needing to clarify something else that she said. "What did you mean when you said he told you to stay away from me?"

"When we met three years ago, while we were watching you skate with the team, he told me that you were off-limits. That you were too old and too much for a girl like me."

My face screws up at that. What the fuck does that mean? "A girl like you?" I scoff, my jaw ticking as I grind my molars. "You're perfect for me, absolutely perfect. Don't listen to him, *dolcezza*. You hear me?"

Her eyes shine with unshed tears, so I stroke her cheek with my thumb soothingly. "Why are you upset? Talk to me."

She sniffs, blinking to prevent her tears from falling.

"Because I never thought this would happen to me, being with someone, hearing words like that. I know that sounds lame, but—"

"It's not," I cut her off. "There's nothing wrong with knowing what you want and waiting for it, instead of settling."

Jasmine's eyes narrow, her lips folding in as she tilts her chin down. "I'm scared because what if he tries to ruin this? The first thing in my life that I'm doing for me?"

"You're an adult. He can't control your life."

I'm poking the bear, hoping she'll open up about her parents and why she feels the incessant need to live up to their demands.

"Rationally, I know that," she starts, pausing as she takes a deep breath, then begins again. "You know that my parents couldn't have any more kids, and that crushed them. They always wanted at least five or six. Once they knew that wouldn't happen, they began to focus all of their energy on me, making sure I was the perfect daughter. It makes me feel this strangling pressure to live up to their demands, to make their wishes for me come true, to make them happy, even if it's not going to make me happy.

"Doing anything for myself always leaves me with guilt, because I'm worried I'll mess up their grand plan for me and ruin their one and only experience they will have with a child. My mother insists that I become a financial analyst or an accountant, something steady that makes good money. She'd never support my true dream of opening up my own bakery." Her voice cracks, a tear making its way down her cheek.

I swipe it away, the sight of her tears making me want to fucking destroy anything that's hurting her. I hate it.

"I'm sorry, *dolcezza*. That's a lot to be dealing with, but I'm sure they want you to be happy, no? Have you tried talking to them about this?" I squeeze her to my chest, putting my hand protectively on the back of her head as I hold her to me.

"I tried to bring up the idea of me owning a business, not

saying exactly what, and they shut it down so fast, claiming it's too risky." She sniffles against my chest.

"You can do anything you want. You're smart, driven, and motivated. You need to decide who you want to live your life for."

"You make it sound so easy," she says as she lifts from my chest, disbelief in her tone.

"It's not, but there's a quote somewhere that says the best things in life are the ones that don't come easily. I usually hate that inspirational crap, but it's true nonetheless. Crossing the line with you wasn't easy. I fucking tortured myself over it for weeks, but when you want something badly enough, nothing else matters."

"For weeks, huh? You like me or something?" She winks, smiling coyly at me.

She's trying to change the subject and I let her. She still has time to think about what she wants to pursue.

I tickle her sides instead, her laughter bubbling out of her as she falls back to the bed, trying and failing to push me away as I hover over her, my hands still making her squirm beneath me.

"You know I do, brat." I laugh, enjoying the sight of her carefree and laughing under me.

"Stop, please," she pants, breathless, so I cease my attack.

Our eyes lock, her lean frame under my bulky, large one. It strikes me then how perfectly we seem to fit together.

Her hand comes up to my beard, stroking it as I've come to learn she likes to do. "I like you, too."

I don't respond. Instead, I show her with my lips how much I like her.

We spend the rest of the day like that, kissing, laughing, and talking in bed after venturing into the kitchen for breakfast where Jasmine makes us pancakes.

It's the best morning I've had in a long time.

Chapter 25

Jasmine

The past week has been different.

School is still school, and I still spend my free time studying, doing videos for my channel, and hanging with Camille between classes.

But now I sleep in Elio's bed every night, where he gives me countless orgasms from his fingers and tongue.

His lips are on mine whenever we're home. We work on my channel, coming up with ideas together rather than Elio doing the internal stuff on his own. It's been amazing, having now reached twenty thousand new followers and making more money from some sponsorships I landed.

I can barely process it still, unable to believe that it finally happened. If you had told me this three years ago, I would've laughed in disbelief.

But somehow, we ended up crossing paths, and I couldn't be happier. The feelings I tried so hard to push away under the guise of pushing him away with my smart mouth are finally able to be set free, and it feels so damn good.

I'm a bit guarded still, don't get me wrong. This is all new to me. And I would be lying if I said this doesn't scare me. I've never felt these feelings before, and navigating them along with my relationship in general is going to be a challenge.

There's so much to figure out, but I'm trying to take it day by day.

I want to enjoy my last year of college while I still can.

Although I wanted to keep our relationship a secret, I did tell Aurora and Camille what's been going on between Elio and me since he cut his work trip short last weekend. I went to Camille's apartment above mine the other day and video chatted with Aurora so that she could find out at the same time.

They both squealed with joy, Aurora chanting that she knew it while Camille kicked her legs against the sofa. To say they were both happy is an understatement.

It's exactly how I feel, wanting to pinch myself to make sure it's real. I finally had my first freaking kiss, with the guy I never thought possible. I can't believe we're dating. The fact scares me when I think about it too much because the things he makes me feel are intense, demanding to be felt even when I try to push them away.

But you want to know what scares me even more? This lunch date I'm on with my parents.

It's been going well so far, as we catch each other up on our lives, but as my mother swallows a bite of quinoa salad, the look on her face tells me that it's about to take a turn that I don't like.

"Jasmine, have you been thinking about where you would like to apply post-graduation? Or are you considering a master's degree? That would be wonderful actually."

Setting my water down, I grapple with what I want to say while I push my spoon around my empty bowl of soup. "I haven't yet. I've been so busy with midterms. Senior year courses are a lot of work. Can I think about it over the holidays and give you an answer after?"

My father speaks up, setting his napkin on his finished plate. "I think that's a great idea, Jas. Sit on it and don't rush it. It is the rest of your life, so think carefully about what you want to do."

I smile at my father, hoping he understands how grateful I am for him. While he still pushes me to be the best and backs my mother up with her wishes for me, he also urges her to look at things differently.

"I suppose that's smart," she agrees, sipping her own water. "I'm really proud of you, my one and only."

My one and only. My mother uses that as a term of endearment all the time, but I don't think she realizes how much it makes me resent it. Because it's the reason I've been forced to do what *they* want all my life. Not wanting to fuck up their wishes for the only child they could have.

"Thanks." I smile back, forcing the cheerfulness I know needs to be in my voice.

Her pager goes off then. "Damn it, looks like I'm needed back at the hospital. Call me, okay? I miss you," she croons, wrapping her arms around me before kissing my father and rushing out of the restaurant.

My father and I follow suit as well, since our lunch is finished. We wrap ourselves up in our jackets, the Colorado chill rampant in late October. We talk on our way to his car, since he picked me up from class to meet with my mother for lunch.

Once we're settled in the car, he asks, "What's this I hear about you going on a date with Adam Wilson?"

"How did you hear that?" My face scrunches at the knowledge that my father seems to find everything out.

"I told you, I know everything." He taps his head and

chuckles. "But seriously, the boys on the team talk in the locker rooms. I heard the tail end of it when I entered the room because they stopped when they saw Elio and me. Hell, he seemed more worked up than I was that they were talking about you. Gave those two extra hell during practice. He's a good friend, looking out for you like I would."

"Well, what did you hear?" I ask, ignoring his comment about Elio, yet secretly loving how protective he is. I'll have to tell him to play it cool, no matter what people are saying, because my father is bound to get suspicious eventually.

"All we heard was that you went on a date with the tight end and that nothing happened. One of my boys started to say how he wasn't surprised, but that's when we came around the corner."

"That's a good summary. We went out, had good food, and talked. We're friends, that's all," I huff, hating that my dating life was a topic amongst students. I guess that's what I get for going out with an athlete, on top of being infamous on campus for being a goody-two-shoes.

"Nothing wrong with that, but a word of advice? Forget boys, Jasmine. They're nothing but trouble at this age, so focus on school."

I want to laugh because he's right. That's why I'm letting his coworker slash friend spend hours between my thighs because he's not their age. He's older and clearly experienced with the way his tongue expertly works me every day.

He drops me off at home minutes later, and I spend the entire elevator ride up thinking about Elio. I know he's seeing his mom for lunch and won't be back for a while since her house is two hours away from here.

I hate how much I miss him, wishing he were here when I push the door open, his stupid cartoons on the TV since it's

Saturday. To avoid thinking about that, I thrust myself into work, spending hours recording and editing myself making banana pudding.

Once that's done and the kitchen's cleaned, I head to my room. It's messy, with clothes strewn about, textbooks on the dresser, and shoes in different spots on the floor. It makes me laugh, knowing how Elio would lose his mind if I did that in his room.

I wonder if he'd put me over his lap again. The thought is a thrilling one, making me bite down on my lip. God, I wish he'd let me pleasure him already. All week he's given me countless orgasms, kissed me senseless, all while he told me no when I offered to get him off.

I understand why he's doing it. He doesn't want me to feel like he's rushing me, but I'm ready. I want the power of knowing I can make him lose control, of bringing him to the edge and toying with him the way he does to me.

I want to see him come undone and know it was because of *me*, my mouth, my hands, my touch. And I think I know a way to get him to snap, let me please him the way I'm finally eager to explore how to.

Chapter 26
Elio

*M*y leg bounces as the elevator takes me up to my apartment, where I know Jasmine is studying.

All day long I wished to be at home with her, my cartoons on while she baked and edited her videos. Don't get me wrong, visiting with my mom was great. We had lunch at her house, where she made us homemade pizza, we caught up, reminisced, and overall had a good time.

But I was ready for dessert.

I enter the apartment and give the girls some love before I go straight to her room, knowing that's where she prefers to study despite spending her nights in my bed.

I peek inside her open door, but she's not at her desk or on her bed. "Jasmine?" I call out, heading down the hallway to my room.

That's when I hear the bubbling of the hot tub jets.

The en suite bathroom door in my room is open, soft music filtering in from it. I walk into it and see Jasmine in the hot tub, her eyes closed, with a content look on her face. I study her for a second, basking in how fucking pretty she is. She must be wearing a new bathing suit because this one seems to be a tube top, with no straps visible.

"Are you going to say hi or just stare?" She giggles, cracking one eye open.

"Hi." I smile.

"Hi." She smiles back, her mocha eyes lifting with the motion.

"I missed you," I admit, wanting her to always know how I feel about her with no confusion.

"You did?"

"I wouldn't say it if I didn't mean it, *dolcezza*."

Her cheeks warm. "What are we going to do when you have an away game next weekend?"

"FaceTime when I'm at the hotel, have phone sex," I suggest, winking at her.

I expect her to blush some more, but she hums, her eyes hooded with lust. "I'd like that, but I think we need to cross something off before we do that."

"What's that?" I prod.

"You letting me please you." She blushes once more, her tongue swiping out to wet her lips.

"Jasmine—" I start to argue, but it's cut short once she stands.

My brain fails to work, my heart beating wildly in my chest at the sight of her naked, perfect body, with droplets of water sticking to her soft skin. I want to lick every inch of her, then fuck her on the counter, but we can't. Not yet.

"I want you, Elio. Teach me how to please you. I want to make you feel as good as you make me feel," she pleads, her trusting eyes on mine as she moves through the water.

She walks over to me, my breath choppy as I fail to tear my eyes away from her breasts. I've seen her naked plenty of times this week, and had my mouth on her nipples more times than I can even remember, but this feels different.

Because seeing her so determined to give me pleasure, wanting my cock and only my cock in her mouth for her first time, is tempting me to let her do exactly that. She's innocent and shy when it comes to being intimate, and she has no idea how sexy it is.

How much it turns me on knowing that I'm the man she trusts, the one who gives her pleasure.

"You want me to teach you how to be my dirty slut, hm?"

Her eyes widen, desire coating her features. I had a hunch she'd like a bit of degradation, since she's always praised and pressured to be good.

"Yes," she purrs, stepping closer.

Once she's close enough, I dip my head and suck a nipple into my mouth, loving the breathy moan that leaves her lips. I lavish both of her breasts, moving from one to the other, giving them both the appreciation they deserve.

She has the best tits I've ever seen.

I pull back, gripping her hair and tilting her head up to mine, taking her lips in a passionate kiss. Her tongue teases my lips first, dipping into my mouth, where she explores. A groan gets caught in my throat, and I force myself to pull away from her.

If she wants to do this, then I need to stop before I devour her instead.

"You want to learn how to suck my cock?"

"Yes, teach me." Her palms land on the hem of my shirt, lifting it up my body.

I help her, tearing it over my head. Her eyes roam over my body appreciatively, and I like knowing that she does it openly now, not like our encounter that night after the gym a month ago.

"Get on your knees for me," I order her, loving how she instantly lowers, her knees hitting the bench in the hot tub.

I undo my zipper, then push my jeans and briefs down. I kick them off and my shirt follows, standing there completely bare to her. My erection stands up proudly, while Jasmine eyes it with a mix of emotions.

Excitement. Want. Curiosity. Nerves.

I climb into the hot tub and sit on the ledge in the corner. I put my hand on her chin, tilting her head up to look at me. "If you don't like it, we'll stop. Okay?"

"Okay. Can I touch it?" she asks, eyeing my cock like it's something to be investigated. It's sexy as hell.

"It's all yours, *dolcezza*."

Her small hand reaches forward, her fingers gently running the length from my tip to the base as her eyes inspect it from different angles. My abs constrict at that. She's barely even touched me and I'm already a goner.

"Is this an average size?" she asks, tilting her head up to me as her hand wraps around my base.

I chuckle at that. "No, it's not. I'm a bit bigger than most."

"It's beautiful," she breathes.

It's the first time my cock has been referred to as beautiful, but I'll take it. I'll take whatever she gives me.

"And it wants to be sucked. You ready to be my little slut?" I thread my fingers through her silky curls.

"Yes." She sits up straighter on her knees, her hand slowly pumping me.

"Don't be afraid to grip me harder," I encourage her, and she responds by doing so, giving me a tighter squeeze as her hand rubs up and down my cock.

"Such a good listener for a brat," I tease. "Stick your tongue out."

She does, looking up at me with those mocha eyes I want to drown in. So trusting, so innocent. I put the tip on her tongue and tap my cock against it a few times as pre-cum drips from the tip.

"Taste me," I tell her, my voice husky.

Jasmine licks the crown of my cock, swallowing my cum, the sight making me nearly lose it.

"Mmm," she hums, wrapping her lips back around my cock without me telling her to. She sucks the crown, making a popping sound with her lips.

"You like that, huh?" I coo, caressing her cheek as she sucks me in again, humming her approval around my cock. "Spit on my cock, get it wet."

She does, wrapping her fist around me to spread it, then places her lips back around me.

"Keep doing that. Hollow your cheeks and take me in deeper. Suck and lick me as you go," I instruct her, gathering her wet strands away from her face.

She does as I say, taking me in deeper, hollowing her cheeks as she pulls back, sucking me so fucking good.

"For what you can't fit, use your hand to pump me," I croak, loving the feeling of her tongue tracing the length of my cock, back and forth.

She wraps her hand around my shaft, pumping me as she takes me deeper this time, my cock hitting the back of her throat already, and I'm not even halfway in.

I let her do this for a bit, getting used to the feeling, her pushing me in a bit deeper each time. My toes curl, my spine tingling as I try my best to fight off coming already.

She pulls back, panting. "Are you okay? Why are your eyes closed? Am I awful?"

I open my eyes to see her looking at me in confusion, with a tinge of hurt. "You're fucking amazing, easily the best blow job

I've ever had. My eyes are closed because I'm trying not to come yet." And it's true. It's the best because she's so determined, into it, and sucking me the way I like it.

"Oh." She laughs, more sure of herself now. "Why don't you want to come yet?"

"Because I want to fuck your smart mouth first, the way I've been wanting to shut you up whenever you were being a brat," I groan as she kisses the tip. She's too fucking sweet.

"Then do it, *roomie*." Her eyes glint with mischief, knowing her little stint of calling me her roomie is going to set me off.

I grip her hair tightly with both hands, forcing my cock into her mouth before she can say something else that's going to piss me off. She gags, so I pull out slightly, but she nods at me to continue.

"Look at you choking on my cock. A needy little slut, aren't you?" I thrust my hips forward erratically, my cock working in and out of her mouth. Tears are leaking from the corner of her eyes, and I'm about to stop until she moans around my cock, the vibration making me tense up with a near release.

Jasmine brings a hand up to her nipple, where she tweaks it with her fingers. I grunt at the sight, loving that she's enjoying this as much as me. Not every girl is into it, but Jasmine seems to love it with the way she's moaning and touching herself.

She pumps me while sucking and licking my cock like it's the best damn thing she's ever had between her lips.

"You're doing so good," I tell her, biting down on my lip. "I'm going to come in your mouth, and I want you to take it."

Jasmine hums, her eyes flicking up to mine as she bobs her head up and down my cock.

"I want it, please," she demands quickly, then wraps her lips back around my cock.

I spill down her throat at that, my spine tingling and my body jutting forward.

"Don't swallow yet," I tell her, letting all of my cum spill into her mouth before pulling out.

She stays still, her mouth full of me. I tilt her head back so that I can get a better view. With my hand around her neck, my eyes locked on hers, my voice is low and rough. "Open, let me see."

Jasmine parts her lips and sticks her tongue out. My cock begins to harden once more because seeing my cum on her tongue is doing something to the possessive beast inside of me.

"So fucking pretty. Now, swallow."

Jasmine swallows, and I groan at the sight. I give her neck a squeeze, eliciting a moan from her. Every time I think she's perfect for me, she goes and proves why.

My fucking dream woman.

I release her, letting my hand fall away as I take her lips in a searing kiss, pulling her naked body to mine, and lifting her out of the tub. She wraps her legs around my waist, her wet body rubbing against mine as she kisses me back just as fiercely.

I plop her down on the sink counter, where I devour her with my tongue. I've enjoyed going down on women before, but with Jasmine, I crave it. Her cunt is fucking delicious.

We shower after, and Jasmine drops to her knees for me again. We're insatiable with one another, a chemistry that can't be explained or ignored. I can only imagine what fucking her will be like, or what it'll do to me.

She's worth the wait to find out.

Chapter 27

Jasmine

"Bullshit!" I shout at the referee, who damn well should have called that ball in on Aurora's serve. Cameron grumbles beside me. He's less vocal when he's pissed, but I know he shares the sentiment.

I'm finally watching Aurora play with Team USA, and I couldn't be more proud. I haven't had the chance to talk to her yet because when I got here, she was already warming up and I can't wait to wrap my arms around my best friend for the first time in four months.

Cameron and I cheer her on fiercely, so damn proud of her for making it here. She's talented, and it shows because they end up winning all three sets, sweeping the other team.

Once they shake hands with the opposing team, Aurora runs directly toward me in the crowd. I stand, running down the steps to meet her at the bottom, where we squeeze one another so tightly I can barely breathe.

"Ro!"

"Minnie!" she squeaks, squeezing me while we rock back and forth.

"You were amazing. And that one call was total bullshit." The sound of my voice is slightly muffled by her dirty-blonde locks.

Her body vibrates against mine as she laughs. "Thank you, and yeah, I heard you yelling. My overprotective bestie."

I pull back, staring into her hazel eyes in person for once. "No one messes with my girl. You know this."

Aurora looks at something behind me, her eyes softening. "Do you mind if I say hi to Cam? He's looking like a sad puppy right now."

I chuckle. "Go ahead."

Aurora jumps into his arms, and he easily lifts her, wrapping an arm around her lower back as he whispers something into her ear that makes her squeeze her body around his and press her face to his chest.

My heart swells watching them, envying the kind of love they have. I want to hope it'll happen, especially with the way I've been feeling with Elio, but I don't want to get too excited yet.

Elio has a home game today, and they've been on a winning streak lately, so he's feeling good about the game despite it being our rival school, the University of Aspen.

The Coyotes and the Foxes have been enemies for what seems like forever, our schools always going head-to-head in every sport possible.

I told Elio about the Halloween party later at Beers n Cheers, but he told me to go have fun as he'd rather have a quiet night in with our girls after the game. I know he mostly said that because he feels weird hanging out at a college bar since he's older, despite him attending classes here.

A quiet night with Elio also sounded good to me, but Aurora and I have been talking about this party for a while and with Halloween being my favorite holiday, I decided to still go out.

I know we can do things without each other even though we're dating, yet I still wish he were coming. I know it's hard since he's gawked at and people tend to not leave him alone, so I get him wanting to stay home.

Aurora, Cameron, and I grab dinner at The Grand Cantina, loading up on chips and guac. It feels so good to see them as we eat, laugh, and exchange stories, reminiscing about our times together at school.

After dinner, we head to her dad's house, who's away on business.

The three of us get ready, Aurora and Cameron in her old room, while I get ready in the bathroom. My costume is genius, or at least I think it is. It cost me twenty dollars, another bonus in my book.

I'm wearing a plaid button-up, tied in the front so that it's more of a crop top, with a black lace bralette underneath. I have on cut-off jean short shorts and I borrowed some cowboy boots from Camille, who has every shoe you could think of, the caramel color of the leather complementing my skin tone.

I'm wearing a cowboy hat on my head, which is what cost me money, and taped to the front of it is a reverse uno sign. Reverse cowgirl, get it? I saw it online and thought it was hilarious.

I'm waiting on the couch in her living room when I hear them coming down the stairs.

"Sorry, we took so long because when Cam was painting my body green, he took a little detour." Aurora waggles her brows.

Cameron grins at her, looking like he could go for round two right now. They're dressed as Gamora and Starlord from the Guardians of the Galaxy. Aurora's body is painted green, a black wig with purple balayage on the ends of her hair.

They really went all out. My little Marvel nerds.

We make it to Beers n Cheers around nine, the place full, with everyone dressed in various costumes. There's Halloween themed music on the speakers, and the bar is decked out in decorations. I spot Camille and Theo in a booth, waiting for us.

Camille is dressed as a mermaid, a starfish bikini top on with a maxi sequin blue skirt. Theo's dressed as a football player—boring.

Theo squeals, literally, when he sees Aurora. He jumps out of the booth and runs toward her, crushing her in a hug. "AV, baby! Holy fuck, I missed you."

"I missed you too, Theo," she tells him as they separate.

Theo's head tilts, giving Cam a cheesy grin. "Ronnie boy! Come here," he booms, giving him one of those guy hand-back clap things.

"I hate that fucking name, but it's nice to see you." Cameron grins once Theo backs up.

"Hello?" I pout, giving Theo a stare down.

"Oh, come on, Jay Bay Bay, you know there's lots of Theo to go around." He smirks, picking me up and spinning me.

I sit beside Camille and Theo, while Cam and Aurora sit on the other side of the table. "Cami, you look so good. Holy shit," I comment. The girl looks good.

She chuckles, sipping her drink. "Thank you."

The five of us are talking animatedly when a waitress comes to the table, halting our conversations. "Hi, I'm Marcela, your server tonight. What can I get you?" She beams with a smile. I've seen Marcela around when I'm here, but we've never spoken to one another.

This is the girl Theo is pining after, and I can see why. She's stunning with her long brown hair nearly hitting her waist and thick dark eyebrows.

Her eyes are a light brown, lighter than I've ever seen on someone before with freckles covering the tops of her cheeks and nose. I look over at Theo while Aurora and Marcela chat, since they used to work together. He's staring, willing her to look his way, but it seems like she's purposely avoiding him.

Then she takes our orders. Cameron and Aurora order water, while Cami and I split on a bottle of rosé.

Marcela finally turns to Theo. "What would you like to get?"

Theo holds her stare, a sly grin forming on his face. "You."

Aurora giggles, while Cameron and I shake our heads at him.

Marcela visibly blushes, not looking at him as she stares at her notepad. "No, but, um, if that's all, then I'll be back with your drinks shortly."

She begins to walk away when Theo calls out after her. "I'll take a Bud Light, please."

Marcela looks over her shoulder, nodding quickly before turning back around and heading to the bar to tell Craig, the bartender, our drink orders.

Theo suddenly yelps out in pain, gripping his leg under the table. "Cam, what the fuck, man!"

Cameron leans forward on his elbows, pinning him with his stoic gaze. "Don't say shit like that to her. It clearly makes her uncomfortable. She's trying to do her job, so lay off."

Theo makes a strangled noise, waving Cameron off. "She's shy, so I like to push her buttons and make her blush. It's cute."

"It also may be the reason she never gives you a chance. Just saying," Cameron says, wrapping his arm around Aurora's waist and she snuggles into his side.

The conversation is dropped after that, and we all catch up. It's easy and fun, reminding me how much I miss Aurora and

Cameron being around. But I know she's off chasing her dreams and I couldn't be prouder.

My phone vibrates under my thigh, so I pull it out and do my best to stop a smile from spreading on my face when I see Elio's name on my screen.

> **Elio**
>
> I hope you're having fun, but when are you coming home? The girls miss you.

> **Me**
>
> I think it's more than the girls who miss me.

> **Elio**
>
> Your thinking is correct

> **Elio**
>
> I can't do anything without thinking about you now. Home doesn't feel like home without you.

His words nestle themselves inside my heart, making it beat faster than before. I bite my bottom lip as I internally debate whether or not to send him the photo I took earlier in the mirror at Aurora's house.

It's a head-to-toe shot, and I'd be lying if I said my boobs weren't nearly hanging out of my top. I miss him too, and I feel like messing with him a bit. I like when he gets riled up.

> **Me**
>
> Attachment: 1 image

> **Me**
>
> I miss you, too.

Before I can even set my phone down, he calls me. I excuse myself, taking a minute to step outside into the chilly autumn air.

"H-hello," I chatter, my legs already frozen.

"Where are you? Why are you cold?" His voice is laced with concern.

"I'm outside of the bar so I could hear you. Is everything okay?"

"Well, my girlfriend that I can't really be with in public is currently at a bar without me, looking sinful in that damn costume. So no, *dolcezza*, I'm not okay."

I roll my eyes, not that he can see. "I'm fine. Don't worry."

He groans loudly, sighing into the phone. There's a door shutting on his end as his voice comes back on the line. "I know."

"Elio, w-where are you going?" I stutter, my teeth chattering as my lips quiver.

"Jasmine, go back inside, *now*. I'll be there in ten," he demands icily, hanging up the call.

I walk back into the bar, rubbing my hands down the sides of my thighs as I try to warm up. My stomach awakens, those damn butterflies returning at the knowledge that Elio's coming here. But they vanish just as quickly at the reminder that we can't act how we do at home, which is like two teenagers who are obsessed with one another, always making out when possible, never able to get enough.

"You okay?" Aurora asks once I return to the booth, our drinks on the table.

"Elio's on his way. Just a heads-up," I tell them, taking a hefty sip of my wine.

"Good, it's about time I formally meet this guy to see if he's good enough to be dating you," Cameron says so casually, as if he didn't drop the biggest bomb on Theo, who had no idea.

The only ones who know are Camille and Aurora, who told Cameron with my permission.

Dead fucking silence falls over our table. The only sounds are the Halloween music playing, the laughter and conversation milling amongst the crowd. Aurora looks up at him like a deer in headlights, making him turn his head toward her.

Realization dawns over him, his eyes nearly bulging out of his head as his lips form an *O*.

"Oh, shit," he mutters.

"Yeah, what the hell? Dating you? Jay Bay Bay, did you forget to mention this to me or is my letter of acknowledgement sitting in my mailbox?" Theo questions me, one of his eyebrows raised. He's not mad, but I can tell he's slightly hurt that I kept it from him.

"I, uh," I fumble, not wanting to hurt his feelings. "I wanted to tell you, Theo, but it's all new for me. We're keeping it on the down-low because of my father, so not a word of this, understand?"

Theo looks at me in utter shock. "You and Elio fucking Mazzo are dating? This isn't real, c'mon." He chuckles, not realizing that his words are a target to my insecurities.

"What's that supposed to mean?" I place my arms over my chest, trying to comfort myself.

"I mean, that it's unexpected. Last year at the gala it seemed like you couldn't care less about the man, and now suddenly, you're dating? And isn't he way older? And your dad's coworker slash protégé?" he asks, reminding me of all the obstacles in Elio's and my situation.

"Theo," Camille interjects. "Jasmine is a smart woman. I think she knows what she's doing. Clearly, last year they were in a different place than they are now."

I smile at Camille, trying to tell her how grateful I am for her sticking up for me. I take another sip of my wine, the buzz in my veins giving me the courage to keep going with the truth.

"We live together," I admit, causing Theo to gasp. "Which is also a secret. Utter a word of this and I will cut your balls off. He is older, but I'm mature, so it works. And my father is something I'm working on dealing with."

"Oh, man." Theo laughs, taking a sip of his beer. "Coach Park will lose his shit. That guy doesn't fuck around, according to Isaiah. But all jokes aside, I'm sorry. I didn't mean to offend you. I was shocked, but I'm happy if you are."

"That's better," Aurora chimes in.

"Thanks, and I *am* happy."

"Sooo, does this mean you've had your first kiss?" he asks, his voice all teasing as he waggles his eyebrows. He's such a goofball.

"Theo!" Aurora slaps him playfully on the arm. "Leave her alone. It's her business, not yours."

"Ugh, not fair. I already know that both of y'all got the scoop." He points at Camille and Aurora. "Just because I'm a guy doesn't mean I shouldn't know these things too."

We all laugh at that, taking sips of our drinks as Marcela returns. Theo still can't keep his eyes off her, but this time, he doesn't say anything else while we order onion rings, fries, and jalapeńo poppers.

After she leaves, the air in the room changes. The chatter grows quieter and I turn my head to see what has everyone's attention, when my eyes connect with Elio's. He didn't bother to dress up, wearing a black sweater and dark blue jeans with a baseball cap.

He walks over to our table, unfazed by the various eyes on him. His face is stoic, ball cap pulled down to cover his face, letting people know he doesn't want to be bothered.

"Elio Mazzo, what a pleasure to see you again," Theo says, standing to shake his hand. "You're a legend, man. It's fucking wild that you're walking around campus like a normal human being."

"Tell me about it." Elio cracks a smile, clasping Theo's hand in his. "I had to go through a lot of shit to ensure that I wouldn't be bothered while I'm here."

"It's worth it to be here. This school is amazing," Aurora pipes up. "I'm Aurora, and this is my boyfriend, Cameron."

Elio greets them, then turns to Camille. "Nice to see you again."

And then finally he turns to me, at the other end of the booth. "Jasmine," he drawls, his eyes trailing over me like he's peeling my damn clothes off.

I swallow, desire running rampant in my body. "Hi."

"Mind if I sit?" He smirks, walking toward me.

I scoot over, but it's tight. I'm about to grab a chair to pull up, when Elio slides in beside me, pulling half of my leg onto his thigh so that there's more room. I'm about to worry about all the people here, but you can't see anything because of the table top covering our legs.

"Elio," I whisper, low enough for only him to hear.

"Yeah, *dolcezza?*"

"I'm glad you're here," I tell him because it's true. I love that he's here with my friends, and will get to know them.

His minty breath hits my cheek. "Me, too. Now, don't wiggle because we're going to have a problem if you do."

"Hmm, what kind of problem?" I play innocent.

"A hard one, difficult to get rid of unless your lips are involved," he whispers into my ear, sending chills down my spine as his hand clamps my thigh possessively. "If we were on the ice right now, I would've fucking body-slammed these guys into next week for looking at you the way they are."

"I only care about the way you look at me," I whisper back, fighting the urge to kiss him.

"Good," he hums. "Nice costume, by the way. I look forward to putting you in that position, watching your ass bounce up and down my cock as you ride me."

I squirm against him, my body fighting to ignore the lust running rampant in my veins. I suddenly wish we were alone. The reminder of the apartment causes me to nearly jump out of my spot.

"Shit, I haven't paid you yet for this month. I'll e-transfer you now."

His hand on my thigh tightens, his voice low and rough as he whispers in my ear, "You're not paying me anything. You're mine now, which means I take care of you."

"Yeah, but that was the deal in our contract…and people in relationships split bills and responsibilities."

He sucks in a breath, his fingers itching up higher on my inner thigh. "That contract is void, don't you say?" I nod, and he continues. "I don't want it, nor do I need it. Try to send me money, *dolcezza*, and you'll be over my lap in seconds."

I want to argue with him, but I know it's useless. When Elio sets his mind to something, he does exactly that.

My breath is shaky as I speak, "I'm definitely sending you money now."

He chuckles, leaving his hand on my thigh as he falls into conversation with my friends, fitting right in as they talk sports, family, and everything in between. Eventually, Cami, Aurora and I take a trip to the washroom because after what happened to Aurora, we never let her go alone despite her protests.

We're leaving the washroom when Ryker rounds the corner, his eyes instantly finding Camille. He's not in a costume, which doesn't surprise me. His tattooed arms are on display in a black T-shirt, his shoulder-length hair is loose, blue eyes brimming with want as he looks at her.

"Hey, Ryker, how's it going?" Aurora says, oblivious to the stare down between Camille and him.

He peels his eyes away from Camille, looking at his soon-to-be stepsister. "Fine. You?" he says, his tone clipped and gruff.

"Jeez, still grumpy as ever. I'll get you to smile one day." Aurora taps her chin in thought.

"Don't count on it," he replies.

"Maybe you need to get laid, loosen up a bit," she suggests.

He doesn't find it funny or helpful, his eyebrows narrowing at her. "I'm going to forget that this conversation happened," he mutters, barreling past us into the washroom.

Aurora sighs. "He's so damn grumpy. I keep trying to bond with him, but I don't think it'll happen."

Cami speaks up then, "Give it some time."

Before Aurora can respond, Camille squeezes herself between the two of us, looping her arms in ours. "C'mon, let's go back to the table. I need some food."

I sit back down, my leg half on Elio's due to the cramped space. And I don't mind it one bit, not when it's an excuse to be close like this. I've grown accustomed to it at the house, his hands always on my body in some way when we're with one another.

It hits me then, watching him smile and laughing with my friends, how fast I'm falling for him. He's sweet, attentive, confident, smart, and everything I could want in a partner. He makes me feel cared for, and respected like I'm his equal. Hell, sometimes I think he worships the ground I walk on, to be honest, placing me above himself.

Not to mention that I trust him with my body, as he knows how to make me feel desired, how to touch me exactly how I need to be touched.

There's no one else who could affect me the way he does, and that right there is the problem. When this all comes out and inevitably goes to shit, I'll suffer knowing that I will never experience these kinds of feelings again.

Because it's him. It'll only ever be him for me.

Chapter 28

Jasmine

Tonight's the first time I'm attending a hockey game while being a student at RLU.

In the past, I had volleyball, which meant I was too busy to watch my father in action as a head coach. Part of me feels guilty for that, but I knew he understood my responsibilities. Hell, he and my mother remind me any chance they get about them.

I ignore that trail of thoughts, linking my arm through Camille's as we make our way to the seats my father got us. I had to go through him and not Elio to avoid suspicion.

I can barely stand up to my parents about what I want to do with my life, let alone about the man I'm dating, which I'm sure they will lose their minds over.

"Have you ever been to a hockey game before?" I ask Camille while setting our drinks into the holders.

"No, I've always wanted to, but I was usually busy with another sport to cover for the school paper. It's never worked out time-wise." She shrugs her shoulders, popping some popcorn into her mouth.

"I appreciate you coming with me anyway." I smile at her while grabbing my own handful of popcorn and shoving it into my mouth all at once. It's the best way to eat it. Not the most graceful, but the best.

"I'm excited to be here, honestly. Hot guys pushing each other around? Sign me up." She shimmies her body into mine, causing us both to break out in a fit of laughter.

The visiting team from the University of Aspen, the Foxes, exits their tunnel. A few cheers from loyal fans try to outdo the boos from our side, but fail. The atmosphere is already tense.

RLU comes out of their tunnel next, the lights turned down as spotlights flicker across the ice. Their pump-up music bangs out of the speakers and the boys skate out, the green and white jerseys whipping around the ice.

We're seated right next to RLU's bench, giving me a clear view of my father and Elio as they enter it. They're both dressed professionally, wearing suits and ties.

Elio looks sexy as hell in his all black outfit, and I can't take my eyes off of him. As if he senses me, he looks to the left and smiles, giving me a wink before turning and saying something to my father.

My father looks over Elio's shoulder, spotting me. He walks over to the glass separating us and smiles widely. "My one and only is here. About time." He chuckles.

"You better win and show me what your team can do."

"We will," he says confidently, then turns his attention to Camille. "Camille, how are you?"

"Great, it's my first game, so I'm quite excited," she says around a mouthful of popcorn.

"It'll be a good one. These teams always go for blood when we play," he comments. "You ladies enjoy the game." He nods at us, then walks to the other end to talk with a trainer.

Elio comes closer to the glass, keeping his eyes trained on the ice, his voice low as he talks to me. "You look beautiful. How am I supposed to keep my eyes on the team when you look like that?"

I gaze down at my RLU crew neck sweater, tights, and combat boots. It's nothing special by any means. Neither is my hair, my curls falling past my shoulders.

"Thanks." I blush anyways, doing a terrible job at keeping a smile off my face. "You look hot as hell. I can't wait to undress you later."

"Jesus, *dolcezza*," he groans under his breath. "That's supposed to be my line."

"Meh, not my fault your game sucks." I pop my shoulders, a bubble of giddiness filling my chest, knowing that he'll punish me later for that.

"Is this you guys' foreplay?" Camille whispers as she leans toward me.

"Shut up." I push her off me. I catch Elio grinning as he stares at the ice, knowing full well he heard her.

He walks toward my father then, talking with the trainers as the players warm up.

Camille and I settle in with our popcorn and drinks, when Isaiah comes up to the glass.

"Jasmine, Camille, nice to see you girls here." He beams.

"Try not to suck. This is her first game." I point my thumb at Camille.

"I was going to throw the game before, but now, I'll put in some effort, I guess." He winks, ever the charmer, and skates away.

We continue to watch the boys warm up when a purple-and-black jersey glides over to the boards in front of us. Can we get a break?

"If I had known there was a girl as pretty as you at RLU, I

would have transferred years ago," he drawls, eyeing me up and down through his mask.

I ignore him and continue talking to Cami about our plans to go shopping for the holidays soon. He doesn't take the hint.

He taps his stick on the glass. "C'mon, pretty girl, I know you can hear me."

Camille jumps slightly from the noise, and it pisses me off that he's not only bothering me, but her.

"Apparently, you can't, because me ignoring you was a message you didn't receive. I'm not interested," I scoff, looking to the right to see Elio stalking toward us, his jaw clenched tightly.

"That's okay. I like the feisty ones," he purrs, just as Elio reaches us.

"Jacobson, get to your side of the ice, *now*," he says coldly, his voice calm yet lethal.

"I don't take orders from a has-been, but it is time for the game to start." He smirks to himself and skates to his bench.

Elio glares at him the entire time while talking under his breath to me. "You okay?"

"I'm great. Seriously, don't worry about it," I reassure him.

Elio doesn't say anything. He simply nods as the national anthem comes on. We all stand, and once it ends, we relax into our seats as the teams return to their benches.

Minutes later, they're skating to their positions on their side of the ice, gearing up for what is going to be an intense game.

And it is. It's currently the second period, and no one has scored yet. There's been a few close calls, but both goalies are playing their asses off tonight, blocking everything. The players are skating their hardest, and there have been more than a couple dirty hits, some of which have gone unnoticed by the refs.

That is until none other than Jacobson gets a breakaway. He's soaring down the ice, impossibly fast, and he slapshots it into the top right corner of the net. Our goalkeeper's glove barely misses it.

The siren goes off, eliciting a mix of boos and cheers from the crowd.

Jacobson skates toward me, shouting once he's close enough, "Looks like I'm scoring tonight. Hopefully, more than pucks."

Ew.

"Maybe hockey isn't for me." Camille mock gags, making me laugh.

I roll my eyes as Jacobson skates away and look at our bench. Elio glares at him once again, his jaw working back and forth. He walks down the bench line, leaning over to whisper in the ear of one of the biggest defensemen on the team.

I don't think anything of it, turning my attention back to the game.

The guys line up for the puck drop, and Isaiah gets it, passing it to another player on our team. I'm watching with rapt attention as they try to set up a play, when Jacobson tries to steal the puck from Isaiah, slashing him intentionally.

The refs must miss it somehow, because there's no fucking whistle. Our biggest defenseman, Grant, skates over impeccably fast and twists his shoulder right into Jacobson, smashing him into the boards. The crowd goes silent at the hit. It's the worst one we've seen all night.

The refs blow their whistle *now*, calling a penalty on Grant, and the crowd boos. The hit looked clean to me, but I also don't know a whole lot about hockey.

"That looked painful." Camille grimaces as Jacobson is helped up, then he skates off by himself to sit on the bench.

My brain turns things over in my head, and I quickly look over at Elio, who's wearing a shit-eating grin as he watches the scene unfold. He did this. That must've been what he whispered to Grant.

While I want to swoon over the protectiveness of it, I also want to yell at him. He can't tell his players to pull that kind of stunt for me. It's not cool, and I won't stand by it.

RLU scores twice in the third period, with Jacobson on the bench for the rest of the game. The crowd is electric, losing their minds about the win over our rival school. Camille jumps up and cheers along with them, and I join her, but it's half-hearted, because I'm a bit pissed at my boyfriend.

The team starts to celebrate their win, jumping on one another on the ice, and my father and Elio exit the bench to shake hands with the other team's coaches.

Camille and I begin to exit our row, following the crowd, when I feel his eyes on me. I give him a small smile and a wave, to which he nods. He knows I'm going home with Camille, but he wanted me to make sure I'd say bye when we left.

Due to the thousands of people around, most important of all, my father, a wave is the best he can get. It might be all he gets for a while after what he did tonight.

I've been home for an hour and decided to film some content as I wait for Elio to get back from the game.

I'm currently making a dish my *halmeoni* and I made when I was a kid, *Hotteok*, a pancake-like dessert, with a maple cinnamon crumble on the inside. It's easy to make and delicious.

I know I'll have to make more for Chuseok, which is our family's Thanksgiving, but I want some now as I crave the connection I feel to my grandma when I make it.

Peace washes over me as I mix the ingredients, then grab the dough into my hands, making it into the size I want. Once it's perfect, I sprinkle the maple, cinnamon sugar topping on it, and then I fold the dough and close it as I drop it onto the pan.

The sizzle buzzes in my ear, a sound that brings me back to my childhood, the days spent in the kitchen with my *halmeoni*. She didn't speak English, allowing me to only converse with her in Korean. We spent so many days laughing and talking in the kitchen, our special little moments. Tears roll down my cheeks at the memories because I miss her so fucking much, it hurts. She was my soul twin, our personalities one and the same.

I wipe them away as I flip the *Hotteok* over, satisfied with the slight browning. A few minutes later, they're complete. I take a couple of videos and photos of the finished product, and then I dig in.

A moan escapes me as I bite into it, the maple goodness coating my tongue.

"Moaning for me already, dolcezza?" Elio's voice makes me jump, as I didn't hear him enter.

He leans against the island, looking all too cocky and sinful in that damn suit, the top buttons undone now. It's then that I remember I'm mad at him.

"Wait, why were you crying?" He straightens and comes over to me, taking my face in his hands softly as his eyes search mine.

This damn man. Nothing passes by him.

"I miss my grandma, that's all," I tell him, failing to avoid leaning into his touch despite being annoyed with him.

"I'm sorry," he murmurs as his thumb gently rubs circles on my jaw.

I step back and his hands fall from my face, a frown on his lips. "I'm mad at you."

"What, why?" He looks genuinely confused.

"I know you sent Grant over to Jacobson. You didn't need to do that. I can handle myself. Involving players because you're possessive isn't cool."

Elio's eyebrows dip inward, and his steps slow as he walks toward me. My butt hits the island, and I put my hand on his chest, stopping him.

He grabs my hand on his chest and brings it to his lips before letting it fall at our sides.

"*Dolcezza*, you got it all wrong. I told Grant to take him out if he messes with our guys, and Jacobson did. He was playing dirty with that fucking slash on Isaiah, which went unnoticed by the refs. Did I make a point of saying it after what he said to you? Yes, because you're my girl and no one messes with what's mine. He had it coming to him anyway after the shit he was pulling all game."

I struggle with how to feel because I get what he's saying. Hockey is a cutthroat sport, one of the only team sports where fighting is allowed. I know Jacobson played dirty, but part of me feels bad.

"I don't want to be the reason he got hurt," I murmur.

"You're not, and he's fine. A minor concussion," he assures me. "Do you think he cares about the way he spoke to you? Why do you feel so bad when he didn't give a fuck about being a complete douchebag?"

I open my mouth to respond, but nothing comes out because he's not wrong.

"If I was on the ice and his age, I would've done much worse to him. He got off easy," he scoffs. Elio's hand grips my hip, fingertips digging into my sides. "I care about you so fucking much, it's scary."

My hands reach up to his jaw, pulling his head down to

mine, our foreheads resting on one another's. "I know the feeling," I whisper, my fingers moving to pull at the hair on the back of his neck. He's my first everything, and I want him to be my last. Anytime I think about us breaking up, a painful ache fills my body.

I lean up on my tiptoes and press my lips to his, telling him how much I care about him. It's consuming, like our kiss is. I give and he takes all I'm giving, matching me stride for stride as our lips meld perfectly together.

Elio lifts me on the counter, causing me to inhale sharply. He quickly tears off my sweater and chucks it on the ground. His green eyes darken as they take in my black lace bralette.

"Fuck, these tits," he praises, his hands coming up to grip them. My teeth dig into my bottom lip, a moan slipping through them when his thumbs brush over my nipples.

With my eyes on his, I slip the straps down and yank the bralette down, exposing my breasts to him. Elio likes to be in charge, but so do I at times. His lips are on my nipple in rapid timing, sucking and biting, making my back arch as pleasure dances up my spine.

Elio pulls back, a devious glint in his eyes. I eye him curiously, watching as he brings the bottle of maple syrup over and squeezes it onto my breasts.

"What are you doing?" I pant as he smears the syrup around.

"Having a treat," he says nonchalantly, then leans down, his tongue sucking and lapping up the sticky syrup.

His lips latch onto my nipple, sucking and swirling. My thighs grow slicker at each brush of his mouth over me, and I can't help but moan his name either.

"Elio, fuck," I rasp, gripping onto the counter.

"Maple syrup is good, but on you? It tastes even better," he hums, eyes on me as he takes my other nipple into his mouth.

My lower stomach churns with pleasure, the warmth flooding my body as it builds closer to my orgasm.

"I-I'm going to come."

"Fucking right you are, dolcezza."

Elio continues lavishing my breast as he reaches his hand between us, finding my clit through my tights. All it takes is a couple of strokes and I scream his name as my orgasm hits in full force, my legs shaking as my back bows.

"Oh, my God," I gasp, nails digging into his shoulders.

"I'll be your god anytime," he muses, eyes shining with something I'm not familiar with as he stares at me.

I shake my head at him and push off the counter in search of my sweater.

Elio stops me, scooping me into his arms.

"I'm not done with you yet."

I smirk, feeling a rush of happiness like never before. It's going to be a long night.

Chapter 29

Elio

Dolcezza

What's your favorite dessert?

Me

You.

Dolcezza

Oh I know, trust me. I meant actual food though, babe.

Me

Apple crumble.

I smirk at her calling me babe. It's something she recently started to do, and I fucking love it. Just like how *dolcezza* is no longer a smart-ass remark, but the truth. Because she's my sweetheart, only mine.

If someone had asked me if I thought I'd be flying my private plane to California for the day to pick up a dress my girlfriend saw online at a boutique, I'd laugh.

Brooks' wedding is in a few weeks, and I've asked Jasmine

to come with me. She was thrilled, claiming it'll be her first time leaving the country. That fact prompted me to stay up long after she'd fallen asleep as I planned a vacation for us once we graduate, which will be her Christmas gift.

Jasmine talks about visiting Europe all the time, so that's where we're going for a two-month-long vacation.

She's been looking for a dress to wear for a while now, coming up short every time, because she can't find *the one*. I wanted to tell her that it's not *her* wedding, but I refrained because I know she's also nervous about meeting my friends.

I keep telling her she's perfect and that she has nothing to worry about, yet she still does because that's how my girl is.

Jasmine finally fell in love with a dress she found at a boutique online, her face lighting up with excitement, only to fall with disappointment once she realized how expensive the dress was, and the fact that they didn't ship orders from California.

I said to hell with all of that. If she wants the dress, she's getting it. No matter how expensive or far away it is. Based on the picture she showed me, it's going to look fucking stunning on her.

I don't know how I'll be able to not rip it off her body immediately, but I'll do my best to try.

It's Sunday, which means it's a day free of practice and games for me, making it easy to fly there and back in one day. I told Jasmine I was going out with Brooks for some wedding duty stuff, which isn't a total lie, since I'm getting her a dress for the wedding.

I called the boutique ahead of time, asking them to hold a dress in her size. I ordered her a pair of matching heels, black with gold spiral straps, which should be arriving tomorrow.

I like spoiling her, because not only does she deserve every fucking thing in this world, but because I take great pleasure in knowing I'm the only one who's ever done that for her.

My trip was a short one, and six hours later, I have her dress hanging in the back seat.

My mind wanders as I drive back to the apartment.

We've been dating for a month now, and to say I'm happy is an understatement. Next week, I'm taking her home to meet my family for Thanksgiving, and two weeks after that, we're going to the wedding together.

She hasn't told her father yet, and it bothers me a little. I'm ready to tell him, ready to start living our life as a couple in public. But I know she's not, so I don't push it. I'll take what I can from her any day of the week.

I greet Colin, the dress bag over my shoulder as I head up to our apartment. I push the door open, my heart swelling in my chest at the sight before me.

Jasmine's asleep on the couch, her curls splayed on the pillow, hands under her cheek and her knees curled up toward her chest. The cats are by her feet, all three of them cramped up together.

But what gets me, besides the sight of her existing, is that she's wearing one of my old jerseys. It looks massive on her, swallowing her up whole. I don't know what prompted her to wear it, but I'm not complaining.

Seeing her in my jersey is doing something to the possessive part of me, making me want to bend her over the side of the couch and claim her with my cock once and for all. I shake the thoughts away, softly shutting the door behind me.

My girls awaken, stretching and sauntering over to me. After giving them some love, I place the dress over the back of the couch and walk over to Jasmine, who's still sleeping.

I crouch down, putting a strand of dark hair behind her ear as I press my lips to her forehead. Jasmine stirs, her lashes fluttering before her mocha eyes meet mine.

"Hi," I whisper.

"Hi," she croaks, her voice gravelly from sleep.

"Why are you wearing my jersey?" I inquire, my voice soft.

"Call it curiosity."

"About?" I ask her, smoothing the hair away from her face.

"How you'd react to me in it."

"I fucking love it. Makes me want to throw you over my shoulder." I smirk as the possessive beast inside pumps its chest.

It's then that I smell apples, a sweet, sugary scent following after it.

"Did you make me an apple crumble?" I ask.

She shrugs, a pink hue on her cheeks. "I wanted to do something for you, since I can't buy you anything. It's random and probably weird."

"*Dolcezza*, it's not weird. You're showing me affection by doing something for me. It's normal and appreciated. I'll try some later."

"Later?" She crinkles her nose at me.

"Yeah." I stand, walking over to grab the dress bag off the couch. "I want to show you something first."

Jasmine cocks an eyebrow, tilting her head as she leans up on her elbow. "Elio, what did you do?"

I unzip the bag, my eyes never leaving hers. "You wanted something, so I got it."

The burnt orange dress peeks through the opened zipper, eliciting a gasp from Jasmine, who is now rushing over to me. "How did you do this?" she marvels, running her fingers over the material of the dress. "Did you pay them to ship it here?"

I shake my head at her, placing the dress carefully on the couch. "I may have lied about what I was doing today and I apologize for that, but I knew you'd give me hell for going."

"*Going?* Elio, tell me you didn't," she breathes, looking incredulous.

"I did. I flew there this morning, got the dress, and flew

back. Oh, and your shoes should be here by tomorrow. I think they complement the dress really well, or at least, that's what my sister told me."

Jasmine folds her lips together, her eyes bouncing between mine as she struggles to hold onto her annoyance with me doing this for her. Her eyes shift to the dress on the couch, causing her hold to break, a wide grin spreading across her face.

She closes the space between us, standing on her tiptoes to wrap her arms around my neck. "Thank you, babe. I love it, even if it's a little much that you did all of this for me."

I wrap my arms around her waist, tugging her to my chest as I crane my neck down to look at her. "There's nothing I wouldn't do for you."

As the last word leaves my mouth, her lips crash onto mine. She kisses me fiercely, pouring all of her appreciation into it with a hint of hunger for more. I cradle her head with one hand, the other gripping her ass, and I explore her mouth with my tongue.

Breathless, she pulls back, staring up at me with the utmost trust in her eyes. "I'm ready."

"What?"

"I'm yours, and I want to feel close to you. I'm ready. Please," she states, nothing but a firm confidence in her tone.

I cup her chin, studying her for a beat. "Are you sure, *dolcezza?*"

"I'm sure. We can eat the apple crumble later to celebrate," she teases, her eyes glittering with an eagerness I've yet to see from her.

I'm slightly nervous. I don't want to hurt her, but I know it's going to hurt regardless since it's her first time, but I'm glad it'll be with me.

I crouch down, wrapping my arm around her legs as I hoist her over my shoulder. "I'm ready to eat something else first."

She bursts out laughing, the sound vibrating against my chest, making me warm from the inside out.

I'm so fucking in love with this girl.

And I'm ready to make her mine, completely.

Chapter 30

Jasmine

lio tosses me on his bed, my heart thumping rapidly in my chest. I'm ready for this, but it still doesn't take away the slight anxiety for my first time.

I have no idea what it's going to feel like, despite having read about it in books. Will it hurt and I'll feel nothing but pain the whole time? Will I enjoy it? Will I even have an orgasm? Those are things running through my mind when Elio lies down beside me.

"What are you doing?" I question him, leaning up on my elbows.

"Waiting for you to come sit on my face," he states casually.

"You don't actually want me to do that to you, right?"

"I said come put that pretty cunt of yours on my tongue." His voice is smooth yet demanding, making my body respond instantly.

I crawl over to his lap, where I straddle his waist.

"My face is up here," he says, grabbing my hips and pulling me up where I hover above him. Lifting one hand off of my waist, he trails it up my thighs, looking for panties that aren't there.

I giggle, and he groans. "You haven't been wearing panties this whole time?"

"Nope, didn't feel the need to when your face ends up between my thighs whenever we're home anyway."

His fingers find my entrance, two of them entering me and curling as he thrusts them in and out. I buck forward, my hands finding the headboard. "Good, because once I've fucked you, you're really not going to need them, *dolcezza*. When we're home, I want you in nothing but my shirt. That way when you're being a brat, I can easily slide my cock inside of you and fuck you like you need to be."

Elio's words make the pit of my stomach warm, my pussy dripping around his fingers. He removes them and sucks them into his mouth before gripping my hips and pulling me onto his face.

I'm about to lift up when he tightens his grip, holding me there as he licks my slit, the roughness of his beard rubbing against my thighs.

Oh. My. Fuck.

My head lolls back, my eyelids fluttering as pleasure takes over my entire body. He sucks my clit into his mouth, hard. It's almost too much, but since he's holding me to him, I have no choice but to feel all of it.

It's intense this way, so much so that I come within a minute.

"Elio!" I moan, my orgasm crashing through my body on a rampage, ruining me from the inside out.

I move down his chest, sitting at his waist as I try to catch my breath. Elio smiles at me, my arousal glistening on his face. It's sexy as hell, especially when he wipes it with his hand, then licks it off.

"As much as I want to fuck you in my jersey, I need to see you the first time I fuck you." His voice is rough as he takes the hemline of the jersey into his hands, lifting it over my head and tossing it on the floor.

He sits up, taking a nipple into his mouth, sucking on it before swirling his tongue around , right before biting it. I yelp, but then he soothes the sting with his mouth, pressing kisses all over my breasts, repeating the same pattern to my other one.

His mouth pops as he pulls on my nipple with his lips, making me moan and squirm in his lap.

"I fucking love your tits," he murmurs, right before sucking hard at the underside of my breast, no doubt leaving a mark. He likes to do this often, marking me with his lips where no one will see but him.

I pull his head up to mine, needing his lips immediately. We kiss passionately. His lips are firm against mine, knowing how to lead and set the pace as I kiss him back with just as much fervor.

I trail my fingers until I reach the bottom of his shirt. He pulls back, yanking it over his head with one hand. The move shouldn't turn me on, but it does. I crawl off of his lap, moving to kneel beside him as I undo the zipper on his jeans, his erection nearly bursting through the material.

He moves to stand at the foot of the bed, pulling his jeans and briefs down in one go, leaving him bare. His lengthy cock is rock-solid, the vein on the underside prominent.

I crawl toward him at the edge of the bed, watching as his eyes hood with lust.

"Who would've thought daddy's perfect girl would be crawling on her hands and knees to me, her cunt dripping at the thought of putting my cock in her mouth," he drawls, running one hand up and down his cock.

I stop once I reach him, peering up at him through my lashes. "Let me make you feel good," I plead.

His jaw clenches. "Fuck, those words have never sounded

better. But, *dolcezza*, if you put me in your mouth, I'm not going to last very long."

"Oh." I giggle.

Elio crowds me, making me fall onto my back as his body hovers over mine. "That's funny to you? The way you own me?"

My laughter ceases, my breath catching in my throat. "Take me how you want then. Ruin me."

His head drops, his forehead resting against mine. "Not for your first time, okay? I need to be careful with you. We can work up to that."

"Okay." I nod. Elio rises, making me frown at him.

"Getting a condom. Give me a second."

"If you're okay with it, we don't need it. I'm on the pill and obviously have never been with anyone," I ramble, feeling like an idiot for even bringing it up.

"My last tests were clear."

"I want to feel everything with you, especially my first time."

He crawls back on top of me, a cocky grin on his lips. "You want to be filled with my cum, don't you?"

I nod feverishly. "Only yours."

"Damn fucking right," he growls, taking my lips in a bruising kiss. He kisses me until I'm panting beneath him, my hips arching to meet him as his cock slides against my belly.

"Elio, I need you inside of me. My pussy aches for you," I whimper, gripping his back with my hands.

He kisses my forehead then lifts his head, his deep green eyes filled with desire. "I'm going to take care of you. Do you trust me?"

"I do."

He positions himself between my legs, then uses his hands to spread my thighs farther apart. He rests on his haunches, gripping his cock as he brings it to my slit.

I gasp as he rubs the wetness from my entrance up to my

clit using the tip, spreading it and making me moan at the feel of his cock against the most intimate part of me where no one else has been.

"Ready?" he asks, his eyes softening as they look at me.

"Yes."

He keeps his eyes trained on me as he slides the tip inside of me. I tighten around him, feeling a pleasure like no other unfurl in my stomach.

He stops, one hand on his cock, the other planted beside my head. "Are you okay?"

"Yeah, it's a different feeling, but it's a good different. I like it. Keep going," I urge him.

Elio inches forward, slowly sliding himself inside of me. I wince as the pain kicks in, my pussy feeling like it's being stretched beyond its capacity.

"Do you want me to stop? I'm less than halfway," he asks, his voice laced with concern.

Less than halfway? Is he fucking joking with me? Where is it all going to go?

I shake my head at him despite my internal worries, moving my hips to take more of him. "No, keep going until you can't. It's going to hurt, but I need you to fill me."

He grimaces, not liking that he's hurting me as he presses deeper inside until his balls hit my skin. I inhale sharply, a mix of a whimper and a moan leaving my lips in the next breath.

Elio grunts, lowering himself so that his face is above mine, his other hand coming to rest beside my head. We're both breathing heavily as he lets me take a minute to feel everything that I need to.

It hurts, I won't deny it. His cock is massive, and I've never been stretched like this. But it also feels really good at the same time.

It's a dichotomy, pain and pleasure wrapped into one.

"You okay?" he pants, pressing a kiss to the tip of my nose.

"You just had to have the biggest cock, didn't you?" I groan, needing this ache to go away.

He chuckles, but it's short-lived. "You're soaked and stretching around me. Give it a few seconds."

I do as he says, the two of us staring intently at one another, neither of us moving a muscle until his lips come crashing down onto mine. His hips move of their own accord, his cock thrusting inside of me.

I expect pain to pulsate through my core, but it's pleasure instead. I moan against his lips, wrapping my legs around his waist to pull him in tighter to my body.

"Sorry about that," he apologizes, then laughs. "I'm usually not this soft in bed, so don't expect it again. Next time, it'll be a different story."

I move my hips against his, rocking on his cock.

He groans. "Jasmine, I'm trying to take this slow and be gentle."

"At least move, dammit," I grumble in frustration. "I need to feel you move inside of me."

He rolls his hips against mine, setting the pace as his cock rocks in and out of me. His eyes are on mine, his body slick with sweat as he moves in and out with a perfect rhythm.

I moan as his cock hits a spot deep inside me. He grunts, doing the same move but harder this time, making me see fucking stars. The way he rolls his hips has his shaft rubbing against my clit, making my spine shiver at the sensation.

His lips find my neck, kissing and sucking the soft skin there as my fingers thread through his hair, tugging as he rocks in and out of me.

"I need to fuck you," he groans. "I'm trying to be gentle, but fuck. It's killing me."

"Then don't be. Fuck me, *roomie*," I entice him.

His eyes darken as he leans up and unwraps my legs from around my waist. "Roomie, huh? I think someone needs a lesson, don't you?"

"Yes," I moan as he flips me over so that I'm lying on my stomach.

I barely have time to think before he's lifting my ass into the air, my chest on the bed as he slides into me. I cry out, his cock feeling even fuller this way.

Elio wraps my hair around his fist, yanking my chest up, and I place my hands on the bed. "Is this what *roommates* do?" he snaps, using my hair to help him thrust in and out of me at a pace that has my eyes rolling and toes curling. It's rough, yet precise, skilled and measured thrusts of his cock. "My cock is the first and last one you'll ever feel inside of you. Does that sound very roommate-like to you?"

"No," I whine.

"That's what I thought. I'm the only man you need, the only cock you'll come on. Tell me you understand this," he grits.

"You are the only man and cock I'll ever need."

His other palm lands a smack on my ass, my pussy tightening around his cock as I sigh his name. Elio does it again as his cock brutally works me from behind, his hand still fisting in my hair.

"Come on my cock, Jasmine. Let me feel that cunt squeeze me," he demands, his words setting me off as my orgasm ripples through me.

I moan and writhe, my body shaking with the aftershocks as his name continues to fall off my tongue. He pulls out, rounding the bed to stand in front of me. His cock is inches from my face, coated in my arousal.

He grips my cheeks, pulling my mouth around his cock. "You know I don't like messes, *dolcezza*. Clean it up like the dirty slut you are."

Holy. Fuck.

My core hums at his words, loving them for whatever reason. I happily suck his cock, tasting myself as I lick up the evidence of my orgasm.

"That's my dirty girl," he says, his words coated in filth.

He doesn't let me do it for long, pulling out of my mouth abruptly. He gently pushes me onto my back, crawling between my thighs again where he slides into me much more easily this time.

Elio slaps his hips against mine rapidly, his jaw clenching as he swears under his breath. "Your cunt is fucking made for me. You feel so good, Jasmine."

It doesn't take long for another orgasm to build as he begins to stroke my clit. That familiar warm feeling spreads throughout my body as he fucks me into oblivion, taking him right with me as we come at the same time, our moans and yells filling the air.

I feel him spill inside of me, and I gasp at the feeling. It's nothing like I've ever felt before, making me feel like I belong to someone as if he's officially claimed my body.

His movements slow as we ride out our high, our bodies heaving with each breath. Elio brushes a stray curl off my forehead, replacing it with a kiss. "I'm going to pull out," he warns me, sitting up as he then pulls out.

I wince, feeling sore now that the high of the pleasure is gone. Something warm spills out of me, and I quickly realize that it's his cum.

Elio's eyes are glued to my pussy, watching in fascination. "This is mine." His voice is rough, his eyes cutting up to mine. "Your cunt has never looked prettier than it does with my cum dripping out of you."

I blush at his words. "That was fun." I beam, feeling relaxed and euphoric.

"Hold that thought," he tells me, standing to go to the

washroom and returning with a wet cloth. He gently wipes between my legs, then throws it in the hamper. I go to the washroom next and then return to bed, where he wraps me up in his arms.

I rest my arm across his chest, nuzzling my head in between his neck and shoulder.

"So you're okay?" he asks, kissing the top of my head. "I got a little carried away there. I didn't mean to get so rough with you on your first time."

"I wanted it. I'm pretty sure I begged you." I laugh, feeling so light. "I'm perfect, okay? A little sore, but that was to be expected."

Speaking of, I wonder if I bled, instantly feeling embarrassed if I did and if there's a mess on the bed. The chances are low because of volleyball, as athletes usually tear it due to training, but I still feel uncomfortable if I did.

I attempt to pull away from him, but he nestles me tighter against him. "What's wrong?"

"Did I…you know, bleed?"

"No, *dolcezza*, and even if you did, I don't care. It's natural and nothing to be embarrassed about," he reassures me, tilting my chin so that he can press his lips to mine in a soft kiss.

I melt into him, loving how he can be so rough yet so gentle and soft with me. He knows which side of him I need before I do.

Elio then slips out of bed and returns moments later with two plates of apple crumble, making me burst into giggles.

We then proceed to eat in bed, which surprises the hell out of me because of his need to keep things clean. There are crumbs in the bed by the end of our dessert, but he doesn't seem to mind. He pulls my body close to his and kisses me senselessly.

My heart screams at me, telling me that I love him, and this time, my head doesn't argue like it has for the past week. This time, it agrees, making my entire body buzz with the knowledge.

I love Elio Mazzo, even when I know I shouldn't.

Chapter 31

Elio

The next day, I ran practice by myself as Ned had an important faculty meeting to attend for all head coaches.

I didn't think I'd enjoy it, but I found myself in the zone, my mind empty except for what was right in front of me. It's moments like those that make me believe I'm right where I need to be.

I still don't know what I want to do post-graduation. I have the money and the intelligence, and soon, the degree to prove it, but there's no spark of passion to expand on. I love coaching, but my body is itching for more. I want to find a driving force like playing hockey did.

"Coach Mazzo." Isaiah coughs, clearing his throat as he approaches me while I store equipment away.

"Mind giving me a hand, Thomas?" I ask because when Ned is here, cleanup goes a lot faster.

"Sure." He jumps right in, helping me cart off various things to the storage room without missing a beat. He's a hard-working athlete, having listened to my advice about improving his stamina. He's gotten faster on the ice, which has resulted in more confidence for him and upping his overall abilities.

I lock the room once it's all put away and turn to him. "Thanks for helping, Thomas, appreciate it."

"No problem, Coach." He smiles, but it doesn't last. "Hey, can I talk to you?" His voice shakes.

"Yeah, let's go to my office." I do my best to sound calm, but internally, I'm stressing the fuck out. What is he going to say? I've never done this side of coaching yet, the interpersonal stuff, and I have no idea if I'll be any good at it.

Once we're in my office, I offer him a water, which he takes, and then we both stand there in silence.

"What did you want to talk about?" I prod, noting how his knee is bouncing and that he keeps running a hand over his brown mop. He's nervous and it's making *me* nervous.

"I have to quit the team," he says, nearly knocking me on my ass.

"What? Why?"

He can't quit. He's made so much progress already and he's easily the best player on our team.

"My mom's business isn't doing well, and she can't afford all the bills. I need to quit the team, drop out of school, and get a job to help her out so my siblings don't have to go through that. I can't even attend school without my hockey scholarship." He's breathing heavily, nearly hyperventilating.

"Hey," I say as I walk over to him. "Look at me."

Brown eyes flash to mine, so much worry and uncertainty in them.

"Tell me five things you can see right now."

"You," he exhales, eyes searching the room. "The door, your desk, a water bottle, and your computer."

"Good, now take a few deep breaths," I instruct him, watching with relief as he begins to calm down.

"What's your mom's business?" I ask out of curiosity. He's not leaving this team nor this school. I'll make sure of it one way or another.

"She owns and runs a music school. The landlord increased rent, and she refuses to upcharge families to account for it. It doesn't help that she's had a lot of kids drop out recently, too," he explains, looking so damn lost.

"Do you mind taking me there?" I say before I think it through.

"Why?"

"Because I want to meet your mom and get to understand her business. You're not quitting."

"But—"

"Thomas, this team needs you and you'd be stupid to waste your potential now after all the years of hard work you've put in. I refuse to see that happen. You're going places, and I'm going to help you get there, okay?"

"Coach." He looks speechless, his brown eyes glassy.

"Don't thank me yet. Let's go meet Mama Thomas first."

Tammy Thomas is a bright, warm woman who wants nothing more than to pass on her love of music to the next generation.

We caught the tail end of her class and I could see how much she adores what she does. It was in the gentleness she corrected students with, the love in her eyes as she watched them play and the way she moved around the room to the beat.

After talking with her about her business for an hour, it was clear to me what the issue was. For one, she needed to get out of the area she was in. It wasn't a great location, and she needed to be more accessible to kids to commute to.

She also needed a social media presence, since she had none at all. I mentioned a grant I knew of that one of my old hockey buddies has for music schools, since his mom was also a music teacher.

Tammy was more than grateful when I told her not to worry about a thing because not only was I going to put a good word in with my teammate, I was going to find and buy her a new location and create her social media presence.

The conversation lit a fire in me, this innate desire to help her and their family, and I think that's what got me. Hearing all about the Thomas household from Isaiah and his mother this afternoon reminded me of my own family.

I knew I was enjoying helping Jasmine with her business, but I thought it was because it was *her*. Maybe this is what I'm meant to be doing. Helping small businesses.

Isaiah would stay at RLU, on our team, and his mom was going to have a kick-ass music school soon.

I'd make sure of it.

Chapter 32

Jasmine

*P*ine trees pass by in a blur as I drive toward my parent's house on the outskirts of town.

My mother texted me last night, asking if I'd come over for a visit. I didn't want to, which sounds awful, but I know it's going to turn into her pestering me about my life.

I narrow my eyes as I pull into the driveway, thinking I must be imagining Elio's SUV parked in my usual spot.

Why the hell is he here?

Don't get me wrong, I want to see him. He's my boyfriend. But not here. Not where we have to pretend we're nothing but acquaintances.

I turn my car off, then slide out and nestle myself in my trench coat. The November chill is biting today, making me hurry up the steps and to the front door.

"Mom?" I call out, hanging my jacket up in the foyer.

"In the living room," she shouts back.

I kick off my booties, still feeling cold as I wrap my arms around my body. Not that it's cold in here, but this house is so pristine and elegant that it feels that way.

Passing the mirror in the foyer, I stop to adjust my outfit. I have on a black long-sleeved bodysuit, with a brown leather skirt. Elio and I were supposed to have a date night at home when I got back, which meant I had to get all dolled up to come here so that when I got home, I looked like this.

Now, I can't wait to watch him try and hold it together in front of my parents while I look this good. It gives me an extra boost, making me smile as I make my way toward the living room.

My knuckles knock on the ajar door, drawing three sets of eyes my way as I enter the room.

My parents look elated to see me.

And then there's Elio. His deep green eyes darken, roaming up and down my body hungrily. I've seen that look before, when his head is between my thighs, and he's about to devour me. Too bad that can't happen right now.

"Mom, *Appa*," I greet them with a smile. "And Ethan, right?" I stifle a giggle, knowing he's going to punish me for this later.

"Elio," he corrects me, his tone cool and collected.

I sit down opposite him. He's sitting next to my father, with my mother on my right.

"What brings you two here?" I ask my father because as far as I was concerned, it was supposed to be my mother and me here today.

"I thought it'd be more relaxing to review tapes here," my father replies, taking a sip of his coffee.

"Makes sense," I say while I play with the hem of my skirt. My eyes flit to Elio, only to see his hand balled in a fist while he does anything but look at me.

"We were just catching up with your mother, but we'll leave you two to have girl time," he smiles, kissing my mother on the cheek before doing the same to me.

"Mrs. Park, always a pleasure to see you." Elio hugs her,

then looks at me with barely restrained control. "Jasmine, nice to see you."

Then he leaves, following my father out of the living room and toward the theater room to review tapes.

"Such a good man. I can't believe how big he is now," my mother comments, sipping her tea.

"Uh, I guess." I grab a blueberry scone and shove it in my mouth to avoid smiling. If only she knew how *big* he really is.

"So tell me, how's life going? I miss you." She smiles while reaching out to grip my hand. It warms me, reminding me that even though we don't always see eye to eye, she's still my mother, whom I love.

"It's honestly great. I love this time of year. The crisp air, the color of the leaves changing, comfy sweaters, all the fall foods, and Halloween," I ramble, feeling myself getting giddy. Even though Halloween is over, I am a fall girl through and through.

"You always loved fall as a kid, too. You'd spend hours outside jumping in piles of leaves, collecting your favorite ones to keep in your room. Then you'd wake up sad when they finally decayed." Her hazel eyes sparkle, lost in the memory.

"Yeah, I did," I reminisce along with her, the scene playing out perfectly in my head. My *halmeoni* would always have a snack waiting for me inside, and the fact makes my chest ache since she's no longer here.

"Enough about the past. Let's talk about the future."

There it is.

"Have you thought about what you want to do? It's nearly the end of the first semester, and applications are due in January for positions that start grad school." She claps her hands together in her lap, looking at me expectantly.

I take another bite of my scone, trying to buy myself some more time to think of what to say. "You know how stressful midterms were, and now it's already finals season soon, so it hasn't crossed my mind."

"I know there's a lot going on, but you can't let your future slip through your fingers because you're busy."

"I know, Mother, I know." I blow out a breath, doing my best to keep my composure. We can never have a normal conversation, it seems.

"Once that's in motion, you should let me introduce you to my friend's son," she prattles on, telling me all about this man I have zero interest in meeting.

Sometimes I feel like my mother's personal Sims character, where she dictates and plans my life out for me. I rub my temples, the beginning of a migraine coming on. Thankfully, my mother notices.

"What's wrong, a headache?" she asks, looking at me with genuine worry.

"Yeah, I think I'm going to go lie down in my room for a bit. Is that okay?"

"Of course, go on up. I'll be out in the greenhouse if you need me," she assures me, walking with me to my room, then leaves once she sees that I'm resting on my bed.

Unable to get comfortable considering my outfit, I pull out my e-book app and begin reading where I left off. It was about a twenty-something Margo who has the hots for her dad's best friend, Ford.

"We can't do this," he breathes, *backing up for every step I take toward him.*

"Can't do what?" I play coy, running a single finger down his bare chest.

"Margo, you can't be touching me like that. I'm your dad's best friend." He looks anywhere but at me.

"No one can make me come," I whine, stepping into his space,

rubbing my bathing-suit-clad body up against his. He inhales sharply, looking down to see me pressed against him. "I bet you could with all your experience, but maybe I'm wrong."

He grips my chin forcefully, making my thighs quiver. "Make no mistake, I'd make you come ten times over. But I can't."

"Tell me you don't want me, and I'll leave you alone."

War rages in his blue eyes. "I can't do that either," he whispers, reaching behind my neck to undo the tie of my bikini top, letting it fall, revealing my breasts to him. Before I can even process what he did, his lips are wrapped around a nipple.

I gasp.

"Mmm, so perfect," he growls, switching to the other breast as he ravages me.

"I need you inside me, Ford," I pant.

"Such a dirty mouth for such a sweet girl, my sweet girl," he rasps, kissing his way up my neck while his hands grip my ass. "Tell me you didn't let that fucker take your virginity?"

"No, I wanted you to have it. Only you." I jump up and he catches me, my legs wrapping around his waist.

"Damn fucking straight it's mine. If we do this, Margo, you're mine. Once my cock enters you, you'll have no other cock for the rest of your life. Are you sure about this?" he asks so seriously that it makes me more feral for him than before.

Okayyyy, and I'm needy for Elio now. I don't have any vibrators here obviously, and I don't think my fingers will do it for me, not after knowing what it's like to be touched by him.

I want him to fuck me in my parents' home, right here, right now. The fact that they're both home only adds to the heat spreading across my body, knowing how risky it would be.

I send him a text.

Me

Come up to my room, second
door on the right upstairs.
I need you badly.

Elio

What's wrong? I'm on my way up.

I don't reply because he's already in my room, shutting the door quietly behind him. He turns, his eyes going wide when he sees that my fingers are sliding in and out of my pussy. I couldn't wait for him because the ache between my legs was too intense.

"Fuck, Jasmine. What are you doing?" he groans, watching me.

"What does it look like I'm doing? I'm fucking myself until you could get here and give me your cock instead," I pant while growing wetter as his eyes stay glued to my pussy. He loves it, and I love that.

"*Dolcezza*, your dad is downstairs, and your mom is I don't even know where. I told him I had to call my mom. That doesn't give us much time."

"Elio, are you going to fuck me or not? I need you," I whine, rubbing my clit, but it doesn't do me any good. I want him.

"You know I can never say no to you," he groans, unbuckling his belt and shoving his pants and briefs down enough to let his hard cock spring free. "Be quiet and take it like a good little slut, got it?"

I nod fervently as he climbs over me, his lips crashing on mine as he slams his cock inside of me with no warning.

"Fuck," I yelp, making Elio's eyes widen. He looks around, seeing the panties I discarded beside me. Elio grabs them, balling them up.

"Open," he whispers, and I do. He puts my panties in my mouth, ensuring I won't be making any more noise.

And then he unleashes himself on me, pounding into me like never before. It's nearing painful, but I love how deep he is, how full I feel of him. Fuck, why is that so hot?

"I love fucking you," he grunts. "My little slut is doing so good." His voice is raspy as he looks between us while his cock slides in and out rapidly.

I dig my nails into his biceps, holding on for dear life as he fucks me. I can feel my orgasm starting at the tips of my toes.

"Ethan, huh?" he bites out, thrusting into me relentlessly. "I wish I could spank you right now because you know exactly whose cock you come on every morning and night."

I moan around my panties and reach up, resting my arms around his neck as my fingers tug at the hair on the back of his head. Elio brings his hand between us, stroking my clit with precise flicks that he knows drive me insane.

"Come for me before your parents find me fucking their precious girl. Show me what a good little slut you are."

His words cause my orgasm to shoot through me, warmth spreading in its wake as I come so hard I nearly black out while my pussy squeezes him inside of me. Elio follows me, coming inside of me as his hips jerk roughly against mine.

He pulls out quicker than I'd like, pulling my panties out of my mouth.

"You did so well," he whispers, kissing my cheek before getting up and tucking himself back in his pants. "You okay?"

"More than okay, thank you. I needed that."

"That was so fucking hot," he muses, fixing his shirt and making himself look as if he didn't rail me while my father is waiting for him downstairs.

I can feel his cum leaking out of me, and it makes me want

round two. There's something about it that makes me feel feral for him, seeing his seed on me. It's possessive and raw, like nothing I've ever felt before.

"Fuck, *dolcezza*. I love watching my cum seep out of you, but I need to get back. Push it back inside you. I want you to feel me when I'm gone," he orders me, then opens the door and walks out of my room.

I do as he says, leaving me breathless and needy for more because that man has quite the mouth. Who needs fictional men when my real-life man has a mouth like that?

I've never felt luckier.

"Pass me the salt," I instruct Elio.

He leans over the island, grabbing the salt for me.

We're making Kimchi together, in honor of what would have been my *halmeoni*'s birthday today. It was her favorite dish.

She taught me her secret recipe, and it's the one I've used ever since.

"Now, you're going to sprinkle some on the cabbage," I tell him as I pass the bowl of chopped cabbage to him.

"How much exactly?"

"Honestly, we never measured things out exactly. As my grandma would say, use your heart."

Elio smiles as he begins to sprinkle the salt over the cabbage. "Our cultures are similar that way, leading with our hearts in the kitchen."

I smile back at him, watching as he carefully carries out each task that I taught him.

"What's next?" he asks excitedly.

Elio and I have been cooking a lot together, teaching each other about our culture through food. We'll rotate, where he teaches me how to cook traditional Italian meals, and I teach him how to cook traditional Korean meals, along with some American meals I learned from my mom.

"Massage the salt into the cabbage."

Elio grins. "Watch these hands work their magic."

I giggle at that, knowing his hands are quite literally magic with the way they work my body.

After a few minutes of him massaging the cabbage, we move on to the next step.

"Next, we need to make the paste while the cabbage sits for a while," I tell him as I line up the ingredients for him to put into the blender.

As we work together to combine the paste with the carrots, green onions, and cabbage, a similar sense of peace settles over me.

The one that used to fill me when I spent time in the kitchen with my grandmother. I rub the heart on my bracelet, a small smile on my lips as a tear strolls down my cheek.

"안녕하세요 할머니, 보고 싶어요," I whisper.

Elio comes up behind me, wrapping his arms around my waist as he kisses my cheek.

"What did you say?" he asks.

"I was saying hi to my grandma, and that I missed her. I could feel her here with us now." My eyes water once more.

His grip on me tightens, his voice like silk in my ear. "Can you tell her something for me?"

I nod, unable to speak.

"Tell her that her granddaughter is the most brilliant and beautiful person, and I thank her for having a hand in that."

And now I'm sobbing.

With a shaky breath, I whisper, "할머니한테 내 여자친구는 굉장히 좋은사람이고, 또 부자예요 할머니, 잘 키워주셔서 정말 감사합니다."

Contentedness washes over me as I feel her love coursing through my body. This is why I bake, for the connection I feel to her each time I do. It's something I never want to lose.

It's a part of myself, and I'm terrified to let it go.

Chapter 33

Elio

The morning sun peeks through my office window, where I'm finishing up what needs to be done before the short break we get off of hockey for Thanksgiving weekend.

Ned is across the hall, working to get things done as well. He and Paul, the dean, are heading to the football game today, while Jasmine and I are traveling to my parents' house for Thanksgiving dinner.

She's nervous as hell to meet them, along with my sisters, their spouses, and my niece and nephew. They're going to love her as much as I do. I haven't told her yet, not wanting to scare her off since this is all new to her.

It worked out well for us that her dad already had plans today, and her mom is working a twelve-hour shift at the hospital, so they're having their own family Thanksgiving tomorrow instead. Jasmine is mine for the day, and this way, she doesn't have to lie to her parents.

I'm finishing up my work when I hear her voice carrying down the hallway. Through my office window, I can see that she's here to see her dad.

We're supposed to leave here in an hour, once her dad is gone for the day. I had a driver of mine drop her off so she didn't walk here by herself and so that she could avoid leaving her car in the parking lot overnight, raising suspicion.

I get up out of my chair, opening my door slightly so that I can hear their conversation. Call it overprotective, but I know how her parents make her feel at times, and if he starts making her uncomfortable, I'll come up with some way to get her out of there.

I can't hear much honestly, a random laugh here and there. A few minutes later, Jasmine and her dad exit his office. I watch from my peripheral vision as I pretend to be busy on my computer since they can see right into my office.

"It was nice to see you, Jasmine. I know you've been working hard, but your mother and I miss you. I think having you around the house all summer made us realize how much we missed you living at home," her dad says, looking at her like she's his entire world.

"I miss you both, too." She smiles, but it doesn't reach her eyes. "I'll see you tomorrow, okay? I have to go to the washroom and then I'm heading home. Have fun at the game, and tell Paul I said hi!"

"All right, I will. Drive safely tomorrow, and have a good night, Jas." He pulls her into a hug, then parts, heading down the hallway as Jasmine walks in the opposite direction toward the washroom.

She's stalling, waiting for him to leave and then she's coming to my office so we can get on the road. Jasmine enters my office after a few minutes, looking fucking edible in her loungewear, a gray cropped hoodie and matching gray sweats.

She plans on changing before we get to my mom's, wanting

to be comfortable during the car ride. But truthfully, she looks good like this. Just the way she is.

I stride over to her, not even saying hello as my mouth crashes onto hers, pushing her back against the door as I lift her and wrap her legs around my waist. She gasps in surprise but quickly reciprocates my need, kissing me back.

We're insatiable with one another, the pull too fucking strong to ignore when we're in the same room. I break away from her lips to close and lock my door, then shut my blinds, all while keeping her in my arms.

Jasmine's chest is heaving, her lips swollen and eyes glazed with lust. I put her body back against the door, taking her lips in a punishing kiss, my lips rough and demanding as my tongue prods between her lips seeking access.

She grants it, letting me taste her and tango with her tongue as we kiss passionately. Her hands are on my waist, gripping me tightly. I slide my hand down her waist and under the waistband of her sweats, groaning when I fail to find her panties.

My voice is husky and low as I speak while running my finger along her wet slit. "Such a fucking brat."

"I want you to bend me over your desk," she murmurs as my lips bite the soft skin on her neck, followed by my lips pressing soft kisses over the same spot. This girl is trying to kill me with how perfect she is. I've only thought about this exact scenario a thousand times before.

I pull away from her neck, putting her down in front of my desk, and flipping her body so that she's bent over it. I yank her sweats down in one fluid motion, leaving her pert ass in the air. "You want me to fuck you like this, *hmm*? And be my dirty little slut?"

"Yes," she moans in response.

I pull my zipper and jeans down, reaching in my briefs to

pull my raging hard cock out, swiping it between her wet lips, back and forth as I tease her. She groans, annoyed with my teasing, and usually, I'd toy with her more, but I feel the need to fill her right this damn second.

I enter her swiftly, sliding right into the hilt, her cunt choking me. She's so damn tight, wet, and warm. It's my favorite place to be.

I set a punishing pace, my hips snapping wildly, thrusting into her with abandon. If it weren't for my hold on her hips, she'd be halfway onto my desk with the way my cock is pounding into her. She moans and cries out in pleasure, the sounds of my favorite melody in the world.

It's then that a knock sounds on my door.

"Hey, Coach, can we talk for a second?" McCoy calls out through my door.

Jasmine's head whips around to mine, her eyes wide, lips parting, but no sound leaves her.

"Yeah, give me a few minutes, on the phone," I bite out, lying through my teeth. I don't know why the fuck he needs to talk to me now, but he interrupted my time with Jasmine, and that's time I don't like to waste.

Jasmine tries to get up, but I push her back down onto my desk, my hand moving to cover her mouth. "No, lie back and take my cock like the good girl you pretend to be," I whisper, my words a demand.

She moans against my hand, her hips pushing back against mine as she takes control for a bit, moving her cunt up and down my cock. I let her, enjoying watching her ass bounce each time her hips meet mine.

I grab ahold of her hips with one hand, the other still covering her mouth as I take control, fucking her roughly and deeply with each hard thrust of my cock inside of her. Her cunt squeezes me, wrapping around my cock so tightly that my own orgasm hits me, both of us muffling our sounds as I spill into her.

I stay there for a few beats as our breathing comes down. I pull out of her, loving the way my cum drips out of her. It's the most beautiful thing I've seen second to her.

I pull her body up, along with her sweats, and kiss her neck gently, her body melting against mine. "I'll be right back. Hide behind my desk."

"I need a tissue or something, I can feel you dripping all over my thighs."

I grin, kissing her lips sweetly. "Good, that's what you get for wearing no panties outside of the house."

I leave her with that, walking to my door as she crouches down behind my desk.

I swing the door open, my voice cold as I greet McCoy. "What do you need?"

"Do you know if I can practice over the weekend? Will anyone be here?"

Are you fucking kidding me? He interrupted me for this?

"I don't know, kid. Find the maintenance staff and see if anyone will be around to let you skate for a bit," I tell him, backing up to close my door on him.

"Okay, thanks," is all he says, my door closing on him.

Jasmine giggles from under my desk. I walk around to her, putting my hands out to help her stand. She puts her small, soft hands in mine, letting me pull her up to stand.

"Is that what they call a three-pump chump?" Her tone is all tease, a single eyebrow raised.

I scoff at her, shaking my head. "You know damn well it was more than three pumps."

"Oh, I don't know, it ended so quickly it was hard to tell."

"You brat." I chuckle, turning off my computer and the

lights as I shut down for the weekend. "I'll take care of you properly later."

We leave the facility, Jasmine walking ahead of me so that it doesn't look suspicious. We meet in the coach's garage, where no one's around and we can take off.

Jasmine clutches my hand in hers in the center console of my SUV, en route to my mom's house. Little does she know I have a surprise stop for her before we get there. I have a pickup game of hockey with some old friends from high school.

It's our Thanksgiving tradition, getting together on the ice before splitting up to go home for Thanksgiving dinner.

It's time I show her why they called me a legend, even if I can't skate the way I used to.

Chapter 34

Jasmine

The GPS says we're about fifteen minutes away from his mom's house, and my stomach turns upside down at the thought.

It's my first time ever doing something like this and I want them to all like me because if there's one thing I know, it's how important family is.

Elio pulls over into a parking lot in the main strip of his small town, the buildings all different colors, with early Christmas decorations adorning the windows on each one. The lampposts are wrapped in garland, twinkling lights strung from the buildings across the road to the other.

There's an outdoor hockey arena in the center across the parking lot, but what catches my eye is the burnt orange building on the corner, across the road with a For Rent sign in the window.

A vision of my bakery right there on that corner lot hits me, the name "Minniebakes," hanging over the door. The inside is bright, full of white, cream, and pale orange colors. There'd be a bookshelf wall, filled with books for people to donate, return, and read while at the bakery.

I'd have a counter full of goodies for the day, along with preorders waiting to be picked up alongside the back wall. There'd be a lineup of customers, a staff member or two helping me run the place.

"Jasmine?" Elio says, snapping me back to the present.

"Yes?" I swing my head in his direction, my gaze connecting with those dark green eyes I love to lose myself in.

"What was going on in that brain of yours?"

I fold my lips together, then take a deep breath. Elio's become one of my best friends too, which makes it easy to open up to him. "I saw it, my dream career all inside that corner lot. I could see every minuscule detail, could feel the excitement of it in my bones as if it actually happened already. I'd open my own bakery there."

With my admission comes an ache in my chest at the fact that it probably won't happen.

"It'll happen if you want it to, *dolcezza*. It's your choice. Your page has grown, tripling your previous income. By the time you graduate, you'll have enough to buy it on your own," he encourages me. Elio peers past me, looking at the corner lot, writing something down on his phone quickly before stashing it away.

"I have something I want to show you," he tells me before I can question him. He exits the SUV and rounds it, coming to open my door for me. Before I step out, he leans in, pressing his lips to mine, and I kiss him back just as lovingly, whimpering in protest when he pulls back from me.

"We need to be careful. Paparazzi aren't common because it's a small town, but still," he tells me, opening the back seat to grab my winter jacket and a beanie.

I put my jacket on, Elio tugging the beanie over my head as I slide my sunglasses on.

He shuts the back door, moving to the trunk from where he emerges with a hockey bag.

"What's that for?" I ask.

"You mentioned having never seen me play a game before, so we're fixing that."

"But, babe, what about your leg? I don't want you to get hurt." I frown at him, the mental image of it making my insides twist in agony.

He closes the distance between us, his hockey bag over one shoulder as he cups my chin with one hand. "I'll be fine, *dolcezza*. It's a pick-up game that me and some guys from high school do every Thanksgiving. It's nothing serious, and I can still skate. The risks with playing in the NHL were too high, that's all."

"Okay, but be careful, please," I plead, my eyes bouncing between his.

"It's cute when you're being protective of me. I like it," he muses, leading the way as we walk toward the outdoor hockey arena.

There's a bunch of guys on the benches once we get closer, all of them turning to us.

"Elio fucking Mazzo!" one guy cheers, the rest following suit with their own greetings as they all shake hands with him, some hugging him.

Elio greets them, then looks back at me. "This is Jasmine, a friend from school."

I know he's doing it to protect us because if one of these guys wanted to sell the story to a tabloid, they could.

They all wave, smiling at me, except for one, who looks at me more intently than the others. His brown hair is curled around his beanie. Light blue eyes flick up and down my body. "Well, hello there," he drawls.

"Don't even think about it unless you want to be checked

into the boards so hard you miss your dinner, Patrick." Elio stands up taller, his tone clipped.

Patrick waves him off. "Friends' my ass."

I chuckle while Elio places his hand on the small of my back, guiding me toward a bench so I can watch them play.

"Where are their spouses?" I ask, noticing I'm the only person here.

"We make it a rule that no spouses or kids can attend, but you're the exception this year." He smiles brightly at me, pulling my beanie down to cover my ears.

He sits down beside me instead of with his friends, putting his skates and his helmet on.

"You ready to be entertained?" he asks, standing taller than before as the skates give him extra height.

I fake a yawn, patting my hand over my mouth. "You know, I should've brought my notes with me to study if I'd known you were going to be playing."

He rolls his eyes, a deep laugh leaving his throat. It's my favorite side of Elio to see, the playful and happy one.

He skates out onto the ice, joining his friends, who are picking teams. Minutes later, they're facing off, Elio at the forefront, his stick ready as he's bent into position.

He gets the puck and passes it to his teammate. I'm mesmerized by watching how effortlessly he moves on the ice. He's graceful yet rough as he shoves his friends to beat them to the puck. He's faster than any of them, even with his injury, and he proves his scoring skills by making three goals within the first five minutes.

I'd be lying if I said I was

Watching your man dominate the ice, lead his teammates, and demonstrate his strength as he shoves people into the boards has me feeling warm beneath my coat despite the chilly temperature.

240

I'm enjoying myself until a man stands a few feet away near the entrance, leaning against the frame as he watches the men skate around.

He's one of those people who instantly give off a bad feeling, almost like a warning siren.

"Elio Mazzo, the most overhyped athlete on this planet," he mutters.

I glare at him, instantly on the defensive for my man.

"He's not a legend. He's weak for not returning to the game, fucking coward." He shakes his head, his eyes glued to Elio on the ice as he talks to himself.

I've always had a defensiveness in me to protect the ones I love, unable to keep my mouth shut when it comes to defending them. "He's one of the most talented athletes the sport has seen, actually," I speak up, my voice strong and assertive.

The man turns his head to look at me, his eyes lighting up at my words like he wanted to argue with anyone who would listen. "The only thing he was talented at was sticking his dick in all those women."

Fury fills my veins, causing me to stand and walk right over to him. "He's more than the media made him out to be. He's kind, smart, and generous. You should try it sometime."

"What makes you think you know anything? A *woman* is trying to tell me about the sport's greatest failure? Fuck off." He spits, literally *spits* in my face.

I stumble back from the shock of it, my back meeting a hard chest. Elio quickly moves in front of me, still on his skates, and he lunges at the man, knocking him to the ground with one punch that connects with his nose.

"You ever touch or even look at my girl the wrong way again, and you'll be leaving on a stretcher," he snaps, hovering over the man.

His friends pull Elio back, the others picking the man up and escorting him out of the arena, his bloody nose and all.

"Fucking piece of shit," he shouts, yanking his helmet off and tossing it on the ground.

"Bro, chill. He's not worth it. Let it go," his friend tells him, yanking Elio's shoulders to stop him from following them.

I wipe my cheek, feeling the sudden need to throw up at having this man's saliva on me. I run over to the nearest trash can, doing exactly that. Elio's warmth surrounds me, his hand holding my hair back. Once I'm done, I look up at him, seeing the anger that's swirling in his irises, his jaw set more tightly than I've ever seen it before.

"Are you okay? What the hell happened?" he asks, his voice much softer than his face right now.

"I'm okay, but disgusted." I wipe my cheek once more, needing a shower to erase his grime from my skin. "He was talking badly about you, and I couldn't take it. I defended you and he didn't like that."

Elio's rage lessens slightly, but not much as he frowns at me. "*Dolcezza*, I don't care what people say about me. I love that you wanted to protect me, but you put yourself at risk. Who knows what he was capable of? Don't do anything like that again, understand?"

I nod, not arguing with him because he's right. But the feelings overtook me, surprising me because while I've been defensive over my friends before, it's never felt as intense as it just did. It was primal almost, an instinct to protect the man I love so fiercely.

Now I need to work up the courage to say it to him.

I take a quick shower at the hotel Elio booked for us, changing into the outfit I planned to wear tonight.

I'm wearing black skinny jeans with a cream-colored sweater that hangs off of one shoulder, with boots to match. My curls are loose, my face free of makeup except for a pale pink lipstick.

Elio took a while to calm down, and when I attempted to apologize, he told me not to because it wasn't my fault. He's right, so I'm trying to let it go and not feel bad for what happened.

He didn't let go of me the entire car ride, in the hotel and up to our room. The only time he did was to let me shower, since he had to call his mom to let her know we'd be a few minutes late.

I'm never late, so it's stressing me out that we are, but I needed a shower desperately after that incident.

I exit the bathroom, seeing Elio sitting on the edge of the bed with his face in his hands. I walk over to him, stepping into the space between his legs. I cradle his face with my hands, bringing his gaze up to mine.

There's pain etched all over his face as he looks at me.

"I'm okay, babe." My voice is silvery, running my fingers over his beard soothingly.

"You know, I thought being injured and retiring was the worst moment of my life. But then to witness that man trying to hurt you, it made me realize that nothing would ever compare to that feeling. Seeing that, it fucking crushed me." He blows out a breath and leans into my touch. "I love you so much, *dolcezza*. I won't let anything happen to you. I can't. You're everything, my whole heart." His voice cracks on his last words.

The threads of my heart snap, the frays sending warmth throughout my entire body at his admission. He loves me. Elio Mazzo loves me.

I smile widely at him, my cheeks warming. While I feel the same way, I find my throat clogged with emotion, unable to say it back at this very moment. So I crane my neck, pressing my lips to his softly. Our lips move slowly with one another. It's savoring, loving, and sweet.

I use my lips to tell him what I can't say out loud. While I know I love him, I don't know how to say those eight letters yet.

I'm grateful he understands that, not at all upset that I didn't say it back. Elio's confession was him telling me how he feels without any expectations, and I think I love him a little more for that.

We eventually made it down to the lobby several minutes later once he held me in his arms silently until he calmed down, then out to the parking lot where we climbed back into his SUV, driving to his mom's.

Pulling up to the house, my jaw drops at the beautiful landscaping, but it drops even more once the mansion comes into full view.

Elio parks, then we walk hand in hand to the front door. He doesn't bother knocking, walking right in. The first thing I notice is that it's loud, conversations, laughter, and children arguing instantly hitting me. The second thing I notice is how elegant the home is, and the third is the smell of something baked with cheese wafting throughout the house.

A small child runs past us, followed by another, but then they both stop, turning to face us.

"Zio Leo." The girl beams up at him.

"Zio!" the boy shouts.

Elio crouches down to their level. "How are my favorite niece and nephew?" He scratches their heads, muffling their hair in the process. "Jasmine, this is Milo and Mia, and kids, this is Jasmine."

We exchange quick hellos, when a woman walks into the foyer.

"I literally fixed their hair a minute ago," she groans as she pats the kids' hair back into place. Her long black hair is in a ponytail, her eyes match the darkness of mine, and her frame is tall and lean like Elio. She must be his sister.

"Gabriella," he says, standing back up as he wraps an arm around my waist. "This is my girlfriend, Jasmine."

"Ouuuu, Zio has a crush!" Mia giggles, looking no older than five or six.

"Ew, girls have cooties, Zio." Milo fake gags, who looks slightly older than his sister.

"Enough you two, go find Nonna and tell her that we can finally eat," Gabriella instructs them, directing them back to the room they came from.

"It's nice to meet you. You're the designer, right?" I ask.

"Yes, that's me. My twin is the model. I like to design the clothes, and she likes to wear them." She smiles as she takes me in. "You're stunning. Have you ever thought about modeling? I'd love to have you wear one of my pieces."

My eyes widen. "Me?" I choke on a laugh, Elio's warm hand on my back reassuringly. "I'm flattered, but I don't think I'd be a good model."

"We'll see." Her lips grin devilishly. "It's nice to meet you. Finally someone who puts my brother in his place."

"Oh, trust me, I do." I chuckle, sneaking a glance at Elio, who's laughing under his breath.

"What did I miss?" A woman who looks identical to Gabriella, except with hazel eyes, enters the room. "Oh, it's Jasmine. I've heard lots about you. It's nice to meet you. I'm Daniella." She smiles, pulling me into a hug.

I hug her back, pulling back once she does. "It's nice to meet you too. Elio speaks so highly of you all."

"You mean he speaks very highly of me, his favorite sister," his other sister, Bria, enters the room. She looks different than her sisters, her hair a light brown, eyes green like Elio's, and much shorter than her siblings. "It's nice to meet you. I'm Bria." She sticks her hand out to me.

I shake it, smiling warmly at her. "It's nice to meet you too."

"All right, let's move this introduction thing to the dining table. I'm starving," Bria complains, motioning for us to follow her.

We do, passing by various pieces of art down the hallway until we take a left in the middle, entering a grand dining room. There's a chandelier that's probably worth more than my education hanging above the glass table.

Jesus. I knew Elio had money, but this isn't anything I'm used to.

His mother enters from the kitchen, placing a bottle of red wine on the table.

"Ah! *Molto bene*," she yells. "My boy is here."

She rushes over to Elio, taking him into her arms, his large frame swallowing her tiny one. Her hair is lighter like Bria's, falling past her shoulders in curls.

"Hi, Mamma, this is Jasmine. My girlfriend," he introduces me, pulling back from his mom.

She gasps, her hand covering her mouth. "Wow, you are beautiful, darling. It's so nice to meet you."

I blush at her compliment, feeling my entire face turn pink. "That's very kind, thank you. It's nice to meet you too."

"Hey, Papa," Elio says to a man who looks very much like him but is covered in salt-and-pepper hair.

"My son, so good to see you." He grins, kissing Elio's cheek.

"Papa, this is my girlfriend, Jasmine," Elio introduces me for what feels like the hundredth time in five minutes.

"Pleasure to meet you." He grabs my hand and shakes it, giving me a sweet smile.

"It's very nice to meet you." I smile back, leaning into Elio's touch on my lower back.

We spend the rest of dinner getting to know one another, along with being introduced to Caleb, Daniella's boyfriend, and Troy, who is Gabriella's husband.

His family is warm and welcoming. There's never an awkward moment, and the conversation flows easily as we eat. You can tell how much they love one another, and it makes me envy what they have.

Dinner seems to be an important event in their family, as each course is brought out separately, giving enough time for ample conversation in between. This also works out for my stomach because I need the extra time to get ready for the next course. Everything that's been put out has been delicious, from the arancini balls to the lasagna.

My family isn't very big, and I didn't grow up having siblings like Elio did. I've always wanted a big family of my own one day, not wanting my children to grow up the way I did. I felt alone and smothered for most of my life. But I don't want kids right now. I'm almost finished with school and still need to figure out what the hell I'm going to do after the holidays.

Time's ticking on how long I have until I have to make a decision, and I don't know whose path I'll follow.

My parents or mine.

Chapter 35

Elio

*I*n a little over a month, I've managed to secure a prime location for Isaiah's mom's music studio.

It's central, easy to access, and close to neighborhoods with schools, meaning more potential customers for her.

In that time, we've done a complete rebranding, along with creating her social media presence. So far, the response has been great. Her followers are interacting with her content, and many have signed up for spots at the new location, which is opening today.

There's a big red bow at the front, ready for Tammy to cut and signify the beginning of this new journey for her and her family. One that will not only allow Isaiah to keep his spot on the team, but one that will ensure all of his siblings can pursue their dreams too.

I watch with pride from the sideline as Tammy cuts the bow, surrounded by Isaiah and his two younger brothers. It fills me with a sense of accomplishment and joy like no other, seeing how happy they look and knowing I helped get them here.

I've assured Tammy that I'll continue to consult with her

for the first six months to make sure she's on track, since small businesses tend to struggle the first few months of their opening.

It's made me think more seriously about making this my next adventure. Helping small businesses flourish. I've begun working on business plans during my downtime and I'm excited to see where this can go after graduation.

Jasmine's thrilled by the idea, having been nothing but supportive. She wanted to be here today, but due to the press, she didn't come. If her dad caught wind of it, we'd be screwed.

"Coach!" Isaiah yells, catching my attention. "Get over here."

I walk toward the Thomas family, who are all smiles from ear to ear. His two siblings appear to be younger, about ten or twelve if I had to guess.

"Whoa, it's really him," one of them whispers to the other.

Isaiah chuckles. "Yes, this is Elio Mazzo, my coach and the best hockey player to ever exist."

"Wow." They both beam up at me, starstruck.

I bump their fists with a grin. "I may be the best, but your brother here could give me a run for my money if he continues to practice and perform the way he is."

Isaiah pales beside me. "What? Seriously, you think so?"

"I do, I really do. Keep up the hard work, Thomas." I clap him on the back, and then we turn to pose for some photos for the media.

After all that is said and done, Tammy pulls me aside. "Elio, I want to thank you," she cries, happy tears I'm assuming.

"You've done that multiple times. No need."

"I need you to know how grateful I am. This saved not only my business, but my family as well. It broke me when Isaiah offered to quit school to help me out." She pauses, shaking her head before continuing. "Do you know how helpless that made me feel as a mother? I felt like a failure."

"Tammy, look at those boys." I tilt my head and she follows, seeing their wide smiles as they talk. "That is not a failure. The joy on their faces, the good people they are. That's all you. You're an amazing mother and teacher. Don't ever doubt that."

Tammy sniffles, holding back her tears. I pull her into a hug, and she begins to sob against me.

"And for the record, you still wouldn't be a failure even if this didn't work out. You'd find a way to make it work because that's the kind of mother you are. Your worth isn't determined by what you have or can provide. It's about how you love those kids with all that you have. And I know you do."

"Thank you, Elio." She wipes her eyes. "I have no doubt you're going to make a difference with so many businesses, and in turn, their families."

What she doesn't realize is that it's not me changing their lives, it's them. I'm simply giving them resources and the knowledge that I've learned over the years to help them.

I'm no savior. I'm just a guy who wants to help small businesses thrive and do some good along the way.

Chapter 36

Elio

"You okay, *dolcezza?*" I ask Jasmine, who's sitting up straight against the black leather chair in my private plane. We're currently on our way to my friend Brooks' wedding in Bora Bora.

"I've never been on a plane before, so I'm a little scared," she admits, looking embarrassed.

I knew she had never traveled out of the country, but I had assumed she traveled domestically. "Come here." I motion for her to sit next to me.

She hastily shakes her head back and forth. "Nope, I'm not undoing my seat belt. Not a chance."

I reach my hand across the table, intertwining it with hers. "You're going to be okay."

Jasmine nods, giving my hand a squeeze as the jet begins to race down the runway. Her eyes shut as she grips me even tighter.

Knowing her the way I do, I don't say anything. I simply rub my thumb across the back of her hand, letting her know I'm here.

Once we're given the go ahead, I undo my seat belt and

then stand. Leaning over the table between us, I undo her seat belt. "C'mere."

I wrap my arms around her waist, lifting her into the air and over the table. I sit and place her on my lap. She doesn't argue, making herself right at home. Jasmine nestles her head into my neck, inhaling deeply as she takes calming breaths.

I rub my hands up and down her back, trying to soothe her anxiety. We have a fifteen-hour-long flight ahead of us, so I'll have to keep her busy mind off of her worries.

Our classes and exams are finished, making this wedding come at the perfect time. Jasmine studied her ass off, and I rewarded her each night, giving her the appreciation she deserves for working so hard.

It was easy to convince her parents that she was traveling with Camille, telling them that she was visiting her hometown in Europe. Jasmine's parents know Camille is well-off, so they were thrilled when Jasmine told them it wasn't costing her anything either.

Now we have to make sure her parents don't see Camille while we're gone for the week.

"Let's get more comfortable," I tell her and stand with her in my arms, walking us to the black leather couch. It's a perfect fit with her body resting on top of mine.

"What are you doing?" she ponders, resting her chin on my chest.

"Taking a nap with my girlfriend," I respond, pulling the blanket from the top of the couch and wrapping it around us.

It's only four o'clock, but we're going to need some sleep for what I have planned later tonight.

"Elio, I can't nap," she protests, trying to shrug out of my grip on her.

I hold her steady, kissing her forehead, stilling her efforts.

"You can rest your head on my chest. You're going to need your energy for later."

Her mouth parts, eyes filling with desire as they meet mine. "I guess I can try." She grins, her plump lips looking so damn sexy as she does. Her fear seems to have lessened now that we're coasting across the sky.

She settles into me while I run my fingers lightly up and down her side. Her breaths begin to even out, little puffs of air leaving her lips as they part slightly once sleep takes over. I knew she'd be tired. Exams finished yesterday and she hasn't had a moment to relax fully until now.

The cabin lights dim, and I give my attendant a curt nod, letting her know I appreciate it. I close my own eyes, drifting off to sleep with my entire world in my arms as we fly above the rest of the world.

My mind is all over the fucking place, trying to figure out what piece to move in order to make a move on Jasmine's players.

After our nap and some dinner, we started a game of chess.

She's all smiles as she sits across from me, knowing she has me absolutely fucked at this point in the game. The worst part is that I'm trying, really hard actually. She's better than me, and it's sexier than anything since I'm used to being the best at everything.

Jasmine is much more relaxed now, seeming at ease. I think it was the fear of getting in the air from it being her first time, which is understandable.

I'm also loving claiming all of her firsts and I'm only getting started.

I sigh, conceding. "There's no point in finishing this game. You won."

She tilts her head, a challenge in her heated gaze. "C'mon, babe, I never took you for someone who gives up."

"I'm not. I understand that I lost, simple as that."

"Oh, I don't know, I happen to remember that time in your office…seems like you gave up control pretty fast."

I lean forward, resting my arms on the table. "I seem to remember your cunt choking my cock as you came all around it, so I'm failing to see the problem here."

Her eyes don't widen like they usually do at my dirty words, rather they simmer with want.

"But it was only one orgasm…you've spoiled me with multiple each day, so that part was a bit disappointing." She pouts her bottom lip, toying with me.

And it's fucking working.

In one fluid movement, my arm brushes our chess pieces off the table, clattering them to the floor.

"Elio, what the f—" she starts, but I cut her off, standing and rushing her as I scoop her into my arms.

"You want to be spoiled, I'll give you spoiled," I bite out, squeezing her ass in my palms as I walk us to the back of the plane where there's a closed-off bedroom.

Jasmine nips at my bottom lip, a groan rumbling in my chest as her lips take mine in a searing kiss. She's leading, and I'm going to let her. For now.

Her lips are moving over mine with want, making me nearly lose it as she kisses me so fucking well, getting me worked up for her.

I shut the door behind me, then toss her on the white duvet. She giggles, but it's short-lived once I crawl on top of her, her throat bobbing as she swallows hard. I press my lips to hers while my fingers inch into the waistband of her tights, under her panties, which I'm surprised to find.

I don't stop until I reach her slit, running two fingers down to her entrance where I can feel how soaked she is for me. I thrust them inside her, loving the little gasp that emits from her mouth, breaking our lips apart.

It takes me no time to find her G-spot, and I curl my fingers, making her moan and writhe beneath me as I fuck her with them. Jasmine takes her own sweater off, followed by her bra as I continue my movements.

My cock is raging with the need to be inside of her, but I hold off. If she wants more orgasms, I'll be glad to give them to her.

I take her nipple between my teeth, tugging before sucking it into my mouth. Her tits are full and perky, the perfect combination.

"Elio," Jasmine pants, fisting the sheets beside her.

"First, you'll come on my fingers, then my tongue, then my cock. Sound good?"

Her words are jumbled as I fuck her with my fingers, the sound of her arousal filling the room along with her moans and whimpers.

Remembering what I threw in my bag last minute, I pull my fingers out of her and grab it from the duffel on the floor.

Jasmine whines in response. "What are you doing? Get back inside me."

I nearly come in my pants because those are the four hottest words when put together.

I find the vibrator I stole from her collection, a pink bullet-looking one. I turn it on, the buzz filling the room.

"Elio, tell me you didn't steal my vibrator." She chuckles, throwing her hands over her face.

"What's yours is mine, no?" I tease, running the end of the vibrator over her nipple. Jasmine's body jolts, her eyes popping widely.

"Do you wanna play?" I ask, always needing her consent.

"Yes," she tells me easily. Her eyes lock on the vibrator, probably wondering where it is going next.

I run it over her other nipple, humming in satisfaction when her mouth parts with the softest moan. I run it down her stomach, watching as she quivers with each touch. Then I bring it to her inner thighs, which begin to shake.

I fucking love seeing her like this.

I bring it close to her clit, but not close enough.

"Elio. Don't, please," she begs, looking genuinely distressed, so I give in.

I bring the vibrator to her clit while slamming my fingers back inside of her, my cock hardening as her back bows off the bed and she moans wildly.

"Coat my fingers, *dolcezza*. Let me feel you," I order, my voice husky with a burning desire for this girl.

My words set her off, her orgasm squeezing the life out of my fingers as her cunt contracts around them, her cum covering them. I love watching her come undone. It never gets old.

If I wasn't such a possessive asshole, I'd video it, but I'm too paranoid about it getting leaked. And no one sees her like this. No. Fucking. One.

I turn the vibrator off and chuck it to the side. Then I settle between her thighs, planting kisses along her inner thighs before finally making my way to heaven.

I lick her slit, loving the way her hips buck at the feeling. Her fingers tangle in my hair, her legs spreading even wider to give me better access. I purposefully avoid her clit, teasing her entrance with my tongue, lapping at her as I suck, kiss, and lick her from top to bottom.

"Elio, I swear if you don't touch my clit, I'll—"

"You'll what?"

"I…uh. Nothing, okay? Just fucking do it," she belts out in frustration.

I chuckle, her feisty side turning me on more than anything. I bring my tongue near her clit, tracing circles around it, getting close but not close enough. She whines in protest, and I oblige her needs, giving her clit the softest touch with my tongue.

"Are you kidding—" Her annoyance is cut short when I suck her clit into my mouth, hard.

Her second orgasm arrives unexpectedly, her thighs clamping around my head as I continue to suck and lick at her cunt until she relaxes.

Once she's sated, I bring my head up to her body, planting kisses all over it until I reach her lips. Our kiss is sweet, despite the need raging in both of our bodies.

I flip onto my back, lifting my hips to shrug out of my sweats and briefs. Then I toss my hoodie off. Jasmine crawls onto my lap, straddling me. She reaches between us, taking my thick cock in her hand as she lines it up with her entrance.

We both let out the loudest goddamn sigh of pleasure as she slides down my cock. Our foreheads fall together, our heavy breaths mingling together as we try to regulate them.

"Be a good little slut and ride my cock," I order, using my hands on her hips to encourage her as her hips roll against mine.

Jasmine moves rapidly, riding me. Staring in awe, I love the way her tits bounce with the movement. I tweak her nipple with my hand, her head lolling back at the stimulation. If there's anything I've learned about my girl, it's that she loves her breasts to be appreciated.

I trail my hand up her chest, stopping when my fingers curl around her neck. Jasmine gives me a nod of approval, so I apply a light amount of pressure. Jasmine's moan vibrates in her throat, and I hold her a little tighter as I watch my cock disappear in and out of her cunt.

It's the most satisfying thing I've ever seen.

Suddenly, she lifts up, switching positions as she turns away from me. Her head peeks around her shoulder, a smirk on her lips. We've yet to do this position, and I almost come undone at the sight.

Jasmine places one hand on each of my thighs, bracing herself as she begins to lift up, then slams back down on my cock. My back lifts off the bed as pleasure courses up and down my spine, my balls tensing up already.

She feels so fucking good this way, in all ways truthfully, but this is doing something for me. She bounces up and down my cock, her ass slapping loudly against my hips each time.

I join in, giving her ass a slap as she moves. "Fuck, such a good dirty girl," I grunt, giving her other cheek a slap. "Scream my name. Let everyone on this plane know who this cunt belongs to."

Jasmine releases a moan-slash whimper, my name in the mix as she continues to work me so fucking well. I place my hands on her hips, stilling their motion. She looks over her shoulders in confusion, but it fades as I begin pounding into her from below, her eyes rolling into the back of her head as she struggles to keep herself up straight.

My thrusts are relentless, plowing into her hard and deep from below.

"Elio," she whimpers.

"That's it," I praise.

"It's too much. You're so big."

"Take it, *dolcezza*, take my cock pounding into your tiny cunt like you were meant to."

She does as I say, moving her hips in tandem with mine, her fingers on her clit as our bodies working together to bring us to the edge. I lose control, my balls tensing up, my orgasm shooting through my body as I yell obscenities while my cum spills into her.

Jasmine follows me off the edge, her orgasm unfurling once she feels me cum inside, her walls clenching around me, extending the high of the pleasure coursing from my head to my toes.

She lifts up, my cum dripping out of her and onto my cock. Jasmine shifts her body around and wraps her lips around my cock and sucks it off.

This has literally never happened to me before, but that might be the sexiest thing I've ever witnessed.

Jasmine works me up easily, her lips sucking me in deep, her hand around my shaft pumping. What sets off my second orgasm is her hands on my balls, massaging them as she sucks the tip, hard.

I come down her throat, and Jasmine swallows me with a smile on her face. How is she real? How the hell did I get so damn lucky?

I haul her body up to mine and press my lips roughly to hers. Pulling back, I look at her intently. "I love you, *dolcezza*," I drawl, caressing her cheek softly.

"What does that mean?" she finally asks, not reciprocating my words.

I'm not upset that she hasn't said it back yet, because I know she loves me. I don't need words to confirm it. This relationship stuff is still new to her, so I don't want to push her.

"It means sweetheart."

She easily could have Googled it, but knowing her, she'd rather not know until she was ready to hear it.

She crinkles her nose at me. "But you've been calling me that since the beginning of the semester. We weren't friends then."

"I was teasing you, because you were anything but sweet to me. But now it's because you're *my* sweetheart."

Her eyes soften, a sweet smile on her lips. "You're cute, you know that?"

"Mmm, tell me more." I chuckle, running a hand down her naked back.

"You're full of it." She laughs, rolling onto her back.

I get up and grab us a cloth to wash off with. Once we're cleaned up, we snuggle under the covers, her body wrapped up tightly against mine.

Exactly where she was always meant to be.

Chapter 37

Jasmine

I awaken to the sound of waves lapping outside of our cabana.

Birds chirp in the distance, and Elio's heartbeat is soft against my eardrum as my head rests on his chest. I open my eyes, looking out to see the sun slowly rising on the horizon line through the glass sliding door.

Bora Bora is breathtakingly beautiful. We arrived mid-day yesterday and met everyone. The entire wedding party and guests all retreated to their huts immediately after introductions, because we were all exhausted.

Besides, the huts are too stunning and cozy not to retreat right to them. My eyes have been bugging out of my head since we landed, my body overstimulated as it tries to process the beauty all around me from the lush tropics to the crystal clear water.

At the back of our cabana, we have a hammock that sits above the water, along with a ladder that leads right into the ocean. We may or may not have christened the hammock as soon as we saw it, followed by a dip in the cool water to refresh our bodies.

Later that evening, we all met at the resort's dining hall for dinner.

I was surprised by how natural being around his friends felt, who were all older and somewhat well-known. I know it sounds silly, but it really is weird when you realize they are normal people.

I'm not as nervous as I anticipated I'd be, instead a sense of belonging flows through me.

I mean, not in this luxurious hut that probably cost more than my monthly income, but with Elio and his friends. It's the same feeling I got at Thanksgiving dinner with his family, like I'm finally where I'm meant to be because when I'm with Elio, I'm living for me and no one else.

There's a knock on the door, so I extract myself from Elio's embrace, wrapping my silk bathrobe around my waist as I make my way to the door.

I open it to see a staff member with a tray of covered food for breakfast. "Breakfast for you, Mrs. Mazzo."

I don't even bother to correct him, because I like the way it sounds. "Thank you," I tell him, tipping him with the cash from my wallet.

He thanks me then heads off, while I shut the door and set the tray down on the coffee table in the living room.

"Morning, beautiful," Elio calls out from the bed, stretching his arms out, his chiseled chest poking out from under the sheets.

"Morning, babe." I smile at him, my eyes hungrily watching his every movement.

"What's that?" he asks, voice raspy from sleep as he gets up, throwing a pair of shorts on from the floor.

"Breakfast. A staff member brought it over," I tell him, removing the lid from one of the plates, revealing a plate of crispy bacon.

My mouth waters. There's also a plate of mixed fruits, toast with various spreads of jellies and nut butters, and finally, a plate of scrambled eggs.

Although I can't eat them, I don't mind if Elio does. I only have a bad reaction if I ingest them, not if they're near me. But ever since that first morning, he's yet to buy any more eggs for our fridge at home.

Elio scowls, quickly picking up the plate of eggs and literally runs to the opposite side of the open space with them.

"Elio, I'm fine. You can eat them. Don't waste the food." My voice is gentle as I slowly approach him.

"I don't care. I don't want anything that could hurt you near you. I told the staff you had an allergy. I'm pissed off they weren't careful." His jaw clenches.

"That's sweet, babe, but you need to relax. Don't yell at them," I plead, feeling bad for the guy already.

Elio shakes his head while dumping the eggs into the trash, which he then proceeds to leave outside the door of our cabana. He storms back into the room, sitting next to me on the couch while I grab two pieces of toast, slather them with raspberry jam, a few pieces of bacon, and fruit.

"Are you going to be okay?" I tease, popping a strawberry into my mouth.

"I'm glad you find your safety funny," he mutters, grabbing some bacon, fruit, and three pieces of toast and almond butter spread.

"I don't. What I find funny is how overprotective you're being. I'm fine. There's no harm in them being around me."

"Logically, I know that, but emotionally I can't handle the thought of anything happening to you." His words warm my chest, making their way to my heart.

I put my plate down on the coffee table, along with his as I straddle his lap. I stroke his beard with one finger, smoothing the crease in his forehead with the other. "I'm going to be okay. I appreciate you caring about me so much. It does something to me, you know," I bite my lip, rocking my hips against his.

"I'm going to take the utmost care of you," he states. "But first, let's eat so I can get to my dessert."

I've never inhaled my breakfast so quickly in my life.

Elio planned the entire day for us, which has been without a doubt the best day of my life.

After breakfast, Elio followed through and had me for dessert, which led to us having sex in the water this time, since our cabana's back end is secluded.

We then finally made it out of the room, where we went on a hike, trailing through the island's lush tropics. At the top, we explored an extinct volcano with our guide. On the way down, we rode an ATV, and I laughed the entire way down from pure joy coursing through my body.

Elio rented a jeep and drove us around the island as we explored its depths and culture beyond the resort. We had lunch at a food truck, sitting on a picnic bench as locals offered us various fruits to try from their stands.

After lunch, we ventured to the beach, where we rented a jet ski to take out. Elio and I raced and tried our best to spray one another on them. We finished up the day by getting to pet stingrays.

All in all, it was amazing. So full of life, color, new people, and experiences.

When we got back to our room, we took a nap, my body demanding some rest from the eventful day. Elio and I slept for about an hour, and upon waking up, he told me I had an hour to get dressed and ready for dinner, the two of us.

The wedding is in two days, so this is our last night to ourselves until then, as we have the rehearsal dinner tomorrow and Elio needs to do his groomsmen activities.

I'm finishing the final touches on my hair, curling the ends as I let it flow freely. My face is bare as per usual, with only a nude lipstick painted across my lips. My two-piece outfit is a bit much, but I couldn't resist it when I saw it online.

This outfit wasn't appropriate for a wedding by any means, but it's perfect for tonight and I can't wait to see Elio's face when I walk out in this. It's a sky-blue color. The top part is a bandeau, leaving my stomach bare except for a gold chain that crosses my stomach. The skirt hugs my body from below my belly button to my toes.

My sandals match the gold across my stomach, as well as my earrings and bracelet.

I spray some perfume across my chest, neck, and wrists. Giving myself one last look in the mirror, I exit our bathroom, finding Elio leaning against the frame of the door leading to the balcony outside.

He's facing the sun that's lowering into the water, painting the sky with swoops of purple, pink, and orange. I eye him up, taking in his white shorts, rolled up minty blue button-up and white boat shoes.

He looks so damn good, I can feel my pulse already picking up and he hasn't even turned around.

I begin to pad across the floor, stopping once I reach his back. I wrap my arms around him from behind, resting my head against his back. His hands cover mine, releasing my grip as he turns to face me.

His eyes trail my body, rapidly up and down like he's not sure where to look first. His lips part, a shaky breath passing through them. "Wow," he mumbles, looking speechless. "*Dolcezza*, you look fucking exquisite."

My heart lurches forward in my chest, beating rapidly at his silvery words. They cover me up in so much damn love and affection, I can barely stand it. I love him so much, and I think it's about time that I tell him.

But before I get there, he speaks. "Let's get going before I keep you here instead of the dinner I planned."

I chuckle, lacing my fingers with his as he walks us out of the hut, onto the boardwalk, down a path that leads to a secluded part of the boardwalk.

My breath hitches in my throat at the sight. There are fairy lights strung overhead from post to post, rose petals on the walkway, a bouquet of them on the white cloth-covered table that faces the sunset, a perfect view of the volcano in the distance.

He pulls out my chair for me, his hand on my lower back as he guides me into it. It feels unnecessary to me in a sense. I can sit down perfectly fine on my own, but at that moment, it feels vital.

Like his hands on me are a need rather than a want.

There are two bottles of rosé on the table, and Elio uncorks one, pouring us each a glass. I sip the bubbly sweetness, savoring every drop. This might be the best rosé I've ever tasted, and I don't even want to ask how much it cost. I'm going to enjoy it instead, along with this night with him, considering it might be the most romantic thing he's done.

Although flying on his jet to another state and back in one day to get a dress I like ranks pretty high.

Our conversation is light and easy, and the glasses of wine are going down nicely. Our food was delicious, paired with a local dessert called banana poe, made with no eggs, of course. It was amazing and had me jotting it down in my notes for a possible recreation on my channel.

I'm overall feeling bubbly, content and more happy than I've been in a long time.

"I love seeing you smile, *dolcezza*. Of all the art in the world, that right there is the most beautiful thing." His voice is soft, eyes glistening with so much damn love as he stares at me.

I fork the last bite of pudding into my mouth, letting the sweetness marinate on my tongue while I gather the courage to do what I've been wanting to do. I push my chair back and stand, making Elio's eyebrows rise in concern, but then I settle onto his lap and he becomes content.

I push the single strand of hair that likes to hang over his forehead back, running my fingers lightly over his scalp. Elio sighs whimsically, at peace with me on his lap, my hands tangled in his hair.

It's with a steady breath that I finally open my heart fully to him. "You want to know what I love?"

He nods, his hand gripping my outer thigh while the other palms my back.

"I love how attentive you are to the needs of others, always taking the utmost care of those you love."

Elio grins, looking boyish.

"I love your mind, for how smart and creative it is. I love your body because, well, it's sexy as fuck." I giggle, which makes him chuckle.

"I love how gentle you are with me, how patient and sweet you can be. But I also love that you can be rough with me, while still treating me with respect. You've never once made me feel embarrassed for my lack of experience. Instead, you made me—still make me—feel safe, sexy and cherished."

Elio's forest-green eyes are locked on mine, not missing a

beat as I continue. "I love that you challenge me and how you're helping me grow my business. It means more to me than you'll ever know. I love all the gestures, from flying your damn plane across the country to get me a dress, to taking notes for me when I was sick. The big and the small, they all matter to me. You matter to me, a lot."

His eyes sparkle, drinking me in as he knows what I'm about to say next. And I've never been more sure of anything in my life than these three words attached to his name.

"I love you, Elio Mazzo." My voice is soft, eyes glistening with unshed tears. I usually tease Aurora for being the emotional one, but damn it, Elio broke my defenses down.

"I love you, Jasmine, so fucking much. I want it all with you. A marriage, babies, traveling, helping you run your bakery shop. Anything and everything, I want it with you and only you."

"I do too, all of it and more," I admit. "But no kids right now. I want to start my life first if that's okay."

Elio laughs, the sound vibrating against my ribs. "More than okay. I might be older than you, but I'm in no rush either."

"Oh, trust me, babe, I know. Your body can't keep up the way it used to," I goad him.

A single brow arches, his eyes darkening. "That so, *dolcezza*? I guess I'll have to remind you all night long that my body doesn't just keep up, it sets the pace. It determines when and how you orgasm. It has you screaming my name, and only mine. Remember this when you're begging me to let you come later."

"A reminder is definitely needed." I smirk, knowing we have a very, *very* long night ahead of us.

"How about a reminder of how much I love you?" he asks, reaching into his pocket as he pulls out a green velvet box.

I eye him skeptically, praying it's not a ring...but maybe also hoping it is, because I've fallen so deep for this man.

He hands it to me, the velvet feeling smooth in my hands. "Open it," he urges me.

I do as he says and open the box to find a charm piece like the one my grandma got me.

It's what started this between Elio and me because had I not gotten that gift from her and worn it all the time, including in my videos, Elio would've never learned my secret and used it to get me to move in with him.

Except this charm is a chess piece, a queen. Elio removes it from the box, gently grabbing my wrist so that he can add it to my bracelet. He attaches it to the rose gold chain, his eyes focused.

I admire it on my wrist, watching how it catches the sunrays and reflects the gold back at me. My throat becomes clogged with emotion because this signifies what changed our relationship, one damn game of chess.

It also symbolizes our situation, and ultimately, it was me who brought him to his knees, much like the queen does in chess. All of it is very fitting and I can't handle how fucking cute it is.

I wrap my arms around his neck, squeezing him tightly. "This is so cute. I love it, and you, very"—I kiss his neck—"very"—another kiss to his jaw—"very"—one to his cheek—"much." And finally on his full lips. He kisses me back reverently, like I'm something to be cherished, and it only intensifies the butterflies swirling in my stomach. It's now a damn conservatory in here.

"You're welcome, *dolcezza*, and get used to it, because I'm only getting started with spoiling you." He beams, his face lit up with so much love as he looks at me.

"I think I could get on board with that. In fact, I know how you can start."

"How's that?" he hums, running his hand up and down my thigh.

"With your lips all over my body, specifically, my pussy," I whisper, my cheeks tinting at the use of such a bold sentence, but I'm starting to get more comfortable telling him what I want.

"Done," he says, standing abruptly with me in his arms.

I clutch onto him, giggling as he nearly runs us back to our cabana.

He's everything I thought I'd never have, and I'm so damn grateful, because I've never known a happiness quite like this one.

Chapter 38

Elio

*T*his day has been exhausting.

Being a part of the groomsmen required me to get up early and meet the guys for haircuts at the resort's salon. After that, we had brunch, followed by getting ready for the wedding.

We've taken what feels like a thousand photos with the photographer, and quite frankly, I'm over it. Don't get me wrong, I love these guys, especially Brooks, but this photo crap isn't for me.

I also miss my girl, who's spending the day at the spa and getting ready with the girls, despite her not being in the actual wedding. Jasmine gets along with everyone, and I know she's making friends with the other girls, so that eases my worries a bit.

We're all near the altar, conversing as we wait for the ceremony to officially start. The audience is small, consisting of Brooks' and Stephanie's immediate family.

Jasmine will be among them, and the thought makes me eager to see her. I pull out my phone because I can't go any longer without some form of communication with her.

Me

When are you coming here?
I want to see you before the
wedding starts.

Dolcezza

I'm finished getting ready, the girls
have about a half hour before they
need to line up for the ceremony.
I'll come now.

I pocket my phone, heading towards the end of the boardwalk that is doubling as the aisle. Yeah, Brooks paid for the resort to build a floating boardwalk complete with a floral archway for their wedding.

We're all standing on it, while the guests will be sitting on chairs in the sand. It's over-the-top and very fitting for Brooks.

As I'm about to take my shoes off and walk through the sand, I see Jasmine exiting the resort, walking toward the ceremony. My breath hitches at the sight of her, my cock twitching in my pants, my palms itching to touch her while my heart thuds wildly in my chest.

Sei la mia vita.

The orange dress I flew to get for her was worth everything I had to do to get it. The satin material clings to her body, and the corset-style top accentuates her lean waist, while hoisting her breasts up more than usual.

The shoulder straps hang off of her shoulders, and the skirt is mid-length, a slit running up her thigh.

Jasmine stops in front of me, and without any warning, I pull her into me, crashing my lips onto hers. Her lips part, letting me explore her with my tongue as our kiss quickly turns less appropriate for the setting.

Brooks whistles behind me, making me reluctantly pull away from her. I intertwine my fingers with her, holding her arms out to the side as I check her out more thoroughly.

"There's not a single word in any language that could describe how beautiful you look tonight. Nothing could capture it right."

Jasmine's face softens, her head tilting as she smiles shyly at me. "That is, wow. I have no words honestly, except for that I love you, babe. Thank you. You look insanely good right now, too. It's unfair."

I smirk, pulling her back into me so that I can whisper in her ear. "Why's that?"

She leans up on her toes, trying to whisper in my ear, so I lift her by her ass so that she actually reaches it. "Because I want to put your cock in my mouth so badly, and then in my pussy. Where it belongs."

Jesus. Christ.

It takes everything, literally everything in me not to harden at those words. I've corrupted her, and I'm not a bit sorry about it.

I lean my forehead against hers, breathing in her familiar scent of peaches and flowers. "Fuck, I love you. I want to say screw this wedding and have my way with you instead."

Jasmine smiles up at me, a teasing glint in her eyes. "Later, babe. I promise I'll be a good girl for you."

"Funny thing is, I prefer it when you're not," I tease her right back.

"I can do that, don't you worry." She smiles, kissing me on the cheek before turning and making her way to her seat.

I make my way back to the altar, standing with the guys as the procession music begins to play. The bridesmaids make their way down the aisle, but all I register is a blur of blue because my eyes are on Jasmine.

I only avert my gaze once Stephanie starts to walk down the aisle, her tight lace gown trailing over the sand as she does. Brooks doesn't hide his emotion, tears leaking down his cheeks as he takes in his soon-to-be wife.

I imagine Jasmine walking toward me in a white dress and I nearly get choked up at the image.

The ceremony is beautiful, my best friend professing his love as he marries the girl who caught his heart when he was sixteen, and it makes me happy for him. After they say I do, we follow the couple to the tented area farther down the beach where the reception is.

I walk hand in hand with Jasmine, both of us silent as we take our seats with our name cards on a table near the front. Brooks and Stephanie are sitting at the front, allowing their bridal party to sit with their loved ones rather than separated at the front.

There are lights strung above us, wooden wicker chairs with white tulle, tables covered in white and filled with various floral arrangements in the middle. In the middle of the sand is a makeshift dance floor and DJ setup. Like I said before, Brooks spared no expense and went all-out.

Jasmine and I chat with the people at my table, two of my old teammates and their wives, while dinner is served. I already talked to the chef earlier, ensuring there is nothing egg-related being served or near the dishes they made.

After various speeches and dessert, the dance floor is opened up to the newlyweds. We stand to watch them dance, a tear slipping down Jasmine's cheek as we do. I pull her in front of me, wrapping my arms across her chest as she leans into me.

"This will be us someday, dolcezza," I whisper against her ear.

She cranes her neck to look at me, her mocha eyes filled with love. "It will."

I press my lips to hers in a sweet, gentle kiss. It's loving and slow, not rushed and crazed.

The DJ announces that the floor is now open and switches the melody from a classical tune to a more upbeat one, encouraging everyone to join them on the dance floor.

Jasmine grabs my hand, pulling me toward the makeshift dance floor, when I halt my footing, staying exactly where I am.

"I don't dance, Jasmine."

"That's okay." A defender who was new to the team my last year playing with them, Wyatt, steps in. "I can take her out there if you don't want to."

Jasmine's lips fold together, seeming uncomfortable at the intrusion.

I guide her body back into my side, placing a possessive arm around the small of her back. "No, thank you, I got her."

Wyatt throws his hands up, taking a step back. "I meant no disrespect. Dancing is just dancing and your girl wanted to do that."

"And a punch to the face is just a punch to the face, isn't it?" I scowl, not caring that I'm overreacting a tad.

"Thanks for the offer, but if I'm not dancing with Elio, then I don't want to dance at all," Jasmine says, placing her small palm on my chest.

"No worries, have a good night," he says, walking away to join the rest of the group on the dance floor.

Jasmine spins in my arms, pouting as she peers up at me. "You really won't dance with me?"

A grin creeps up my lips, hitching them up to the side. "I was messing with you, *dolcezza*. I dance. I simply wanted to make you beg for it."

Her lips part in shock, the gloss on her lips making them look delectable. "You're an ass."

"C'mon." I grab her hand in mine, leading her to the dance floor.

I keep her hand in mine, twisting her body so that it's flush to mine, her back to my chest as the music is definitely grinding music. Jasmine wastes no time, swaying her hips to the beat so damn seductively that I harden immediately in my pants.

It's a good fucking thing she's dancing on my cock because it's concealing my raging erection.

My hands trail down her waist, moving to her hips, where I grip her tightly as she grinds against me, her ass pressing against my cock just right. My lips find her neck, kissing the sensitive skin as she rolls her body on mine.

Jasmine's hand comes up, wrapping around my neck and tugging at my hair as her ass grinds harder against me, more sensually than before if that's even fucking possible.

"Keep dancing like this, and I'll be fucking you against the closest thing I can find," I whisper against her neck, my breath causing her to shiver.

"Please, I need you," she whimpers. Jasmine usually doesn't beg this quickly, so I know she must be more turned on than I imagined.

I lead her off the dance floor, throwing her over my shoulder once we're out of the tent.

Jasmine laughs, the sound so damn sweet as it mixes in with the crashing waves of the ocean. I walk toward the boardwalk, going under it instead so that I can prop her against the poles holding it up.

It shields us and is close, making it the best option.

I slide her down the front of my body, placing her in the sand so that I can quickly undo my zipper and pull my cock free.

Jasmine's knees hit the sand, her hand wrapping around the base as she wraps her lips around my cock. Her mocha eyes peer up at me through her long lashes, looking so fucking beautiful as her head begins to bob up and down my length.

I throw my head back, enjoying the feeling of her warm mouth wrapped around me. I thread my fingers in her hair, moving her head along my cock at a faster pace. Jasmine hums in approval because if anything, my girl loves it when I take control, giving her mind a break.

"You love sucking *my* cock, don't you?" I drawl, our eyes connected as she licks the tip then continues down the underside of my length.

She shakes her head, drawing back from me, my tip mere centimeters from her lips.

Brat.

"Don't lie to me, *dolcezza*, touch your cunt and prove me wrong then."

Jasmine does as I say, her hand trailing underneath her slit until she reaches her destination. I know she finds herself soaked the moment it happens, as her eyelids flutter, cheeks tinting pink as her fingers begin to move in and out of her.

"Show me," I bite out. "Show me how much you love sucking my cock. Let me see how wet you are."

Jasmine removes her hand, showing me her two fingers that are shining with her arousal. I lean forward and suck them into my mouth with a groan. "So fucking sweet for a liar, *dolcezza*."

I surprise her by shifting my hips forward, my cock entering between her lips. I fuck her mouth wildly, my hips snapping of their own accord as Jasmine moans around my cock.

"That's it, take my cock so deep down your throat that the only thing you'll be able to do for weeks is feel me there."

Jasmine's mouth tightens around my cock, sending chills up my spine.

I roughly pull out of her and haul her up to me, wrapping

her legs around my waist as I lean her body against the pole. I inch my hand up her thigh, trailing higher and higher until I reach her panties where I rip them with one tug, storing them in my suit pocket.

"Elio." Jasmine's voice is frantic, her nails digging into my shoulders through my jacket. We have far too many clothes on for my liking, but it'll do because I quite literally can't go another second without being inside her.

I slide into her easily, her wet cunt taking me so well as it stretches around me. I rock into her, warmth spreading across my chest as I do. I've never had sex with someone I love because I've never loved anyone the way I love her, and each time it makes my heart squeeze in my chest.

"That trip was worth it. Watching your tits bounce as I slide my cock into you over and over again is fucking perfect." I grunt while Jasmine moans, her body rocking up and down the pole.

There's nothing sweet, slow, or gracious about this. We're fucking wildly, my hips snapping frantically while Jasmine's hips are meeting my every thrust the best she can. I can barely keep up with myself right now, so I don't expect her to.

I adjust my hold on her so that I can slide my hand up to her neck, where I wrap my fingers around it and apply enough pressure to make Jasmine moan loudly.

I press my lips to hers to conceal her noises, our mouths moving over one another passionately, losing ourselves in each other completely.

"I love you," I breathe against her lips.

My words set her off as her cunt tightens around me, her body shaking. "Elio!" she screams into my neck to muffle the sound.

I pump into her once, twice, and with one final brutal thrust,

I come undone. My legs shake, my cock throbbing as it releases inside of her as I pant, completely breathless.

Jasmine plants kisses along my neck, working her way up my jaw, then finally to my lips. "I love you too, babe."

"I know." My voice is hoarse, barely a whisper as I press my lips to her forehead.

If there's one thing I know for certain, it's that our love is coveted, real, and forever.

No matter what happens next.

Chapter 39

Elio

*C*hristmas came and went as quickly as the snow that fell the night before it.

Jasmine didn't want to tell her dad about us during the holidays, so she spent Christmas Eve at her parents' house, while I spent it at mine, along with Christmas Day. It was torture, only being able to FaceTime her at night, stealing texts throughout the day when we weren't busy with our families.

My family missed her, but understood the situation. They were not the only ones who missed her either, because it was physically painful to be away from her for those two days.

Don't get me wrong, I've been gone longer for away games, but this felt different. After everything we experienced in Bora Bora, I felt closer to her than ever.

God, this fucking girl. She's in my head, heart, and soul. There's not a thing that could ever take her out. She's wedged herself in there with no way to get out.

Jasmine doesn't celebrate the new year with her family since they celebrate the Korean new year in January, which meant we were able to be together on New Year's Eve.

We exchanged our gifts that night. I gave Jasmine her gifts, which included a bunch of new lingerie, partly a gift for me, a couple of new outfits that my sister picked out for her, new highlighters and books, and lastly, a link to a document that outlined our trip to Europe once we graduate.

We're hitting Greece, Italy, Spain, France, England, and the Netherlands.

She hated that I spent so much on her, because she couldn't afford to spend that much on me, but she got over it pretty quickly once my cock was nestled down her throat.

Aside from the mind-blowing blowjob, she gifted me a hoodie, sweatpants, and slippers. It was perfect because she knows how much I love to stay home with her, giving me the perfect outfit to do exactly that.

Honestly, she could've given me a paperclip and I would've been happy with it knowing she spent any fraction of her time thinking of me as she bought it.

While I'm excited for our year ahead together, I know Jasmine is feeling quite apprehensive. She has to decide what she wants to do with her life, since applications for big corporate jobs are due soon if she decides to follow her parents' pathway for her life.

If she decides she wants to live her own pathway and wants that building in my hometown, well, she already has it.

I bought it that day when she mentioned it to me. I called up the realtor when I was in the bathroom at Thanksgiving. I wanted to give her everything, so why not start with helping her achieve her dreams?

She's mentioned talking to her parents about us a few times, but I never push the issue because it's her relationship with her parents, not mine. I know how important that is to her, and I'll never make her do anything she doesn't want to do.

But I'd be lying if I said I didn't wish that she told them already.

I'm sick of keeping her in the dark. I love to stay home for the most part, but I'd also love to take my girl out, show her off, and let everyone know who she belongs to. I want to love her the way she deserves and give her everything she needs, which includes dates out in public, family functions, and everything else that we can't freely do right now.

I push the thoughts away for now as my skates hit the ice, my legs pushing me toward the center of the ice where Ned and the team are. It's our first practice back in the new year, and we're ramping it up with the playoffs not too far away.

Ned instructs them on the drills we're going to run, splitting the group up as they head off to their respective spots. Once the stations are in full swing, Ned skates over to me as I watch the guys work on stick handling.

"How were your holidays?" he asks, crossing his arms over his chest.

"Good, I spent it with my family. How were yours?"

"That's great to hear. Holidays were good. I spent time with my daughter and both my and my wife's families."

"Glad to hear all was well," I say too easily, as if the image of his daughter underneath me isn't flashing through my mind.

Ned and I skate over to the next station, watching as McCoy winds up a shot at the net, only to be blocked by our goalie.

"You know, getting to watch you grow into the person and athlete you are today was pretty special to me. Especially since we couldn't have more kids. You know I've thought of you as my own," Ned comments, bringing his hand up to my shoulder, giving it a squeeze before letting his hand fall away.

"I know," is all I can say because the guilt hits me in a tidal wave. Here he is, reminding me of how influential he was for me growing up, yet last night I was balls deep in his daughter.

Fuck.

We need to tell him. It's going to eat at me until we do. I hadn't felt much guilt so far, but his comment now triggered me, reminding me of why I tried to avoid the temptation in the first place.

Once the grueling drills are over, the boys dripping in sweat, one or two even vomiting, we end the practice. We send the boys to the locker room while Ned and I collect the equipment to drag off the ice before the figure skaters arrive for their ice time.

Once everything is tucked away, we pull out our phones as we walk back toward the hall where our offices are. I see a text from Jasmine, and with my screen brightness turned down low enough, I open it.

Dolcezza

> I may or may not be eating the leftover pasta you made, naked in our bed while I read. Please don't get mad if I make a mess, but I was too tired to sit at the table.

I grin, loving that she said *our* bed. And the tidbit about her being naked? I love that even more.

Me

> If there's a mess when I get home, you'll be on my lap with your ass in the air for a punishment.

Dolcezza

> Attachment: 1 image
> Ooops.

I open the picture to see that there's a red pasta sauce stain on the white sheets, right next to her bowl in the middle of the bed. The image makes me smile rather than freak out because I know she did it on purpose.

Me

I'm going to spank you when I get home while I read a spicy scene in your book. Be ready.

Dolcezza

I'm more than ready babe, if you know what I mean.

Dolcezza

Attachment: 1 image

I put my phone to my chest so fast I barely even saw the image, but what I did see was a picture of her hand between her thighs.

"Everything okay?" Ned asks beside me.

"Yeah." I swallow. "Just lost a bunch of points in my fantasy league."

"The worst," he agrees, his eyes not leaving his phone as he scrolls.

We're about to part ways into our offices when Ned places his hand on the doorframe of his office, halting his movement. "Shit, our games next weekend changed to accommodate the figure skating competition. I need to go tell the boys."

I could stay my course, pack up, and head home to Jasmine, but something propels my feet to follow him. "I'll go with you," I tell him, falling into step beside him as we make our way to the locker room where the guys are probably showering.

Ned opens the door, the boys' voices carrying from the change area. I follow him as we make our way there, when their conversation starts to become more clear.

"She's off the market, man. She's dating Coach," Isaiah says, making the hair on my arms fucking stand.

What the fuck?

"I saw her leaving the building with Elio before the Thanksgiving break. It checks out," McCoy adds.

This is about to go down, and there's not a damn thing I can do to stop it.

Ned stops in front of the boys, who are looking at us with wide eyes.

"Say that again for me, Thomas, because I don't think I heard that correctly," he seethes, crossing his arms over his chest as he looks up at the ceiling for a deep breath before looking back at Isaiah. "Because what I thought I heard is that my daughter is dating the man behind me. The man I raised as my fucking own. The man who is now my friend and coworker. The *man* who I explicitly told to stay away from her."

Isaiah falters, his eyes widening as he looks from Ned to me.

"Uh, sir. I-I don't want any part of this." His voice shakes.

"You should've thought about that before my daughter's name came out of your mouth, because now it's my business and you're part of that business. Tell me I'm wrong, Thomas. Tell me what you said isn't true," he pleads, his voice more tightly wound with anger than I've ever heard it before.

Part of me wants to speak up and say something, but I have no idea what the fuck to say.

"I-I can't do that, sir." His voice is low as he looks from Ned to me.

I shake my head, not at him, but myself. We should've known this was going to happen sooner or later. People talk around campus. It was only a matter of time before this happened.

"There's picture proof, too." McCoy smirks, pulling out his phone. "It's from Thanksgiving. My friend lives in the same town as coach Mazzo did, and he sent me this picture of them outside the ice rink."

He turns his phone around to us, and he wasn't lying. It's a picture, clear as day, of me and Jasmine, her in the SUV as I kiss her. I don't know how the fuck he got this, but it's making my blood boil. No one should have any pictures of Jasmine without her consent, let alone an intimate moment like that one.

I yank the phone from his grip and delete the picture while he protests from the bench.

"Shut up, McCoy. If I find you with another picture of her, you'll be off the team," Ned snaps, and for a moment, I think it'll be okay between us, until he turns to me.

Before I can react, Ned has me shoved up against an empty cubby, his arm digging into my chest as he holds me there. His fist rears back before colliding with my lip.

Truthfully, I could easily push him off me as he's not as strong as I am, but if this is what he needs to do, I'll let him.

Ned delivers another blow, this one to my cheek, and he goes to land another when Isaiah and a few of the guys are pulling him off me.

"Coach, stop!" Isaiah shouts, huffing and puffing as he puts himself between us.

"This has nothing to do with you guys. Leave," Ned orders, but no one moves.

I spit the blood in my mouth on the floor. "It's fine. I deserve it," I admit, making all of their eyes turn to me. "He trusted me and I repaid him by dating his daughter. I'd be livid too."

"How long has this been going on?" he asks, still seething.

"October 15, that's when we officially started dating."

Ned curses under his breath, and then he's charging toward me again. Isaiah remains a buffer between us as Ned shouts at me. "You're no good for her, Mazzo."

This time, I step forward. I want to respect her dad, but I'm also a grown man who's going to defend himself.

"Jasmine is the greatest thing in my life." I grin within the chaos of the moment. "I may not deserve her, but I can guarantee I will do my best to prove it every day."

Ned holds my stare, his dark eyes burning into mine with so much rage.

I don't wait for a response, knowing I said what I needed to say for now since he's still pissed and won't be very understanding anyways.

I turn on my heel and hightail it out of there, right to my SUV. On the drive home, I think about what the hell happened.

Ned knows about us. He punched me, multiple times. The team knows, which means it'll only be a matter of time before everyone on campus knows.

This is not at all how Jasmine wanted this to go down, and as I'm about to call her with my car's Bluetooth, I notice her dad's car behind me at the light.

Fuck.

I call her anyways, despite how much it's going to kill me to hear her frantic voice.

She picks up instantly. "Hey, babe." Her voice is sleepy, likely having fallen asleep in our bed.

"*Dolcezza*," I warn.

"What's wrong?" she gasps, snapping out of her sleepy haze.

"Your dad knows. Long story short, the guys were talking about us in the locker room when your dad and I walked in."

"Fuck," she whispers, the sound of her flipping the sheets off her body rippling through the phone. "What happened? Are you okay?"

Only Jasmine would be concerned about me when her relationship with her father is about to be put through the ringer.

"I'm pulling in, but your dad's behind me in his car. I suggest you come down here unless you want him to also find out that we're living together."

"Oh, my God." Her voice is frantic like I knew it would be, and it fucking guts me. "I'll be down in five."

I pull into my parking spot, catching sight of my bloodied lip in the mirror. It doesn't bother me. I've been in enough hockey fights in my life to not let it. But it might bother Jasmine, and that I don't like.

I hop out of the car at the same time as Ned.

"What are you doing, Ned?" I ask him as we stand off in the parking lot.

"I'm here to talk to my daughter. This doesn't concern you, Mazzo." He stalks past me toward the front entrance, where Colin is watching with apprehension.

"Jasmine is my greatest concern, so therefore, it does concern me. If you're going to upset her, then I'll ask you to leave and wait to talk to her until you've calmed down."

Ned stops in his tracks, turning around to face me. I see a flash of shock cross his face before his anger returns. "Stay out of this."

He begins to turn around, when Jasmine comes flying out the front door, where Colin holds it open for her.

"*Aecha*," Ned breathes.

But she barely glances his way. Instead, her sole focus is on me. "Elio." Her voice cracks, her legs carrying her over to me and past her dad to stand toe to toe with me.

"I'm fine, *dolcezza*," I murmur as her hand lifts, lightly tracing the outside of my swollen lip, then to the bruising I'm sure is on my cheek.

A single tear strolls down her cheek, and I wipe it away gently with a stroke of my thumb. Her features change from hurt to cold within seconds, her jaw tensing, spine steeling as she turns to face her dad.

"Don't you ever lay a hand on him again." Her voice is icy, nothing soft about her in this moment.

"Jasmine," he pleads. "Why him? Do you not remember what I told you that day three years ago?"

"Oh, I do, trust me. It fucks with my head sometimes and makes me feel unworthy. When in reality, it's always been you and Mother who made me feel that way."

I reach for her hand, linking our fingers together, my way of silently letting her know that I'm here for her.

Ned takes a step back, looking sullen. "What? How could you say that? You're our miracle."

"That might be the problem. I've never had any room to breathe my entire life. I can't make my own choices without either of you approving of them first, because I'm so damn scared of letting you guys down, of veering off the path you guys have envisioned for me."

"That's not true. You know your mother and I would support whatever you want to do."

"Really? Then why did we make a deal that I had to quit volleyball to focus on school? I didn't want that, not at all. But I did it for you both because I know I'm your one and only child, your one shot at experiencing parenting. I don't want to ruin that for you both."

"Jasmine, I want you to be happy, and I know your mother has been hard on you, but it comes from a place of love. I'm sorry you've felt this way. I truly am," he remarks sincerely.

"I love you, *Appa*. I really do, but if you can't accept me for me, the life I want to live, and the person I want to spend it with, then I don't see us having much of a relationship going forward.

Elio is a part of my life now, and that's never going to change. I love him," she admits, her hand squeezing mine.

Holy fuck.

I'm so fucking proud of her right now, laying her heart out there while sticking up to her dad.

Ned's mouth parts, inhaling a breath as he eyes his daughter like she's unrecognizable to him. And she may as well be because she's shielded her true self from her parents for years.

And then he turns around, walking back to his car without a single word, and drives away.

Jasmine stares into the distance, her body eerily still as tears begin to fill her eyes.

"Jas," I whisper, giving her hand another squeeze.

Her body begins to shake as a sob rips through her, nearly making her collapse on the ground, but I catch her in time, hauling her into my arms.

I carry her into the lobby and up to our home as her tears soak my sweater, her body shaking against mine. Dropping down onto the couch, I do nothing but hold her tightly as I rub a hand soothingly up and down her back.

She finally spoke up to her dad, and he walked away from her. I don't blame her for feeling this way, and it kills me knowing I had a hand in her pain.

"I'm so sorry," I whisper, my voice hoarse. Seeing her like this is tearing me up.

Jasmine lifts her head off my chest, her teary, broken eyes meeting mine. "Don't be. It's not your fault. *You* did nothing wrong. It's *me*. I can never be enough for them."

I cradle her cheeks as I shake my head. "You don't need to be enough for them. The only person who needs to approve of you, is you."

A silent tear strolls down her cheek that I wipe away with my thumb.

"I know that, but hurting them makes me feel awful. Why does the best thing in my life have to be the worst in theirs? And I know it's a tricky situation, but if I'm happy, it shouldn't matter, right?"

"You've been hurting your whole life, trying to make them happy. How is that fair to you? And it shouldn't, but it was probably a huge shock for him. Maybe he needs some time to cool down, that's all," I opt for some positivity because we're in dire need of it.

She folds her lips together, thinking my words over. After a few minutes, she speaks up.

"I doubt it, but we'll see," she sniffles. "It hurts knowing they can't accept it, but I'm done living for them. I want to focus on the life we're building together instead."

I hate the words I'm about to say, but I know I'd hate myself more if I never offered her this.

"If you need some time apart to think about if this is something you really want, I'll give it to you. I can get a hotel room to stay in."

Jasmine shakes her head profusely. "Absolutely not. I appreciate you asking. I get the intention, but no. You and our future are the only things in my life that I'm certain about."

I smile at that, pressing my lips chastely against hers.

"On a positive note, no more hiding," I tell her, rubbing my nose against hers.

"You're right." Her eyes brighten, lessening the ache in my chest that's been there since she started crying.

"I usually am." I wink, causing her to giggle.

And then she kisses me, and in it, I can feel her love for me. I kiss her back just as lovingly.

Our lips continue to move as I walk us through our apartment, to our bed, where we quickly strip out of our clothes. I slide into her with ease, forgoing foreplay because our need is heightened right now. We could've lost it all today, but we're choosing to weather the storm together.

I'm not rough with her, my thrusts slow and deep as I make love to her, not for the first time, but it feels different. Like she's finally mine, and I can scream it to the world.

Thank fucking God.

Chapter 40

Jasmine

A light buzzing from the side table has me stirring awake. I slide out from Elio's arms around me and swipe my phone from the table.

It's 12:23 a.m., and my mother's name is staring me in the eye. *Shit.*

She must have finished her shift at the hospital and is finally calling me after the disaster that was today. As much as I don't want to have this talk, I know there's no use in avoiding it.

I quickly rise from the bed, pulling my robe on from the chaise at the end of the bed as I answer the call. "Hi," I say quietly into the phone as I make my way to the living room to avoid waking Elio.

"Jasmine," my mother breathes, her tone not easy to decipher.

"How was work?" I yawn while curling up on the couch as the girls hop up to join me.

"I work at a hospital, so the answer is always busy." She chuckles. The sound throws me off. I was expecting her to chastise me instantly, and it has me on edge that she has yet to do that.

"I'm sorry for waking you, dear, but after the day you had, I wanted to talk," my mother adds, her tone blank, not giving me an indication as to how she feels about it.

"Yeah, it was interesting."

My mother scoffs. "Your damn father. I swear I'm going to punch him later and see how he likes it."

Wait. What?

"You're…you're okay with it?" I ask in disbelief.

She takes a deep breath. "Jasmine, look. I know I've been hard on you, but that's only because I care about you more than anything else. I want what's best for you, and if it's Elio, so be it. If that man makes you happy, provides you with security, emotionally and physically, that's all I could ask for."

"Just like that? You know he's older, dad's friend, and famous, right?"

"I'm quite aware, but Elio seems to have his head on right. Your father had a hand in raising him, so I know that to be true."

I shake my head, unable to believe what I'm hearing right now. "He does. He's really great, Mom. I like him a lot."

My mother chuckles. "Yeah, I figured that if you went through all this trouble to be together. I'm also being reasonable about this because I was once in your shoes."

"What do you mean?" I ask, tucking my feet under my butt.

"Your father is older than me. He's not famous, but he was well-known in the athletic community at the time in our town. And he was your aunt's best friend."

Why did I not know this before? I feel like I'm seeing my mother in a whole new light. It doesn't excuse the way she's made me feel over the years, but it's refreshing.

"Wow, we're not so different, it seems."

"We're not, dear. You have my acceptance, and I'll work on your father." She chuckles. "How are job applications going? A coworker's son is in your program and applied to the EY firm. They need two financial analysts. You should apply."

My stomach sinks. I'm happy she accepts my relationship, but having her accept other life choices would be even better.

"It's really late, Mom. Can we talk about this another day?"

"Sure, dear. Rest up, you will need it for your classes. I love you, my one and only."

That damn term of endearment.

"I love you, too. Night." I hang up the phone and toss it on the opposite side of the couch, startling Buttercup by accident.

"Sorry, Cups," I murmur.

I rub my hands down my face in frustration. She said she wants me to be happy but has yet to ever ask me what would make me happy. Instead, she thrusts forward with her own agenda.

A dull ache begins to throb in my head, making me lie down on the couch. As I get comfortable, I hear Elio call my name.

"Jasmine?" he rasps, padding into the living room with nothing on but his briefs.

"I'm here, babe," I call out softly. My headache pounds against my temple, making me wince.

Elio's in front of me in seconds, suddenly more awake than before. "What's wrong?"

"My mother called. She was oddly accepting of us and told me that her and my father's situation was actually quite similar in the beginning. I was happy until she mentioned job applications for a boring desk job I don't want. I started to think too much and now my head is throbbing."

"Come here." His voice is low and smooth, wrapping around me like silk. I reach my arms out to him, wrapping them around his neck as he lifts me carefully into his arms.

As he carries me back to our room, placing me in our bed, I

think of how right my mother was about him. Elio takes care of me in every way possible, and I feel safe with him.

I've never felt as secure with anything or anyone as I do with him.

When he leaves to grab a cold cloth for my headache and a pill, I think about how I need to decide what I'm going to do by the end of this month.

Will I apply for that stupid desk job? Call that realtor about the bakery? Will my father ever forgive me? Or will I push away the little family I have to be happy with my life?

So many questions, and for once, I don't have any of the answers.

Chapter 41

Jasmine

I don't think I've ever seen Elio more excited than he is right now.

We're currently out to breakfast for the first time as a couple in public, and despite him being retired, he does get stopped quite a few times by fans and photographers here and there.

Elio's so damn happy that we can finally be a couple out in the open. He hasn't let go of my hand since we got out of his SUV, and even now as we sit across from one another at the bistro-style table, my hand is firmly interlocked with his.

I order vegan pancakes, while Elio orders toast, hash browns, and bacon. I told him he could order eggs, but he refused.

His stubbornness to keep me safe is starting to become more endearing. God, this man is cute. I never thought I'd use that word to describe Elio Mazzo, but truthfully, beneath all of his exteriors, he's a total softie.

Neither of us felt like cooking this morning after last night's events, so we decided to venture out for breakfast. We're at a cozy café down the road from the hospital, which only reminds me of my mother and our conversation from last night.

My head threatens to throb at the memory, but Elio prevents that from happening.

"*Dolcezza*," he muses, rubbing a hand across his beard.

"Babe," I hum, smiling at him like a girl in love. Because I am, very much so.

"Your page hit a hundred thousand subscribers today."

I nearly spit my maple-flavored coffee out. "What? Seriously?"

Elio smiles proudly. "Yeah, I checked it when you were in the shower. You also got a couple of emails from potential sponsorship deals. Two of them are good offers that I think you should take."

"Holy fuck," I mutter, sitting back in my chair.

He chuckles, taking a sip of his water. "I'm proud of you, Jasmine. Your talent makes my belly very happy."

"Thank you." I pucker my lips and give him an air kiss.

Elio leans forward, his body nearly on the table. He presses his lips to mine, the roughness of his beard rubbing against my jaw as he kisses me so damn sweetly.

"I needed a real one." He smirks, leaning back in his chair with a satisfied look on his face as he openly stares at my cleavage that's on display from my tank top and cardigan that I'm wearing.

I shake my head at him, sipping my coffee when our food arrives.

The waiter places our plates down, and we thank him with a smile.

We dig into our food. Elio crunches a piece of crispy bacon between his teeth while I cut into my blueberry pancakes. I then pour a hefty amount of maple syrup on top, causing Elio to shake his head and chuckle at me.

"Mmm," I moan around the fork in my mouth. These are the best vegan pancakes I've ever had. They're so fluffy and taste exactly like—

Wait.

I drop my fork, the metal clattering against the porcelain plate.

Distantly, I hear Elio saying my name, but all I can focus on is the itchiness that's spreading across my chest as my throat starts to tighten.

"Elio," I croak, my voice barely audible as my eyes snap up to his.

He stands instantly, knowing exactly what's happening. He's always been overprotective about this, and his worst dream came true.

Elio empties my purse on the table, looking for my EpiPen, and when he finds it, he quickly jabs it into my thigh.

Immediately, my throat opens back up, my other symptoms slowly fading as well. I take deep, calming breaths as I try to ignore the craze that's circling us. The waitress is asking someone to call 911. Everyone in the café is staring. A couple of people are even recording us.

"Jas, we need to get you checked out to be safe," Elio says calmly, despite his eyes telling a different story.

I nod, unable to speak at the moment from the whirlwind of the last few minutes.

I'm in his arms before I can register what's happening, clutching onto him as he begins to run with me in his arms.

"Those fucking idiot chefs," he grunts, the shops passing by in a blur as he moves quickly with me in his arms. It's then that I remember his leg, and I start to feel bad.

"Babe." I cough. "Put me down. Your leg."

"There's not a chance I'm setting you down anywhere until I get you to the hospital."

I don't respond, knowing he needs this. I try to keep my breathing even, despite the anxiety that's running rampant throughout my body.

I haven't had a reaction like this ever, and it scares me.

Within five minutes, he's running us into the lobby of the emergency room, Elio out of breath as I try to catch mine.

"My girlfriend had an allergic reaction. She needs help," Elio shouts, his voice ridden with worry.

Moments later, I'm in Elio's arms as we sit on a gurney while we wait for the doctor to come. He hasn't let go of me, and I'm thankful for it. His touch soothes me in places he can't actually touch.

Once the doctor arrives, she goes through a standard checkup, running various tests to ensure I'm okay. She deems me to be fine, even after Elio asks her countless times if she's sure. The doctor tells me to get some rest and to be careful when eating out, with a reminder to ensure my EpiPen is always with me.

We eventually return home, Elio taking the utmost care of me as I rest in bed. While I do feel better, my thigh is sore from the EpiPen and overall, my body feels tired from the events of the day.

As I drift off to sleep, the one thing running through my mind is how badly I want to reach out to my father, who always made me feel better when I was sick. But I can't, and that fact hurts me more than anything else I've had to deal with today.

Chapter 42

Elio

*T*his has been the longest day of my fucking life.

Logically, I knew she was okay, but seeing her reach out for me in desperation with fear swirling in her eyes at the café? Yeah, that broke me.

She is safe now, napping in our bed.

As for me? I can't rest. My blood is boiling too much to do that.

Instead, I make a call to the place we ate at, and let's just say, I'm not very fucking nice. I know mistakes happen, but that's one that could cost someone their life and I don't fucking mess around with that. Especially when it's the girl who holds my entire world in her heart.

I'm about to begin making cacio e pepe spaghetti when my phone pings with a text from Brooks.

Brooks

Hey, have you seen the internet today? You'reall over it.

Attached is a video link, and once I click on it, my grip on my phone tightens. Someone recorded us at the café this morning and posted it online. Whoever recorded it must have had their phone out at the right time because you can see everything. The moment her fork clatters on the plate, me dumping her purse and jabbing the EpiPen into her thigh.

Fear trickles down my spine watching my worst nightmare once more, but anger follows it knowing that the video is also out there for everyone else to see. It hits me then that if this has gone viral, I have no doubt her parents must have seen it by now.

Fuck.

Before I can think of what to do, my phone starts to ring, Colin's name popping up on the screen. I answer it, wondering how this day can get worse.

"Mr. Mazzo, I'm sorry to bother you, but there is a couple here requesting to come upstairs."

Well, there's my answer. It *can* get worse.

I already know who it is. Her parents.

I don't want them upsetting her after the day she's had, but I imagine as her parents they need to hear what happened. I decide to head down there instead. That way I'm not overstepping by allowing them into our home when I'm not sure she wants them there.

Using a sticky note, I leave a note on the bedside table, telling her where I am in case she wakes up and I'm not there.

I head downstairs, and as the elevator begins to descend, my anxiety increases. I have no idea how this is going to go. Once I'm in the lobby, I spot Jasmine's mom, sitting on the couch.

"Mrs. Park," I greet her, noting that Ned is missing.

"Call me Madeline, please, and sit. Ned's taking an important call outside."

I do as she says, sitting across from her as apprehension fills me.

"What happened?" she asks calmly.

"She ate pancakes that she thought were egg-free, but turns out the chef made a mistake," I grumble.

"Idiot," she mutters.

"The doctor said she'll be fine. They ran a bunch of tests and want her to rest."

"Oh, thank goodness," she breathes, eyes shut tightly for a beat. "Thank you so much for saving my daughter."

"Don't thank me for that. It's what needed to be done. I'd do it again, over and over," I tell her, my leg throbbing at the strain from running today. I rub it, hoping to relieve the pain.

Sure, I work out and even skate from time to time, but that random high sprint run I did? Not ideal for the ligaments around my knee that have already been torn to shreds once.

"Your knee bothering you?" she asks, observing my every movement.

"I'll be fine."

"If it was torn, you'd be on the ground in a fetal position, so I'm going to assume it's strained from the running. But if the pain doesn't go away, go back to the hospital to get it looked at, okay?" Her doctor's voice is on, sweet yet firm.

"Will do." I nod, taking her in for the first time.

It strikes me then how oddly calm she is considering what happened.

"How are you so calm right now?" I ask, perplexed.

Madeline scoffs, shaking her head. "I'm not, not at all actually. Doctors are trained to hide their emotions because we can't freak out. It would worry our patients. I guess sometimes I forget to turn it off."

I nod, understanding what she means. "I'm sorry this happened," I apologize, feeling like I failed her by letting her daughter end up here.

She turns to face me head-on now, a no-bullshit look on her face. "Elio, it's not your fault. You didn't make the pancakes, so let it go. She's okay, and that's what matters."

I inhale a deep breath, doing my best to let her words seep in and rid me of the guilt I feel for this happening.

Ned comes bustling around the corner, into the lobby, where he stops in his tracks once he spots us. His eyes are red, and bags rest underneath them, not looking his best.

A sick part of me is happy to see it, knowing he still cares about Jasmine despite everything that happened.

He sits next to his wife, his eyes downcast as he takes a deep breath.

Madeline places her hand on his shoulder, giving it a squeeze. "Ned, let's go. Get on with it."

This ought to be good. I hope.

"I'm sorry, Elio. I shouldn't have let my anger get the best of me, and hitting you was way out of line, especially in front of our team. Even if what you did *was* wrong."

Madeline coughs, and he sighs.

"But if you make my daughter happy, then I have no choice but to accept it because her happiness is all that matters."

A wave of relief crashes through me. It's not what I was expecting to hear, and I'm thankful for his acceptance because I know how much it'll mean to Jasmine.

"If you break her heart, Mazzo, we'll be having a different conversation. Got it?" he asks, his eyes boring into mine with a seriousness I've only seen on the ice.

"I won't. I promise you that."

Ned clears his throat. "And, Elio, thank you for saving my daughter."

My head tilts as I look at him, seeing a man who cares deeply for his child. I can't fault him for that. Instead, it makes me happy knowing that her parents care about her because not everyone is fortunate in that department.

"Always." Then it's my turn to clear my throat. "Ned, I truly am sorry. I love your daughter more than anything in this world and I'm going to care for and protect her with all that I have. Every day."

Ned sighs, folding his hands over his stomach. "That's the only thing that's helping me find some sort of acceptance."

"I understand."

"You know, Elio, I do love you like my own. I practically raised you over the years on the ice, and I know you're a good person. But when you have kids, it's hard to let them go, and you'll look for faults in anyone they want to be with to make sure they find someone who's perfect. The truth, though? No one is." He swallows. "I'm slowly learning to let her go, but it's hard."

I nod, understanding what he's saying. Because the thought of a little girl who's half me and half Jasmine makes the protective beast inside of me light up.

"You don't need to let her go, but she needs space to bloom on her own. She's an adult, who's more than capable of making good choices for herself."

Ned nods thoughtfully as Madeline speaks up.

"I understand she's been through a lot today, but we'd like to come back tomorrow to talk to her. Do you think that'd be okay?"

"I'll talk to her, then I'll text Ned and let him know if she's ready for that."

"We know we're not perfect—hell, no parent is. We love our girl, and I think we need to talk," she admits.

I nod along, happy that they seem receptive to listening to Jasmine's feelings. I can only hope their actions follow their words.

We say goodbye, and on my elevator ride back up, I can't help but think of how lucky we were today.

Had she forgotten her EpiPen, what would've happened?

My body recoils at the what-ifs. Jasmine's become my life, our love my favorite thing in it. I've won a championship title, been inducted into a hall of fame, and have more money than I can keep up with.

I have it all, yet she is all I'll ever *need*.

Chapter 43

Jasmine

My eyes struggle to open fully, shutting and fluttering open every few seconds. With one eye open, I glance around the room, noticing the sun filtering in from the curtains.

How long was I out?

My eyes close once more, the urge to fall back asleep strong. I'm nearly drifting off to sleep when I hear Elio's warm voice.

"Jas, you up?"

"Yes. No." I yawn as I roll over to face him. "What time is it?"

"It's past nine. How are you feeling?" he asks as his hand reaches out to stroke my cheek.

"Good. My body is tired, that's all," I tell him, picking his hand up and placing a kiss on his fingers.

Elio lets out a deep breath, sighing in what sounds like relief. "Thank God. You were out for so long. I called the doctor and she said it was normal."

"You worried about me or something?" I tease, injecting some lightness into the conversation.

"Always." He leans forward, pressing his lips to my forehead.

"Is your knee okay?" I ask him, not taking my eyes away from his. I'm so damn grateful to see his beautiful face.

His dark green eyes pin mine with a glare. "It's fine. You're more important."

I shake my head. "That's not how this works. You care about me, and I care about you. Now, tell me how your knee is."

Elio smirks briefly, but then it's gone as quickly as it came. "It's sore, but nothing some ice and rest won't fix."

I grimace, not liking the idea that he's in any sort of pain. "Is there anything I can do to help?"

He shakes his head. "Yes, let me take care of you."

I roll my eyes, but my smile slips through anyway. "I love you."

"I love you, *dolcezza*. What do you think the best moment of my life so far has been?"

I'm thrown off by his question, but I answer it nonetheless. "Uh, probably winning the Stanley Cup?"

He leans in closer, his mouth only inches from mine. "Not even close."

"What was it then?" I ask, my chest rising up and down.

"The night we kissed for the first time."

"That can't be true—"

"It is," he cuts me off. "Nothing has ever felt as good in my life as you do. That kiss was fucking everything to me."

I close the distance, needing to feel his lips against my own this time. He kisses me back reverently, his lips claiming mine as they move over and over again. Elio pulls back, so I pout, jutting my bottom lip out at him.

"Don't give me that look. We need to talk about something first."

My stomach churns.

"What is it?"

Elio proceeds to tell me about how the incident at the café

went viral after someone uploaded it online, and how my parents came here to see me. Not only that, my father apologized to him. And how my mother was oddly calm, explaining that she has a hard time turning off her doctor persona.

I digest what he told me, happy that he and my father are going to be able to move forward. As for my mother, it makes me feel a tad guilty because I never thought of it that way. I'd always assumed that her lack of expression was her being cold, but in reality, she must have had a hard time turning it off.

It doesn't excuse the way she's made me feel over the years, but I do understand her a bit more.

"I'm glad you guys had a good chat," I say, shifting so that I'm sitting up in bed.

"They want to come see you today. It sounded like they wanted to make things right, Jas, but of course, it's up to you."

"I don't know," I mutter.

"Your parents care about you, Jasmine. I think you should tell them about what you really want to do with your life. They'll be more understanding than you think," he encourages me, his voice calling my eyes back to his. I suck in a breath, letting it whoosh through me as I come to terms with what he's saying. A lump of emotion lodges itself in my airway, making it hard to swallow as tears prick my eyes.

"*Dolcezza*, no. Don't cry," Elio curses, cupping my cheek with his large hand.

"I-I don't want to lose them if they don't approve, you know? I want them to support me, and I hate how much I need that from them. I wish I didn't care."

"There's nothing wrong with loving your parents and wanting their support. Your caring heart is one of my favorite things about you. Don't hide it." His voice is like butter, melting away my worries with each and every word.

I smile at him, a lone tear strolling down my cheek. He wipes it away ever so gently, his eyes intently focused on mine.

"Will you stay with me when they come in?" I ask him.

"Anything you want, you know that. I'll text Ned now," he replies, pulling his phone out of his pocket.

We wait in the living room for my parents, playing with the cats as we do. About an hour later, we hear a knock. Elio gets the door, greeting my parents as they walk in.

My breath stills at seeing my father for the first time since he walked away from me, unsure of what exactly is going to happen.

Elio returns to my side on the couch, his nearness bringing me the comfort I need right now.

"Oh, Jasmine, dear." My mother's voice cracks, her hand over her chest as she walks closer to me.

"I'm okay," I tell her as my father comes to stand behind her and lays a comforting hand on her shoulder.

"There is never anything okay about seeing your child hurt like that," my father speaks up, looking distraught.

My eyes snap to his, shocked by his admission.

"But it's okay to walk away from them during a difficult conversation, right?" I surprise myself as the words tumble out, unable to stay quiet.

My father sits on the couch across from me, his hands clasped together. "Jasmine, I am so sorry for that. I'll never forgive myself for hurting you, but I'll spend the rest of my life trying to earn your forgiveness. I was distraught, shocked, and scared. You're my girl, and I felt like I was losing you. I was trying too hard to hold on when you needed to be let go."

Tears stain my cheeks at his apology.

"As long as you're happy, that's all I care about. You have my acceptance, although I don't want to see any PDA. At least, not right now. I can't handle it."

"Understandable." I chuckle as I swipe at my eyes. "Thank you for apologizing. I couldn't imagine a life without us talking."

"I know, Jasmine, me neither."

"Don't scare us like that again. I nearly had a heart attack." My mother sighs.

"Great, that's just what I need. Both of you hurt," my father says.

My mother whispers something in his ear, causing him to turn and smile at her. The sight makes my chest ache because my parents truly love one another and it's something I should be more grateful for. Not everyone grows up witnessing that.

Elio squeezes my hand then, a silent reminder that he's here to support me and the encouragement I need to speak up.

"Mom, *Appa*, I need to tell you something," I announce, my tone stronger than I thought it would be.

Both of their heads whip toward me, but it's my father who looks like he might boil over. "If you say you're pregnant, I might lose it. That's too much in the span of forty-eight hours for me."

I grimace. "I'm not. Don't worry."

"What is it then?" my mother prods.

I inhale a breath, exhaling deeply to try and soothe my nerves. I give Elio's hand a squeeze, and then I finally do it.

"I love to bake, to be creative, and see the joy on people's faces when they recreate my dishes or try one of them. I have an online channel called Minniebakes where I record myself as I make desserts. It's pretty popular now, and I love doing it," I explain, a jolt of happiness hitting me as I talk about my passion.

"But the big dream is owning a bakery, and I think I found the perfect lot for it. I know you both have this idea in your heads of who I am and what you want me to accomplish, but it's not me, and I can't live my life happily like that. *Halmoni* inspired this in me, and that passion never went away when she passed. I know this is disappointing to hear, but after today's events, I now know more than ever that I need to live my life for me."

There, I fucking did it. And it feels damn good like a weighted blanket being lifted off of me.

The silence in the room is almost palpable as my parents stare at me with blank expressions.

My mother is the first to crack. Her eyebrow rises ever so slightly, her face slowly morphing into shock. "You want to own a business and bake?"

Her voice is stoic, so I can't tell where she's at mentally other than that she seems surprised.

"That's what I said, so yes. That's what I want."

"It's risky…" My mother trails off, but my father cuts in.

"But risks come with great rewards. If it'll make you happy, Jasmine, we will support you no matter what. I think it sounds wonderful. *Halmoni* would be very proud of you," he says while resting his hand on my mother's shoulder and squeezing it.

I sigh with audible relief at his words. "Thanks, *Appa*. I appreciate that more than you know."

"It will be difficult, dear, but you can do it. I'll be the first one in line," my mother adds in, surprising the hell out of me.

"Really?" I ask in disbelief.

"You know, when you see something like that happen to your child, it puts things into perspective as a parent. As long as you're happy, you can do whatever you'd like. I'm sorry for ever making you feel differently, and for putting so much pressure on you. It came from a place of fear as a parent, of being a failure. And that was never fair to you," my mother apologizes, her eyes turning glassy along with mine.

"Mom." My voice wavers, teetering on losing it.

"Shh," she says, stepping closer to take my other hand in hers as she kisses the top of it. "We can talk more another time. Your father and I are going to let you rest. Call us tomorrow."

"Okay." I nod. "I love you both, very much."

"We love you more," my father says, leaning in to kiss my forehead before they walk out, hand in hand.

"How did that feel?" Elio asks, running his thumb along the back of my hand.

"Good, really fucking good." I smile to myself, feeling so damn proud that I finally spoke my truth and can start living the life I want.

Running my own bakery. Being my own boss. Seeing the smiles on customers' faces. Living with Elio and starting our life together post-college.

"I'm so proud of you." He smiles, his dark green eyes bursting with so much affection that it makes my heart pound erratically in my chest.

I scoot toward him, hitching my leg over his waist while my arm rests on his chest, fingers toying with the fabric of his sweater. "Thank you." I smirk, lifting my head up to look at him.

Elio pulls me ever so gently into his body so that there's not an inch of space between us.

As we lie there, nestled together as tightly as we can, I think about how grateful I am for this man. Through loving him, I learned not only how to take care of and love someone else, but how to do those same things for myself because of the future I began to envision of our lives together.

I see myself with Elio, running my bakery business and raising a large family. I've seen how Elio and his sisters interact, and I want that.

Not once did I see myself at the damn boring desk job, and this health scare only pushed me to tell my parents about my dream even more. In loving someone, and myself, I learned how to honor who I am and go after what makes me happy.

No matter the repercussions.

I know it's cliché, but people always say whoever truly loves you will stand by your side no matter what, and it's true. I know without a doubt that Elio will be by my side, weathering through any storm, for the rest of our lives.

Chapter 44

Elio

*J*asmine's been trying to get me to fuck her since her parents left. And I've tried my hardest to resist her, because I don't want to hurt her if she's still recovering.

But whatever Jasmine wants, she gets.

"Babe, put me down," Jasmine protests, pushing at my chest as she tries to scramble down my body, but I only tighten my grip on her thighs.

"I can take care of you, hush," I tell her as I begin to walk us to our bedroom.

Once I place her on the bed, that's when I see the scowl on her face.

"What's wrong?"

"Elio, you're in pain and carrying me around when you don't need to," she points out, her eyes on my knee.

"That's where you're wrong. I need to touch you, take care of you," I protest, trying to get the scowl off her lips.

It doesn't work. Her frown deepens, her mocha eyes pinning me where I stand. "Get on the bed," she orders.

I comply, lying down on my side of the bed.

Jasmine crawls over to me, her curls falling loosely down her shoulders as she straddles my hips. There's a flicker of playfulness in her gaze as she pins my arms above my head. Of course I'm letting her, because if I wanted to, I could roll her under me in a second flat.

But I'm intrigued, so I'll let her continue.

Jasmine trails her hands down my arms, over my chest, and across my abs through my sweater. "Keep your hands above your head or else."

I chuckle because her trying to be intimidating is cute as hell. "Or what?"

She answers with a roll of her hips, grinding her sweet spot against my erection that's hardening with every roll. "Or I stop doing this."

I keep my hands above my head, watching her in awe as she grinds herself against me. I enjoy it for about ten seconds. That's when the need to touch her becomes so powerful that I no longer think this feels good because it's more like torture.

My hand twitches above me, and she notices. Stilling her hips, she chides me. "*Ah, ah, ah*, no touching."

Jasmine then brings her hands up under her shirt, whipping it over her head, along with her bra. Her breasts are fucking perfection, her tan nipples hard and begging to be sucked on. She brings her fingers up to them, tugging and squeezing as she continues to grind against me.

When she releases the sweetest moan, that's when I snap.

"*Dolcezza*," I grunt. "I *need* to touch you."

She slows her motions, rocking against me slowly. "Hmm, I thought you *needed* to touch me earlier?"

"I always do," I bite out, trying my hardest not to reach for her, pull her pants off, and put her cunt on my face.

Jasmine grins, a devilish curve to her lips. Oh, fuck me.

"Maybe next time, you'll listen to me." She shrugs, swinging her leg over me as she tries to get off the bed.

Not on my fucking watch.

I sit up and reach for her hips, abruptly pinning her beneath me to the bed, eliciting a gasp of surprise from her.

"Elio," she pants. "I said no touching."

"Yeah, and I'm done with your little game to try and teach me a lesson. If I want to take care of you, I'm going to take care of you. Sore knee or not."

Her mocha eyes fire with the need to fight back, which quickly turns into a blaze of need for something else when I grind my erection against her. Within a second, I have her pants and underwear off, her body writhing beneath mine for my touch, and my touch alone.

"If you want to take care of me, come sit on my cock." My voice cuts through our ragged breaths as I sit back against the headboard.

Jasmine crawls over to me, straddling my waist. Her lips connect with mine wildly, her mouth demanding and taking. It's fucking sexy seeing her so needy for me. She grinds her arousal against me, looking between us as she grips my cock and continues to rock herself against it, coating it.

The sight nearly makes me lose it right there, because there is nothing hotter than knowing she's dripping for me.

With one hand on my shoulder, she uses her other hand to guide my cock to what I pray is her entrance. But knowing the mood she's in, I should've guessed differently. Instead, she rubs the tip against her clit, causing her eyes to flutter as she moans.

"Inside. Now," I grit, with my hands on her hips. I tilt her body then slam her down on my cock.

"Elio!" she whimpers, throwing her head into my neck as I begin moving my hips beneath her.

I usually give her time to adjust, but I'm fucking needy as

hell for her right now. My body is moving without even thinking about it.

"You're massive." She bites down on my shoulder as I roll my hips upward, only increasing the blood that's pumping down to my cock.

I smack her ass, moving my hands up to her hips where I start to move them for her. "When you tease me like that, you get to take my cock however I want it. Let the pain remind you that *I'm* in you so fucking deep. Now, try to be a good little slut and come all over my cock."

Jasmine finally lifts her head from my neck and nods fervently. Always aspiring to do her best. She begins to ride me, swiveling her hips as she locks her arms around my neck.

She feels so goddamn good. It's like nothing I've ever felt before. I'm certain she was made for me.

I lean forward and take one of her nipples between my teeth, loving the loud scream she lets loose. I grunt and move to the other, biting down then soothing the sting with my lips and tongue.

I can feel her walls clenching around me, and it takes everything in me not to go off before she does.

"That's my dirty girl. You can do it," I praise.

"Are you going to fill me up?" she rasps, rocking her hips at the perfect pace.

Do. Not. Come. Dammit.

"I always will, *dolcezza*. Seeing my cum drip out of you is one of my favorite sights on this planet. Come for me. Let me fill that cunt," I pant, breathless as she takes us both higher and higher toward that peak.

All it takes is a graze of my teeth on her nipples, and she's exploding, her cunt tightening around my cock as she convulses and screams my name. I erupt at the same time, jerking forward as my cum fills her while I shout her name just as viscerally.

We remain still for a moment, attempting to even our breaths while our heart rates settle. My hands are roaming up and down her back gently, while hers play with the tuft of hair at the back of my neck.

I kiss her neck softly, inhaling her peach and floral scent as I make my way to her lips. Jasmine moans quietly against my lips, the vibration thrumming throughout my entire body.

Breaking the kiss, Jasmine lifts up, hovering over me as my cum leaks out of her. Her neck is craned, looking down at it with a frown on her lips.

My fingers collect it from her thigh up to her center, where I push it back inside of her. "That better, *dolcezza?*"

"Yes," she hisses, biting down on her lower lip as she hovers over me.

"*Sei il mio mondo,*" I whisper while pumping into her with two fingers, getting her ready for round two. Because I was nowhere close to being done with her.

"What does"—her moan cuts her off briefly, then she continues—"does that mean?"

I sit up and press a kiss to her hip bone, peering up at her with admiration. "You are my world."

A tear strolls down her cheek, a wide smile on her face at the same time. "I love you, so damn much."

Her words set me on fire, fueling my blood with a feeling like no other. She's my present, future, and forever. While I can't wait for what's to come, I'm going to spend every second appreciating this beautiful woman who came into my life and changed everything for me.

I no longer need to look for the next challenge, the next thing because I finally feel sated.

I'm exactly where I need to be for once.

Chapter 45

Jasmine

$\mathcal{I}$’ve never been one to care for Valentine's Day. In fact, we missed the holiday due to midterms and the hockey season, but Elio sent me a bouquet of the books I've been wanting along with some chocolates, and it was perfect.

He's perfect.

But since we missed spending the day together, Elio insisted that we celebrate it today. It's random as hell, since it's March 18, but I'm going along with it to make him happy.

I woke up early this morning to make heart-shaped waffles for Elio and planned on delivering them to him in bed. But he sort of derailed those plans.

I didn't even hear him enter the kitchen while I was bent over looking for a pan in a lower drawer. Then suddenly, I felt his tip prodding at my entrance.

Over the past few months, I've learned about what I like sexually, and this is one of those things. I love when he fucks me by surprise, pushing into me whenever and wherever around the house.

I shiver and moan, instantly wet and ready for him. Once

he feels it, he slams into me and bends me over the counter as he starts off our make-up Valentine's Day the right way.

We end up eating our waffles together at the counter, me on his lap while he feeds me. Sometimes I can't believe who I am now. Who is this sappy, romantic girl who wants to be taken care of all the time?

Love changes you. Don't let anyone tell you differently. But it's a good change. I wouldn't have it any other way.

We shower and get ready for the day, as Elio informs me that he's taking me somewhere. Excited, I dress warmly in jeans, a sherpa sweater, and boots. It's freezing this time of year, and I hate being cold at any cost.

Elio pulls onto the highway around lunch, and I notice we're driving toward the small town he grew up in, Chesterville.

I take the time to send a quick text to Camille, who was traveling with the boys' baseball team for a pre-season game today.

Me

Cami!! He's taking me to his hometown. I have no idea what he's doing, but I'm excited.

Cami

OH MON DIEU! Is he proposing??
Maybe on the ice rink?? AHH!!

Me

I mean...I wouldn't say no. 🙊

Cami

Ahhh I'm so happy for you, Jas!
Let me know asap what happens!

Me

Will do. How's it going on your
end? Have you talked to Ryker?

Cami

It's good, we're still on the bus.
And nope. I'm sitting at the front
by myself. Why?

Me

Just curious, because he seemed
interested at the club. Maybe it's
my romance reader lens looking
into things.

Cami

Definitely.

Why do I feel like that was the most unconvincing text I've ever received?

I tuck my phone away, and a few minutes later, my heart stops when we pull up and park in front of the corner shop that was for sale the last time we came here. The one I saw my dream playing out in.

The one that's sold. *Fuck.*

I feel a piece of my heart dull at the sight. But I could find another place I loved, right?

"I have something to show you," Elio says as he opens my door.

I was so lost in my head that I hadn't even noticed he got out of the SUV. I get out of the car, and Elio takes my gloved hand in his and leads me to the side of the building, toward a door.

Elio pulls out his keys and is about to put one in the door when I finally come to my senses.

I grab his wrist, alarmed. "Elio, what are you doing?"

He grins, one of those panty-dropping grins. "If I remember correctly, it's Valentine's Day, and partners usually buy each other something, right?"

My breath ceases in my lungs while my heart pounds viciously against my chest. "Yes…but why do you have a key for this building?"

"Open it and find out." He shrugs, handing me the key.

With a shaky hand, I take the key from him, open the door, and step inside. My mouth falls at the state-of-the-art kitchen. It looks exactly like the one I pinned on Pinterest…wait a minute.

I rush out of the kitchen and stop in my tracks.

No. He. Didn't.

My eyes blur with tears as I take in the bakery that is set up exactly like I imagined and like the pins on my bakery board.

The counters are white, with gold accents throughout the space. There's a plush seating area near a fireplace, along with a bunch of café-style chairs and tables throughout. There's a brick wall on one side, the opposite a burnt orange, and the wooden floors are stained a honey maple.

A bookshelf sits on one wall, filled with a bunch of romance books. On another wall is an orange ombre of fake flowers in the shape of a heart. It's an ode to my grandma, who gave me the heart on my bracelet that I wear every day.

"This is why our make-up Valentine's Day is today. The finishing touches were only done yesterday."

I spin to find Elio watching me with a glint in his eyes, as mine overflow with tears now.

"Elio," I croak, my voice hoarse with emotions. "This is too much. Let me pay you for it, slowly, because I don't have that money on me right now."

He stalks toward me then, taking my face between his large

hands. "*Dolcezza*, I believe the words you're looking for are *thank you*. Say them and move on, okay? You deserve this."

"But why would you do this?"

"I told you...you're my world and I love you so fucking much. I want to help you reach your dreams, and I have the money to do it. So why not help you get started? Is that wrong?" he asks, seeming a bit worried.

"It's not, babe. I'm overwhelmed, seeing my dream come to life," I sniffle as Elio runs his thumbs under my eyes, wiping the tears away. "I can't even put into words how grateful I am for this, for you. It means everything to me."

"I might have an idea." He raises one brow, forcing a chuckle to bubble from my lips.

"Oh, don't you worry, my lips will be on your cock in a couple of minutes. But I want to give you my gift first. It's going to look really lame now."

"I'll love whatever you give me," he murmurs, kissing my cheek.

I pull away from his embrace, searching for the purse that I dropped when I lost my shit looking around in here. I spot it near the counter and swipe it off the ground, placing it atop the counter. I dig in for his gift and hide it against my chest as I walk back toward him.

I pass it to him and watch as he eyes me in curiosity. Tearing past the wrapping paper, his face lights up with a boyish smile as laughter bellows from his stomach.

"You don't like it?" I frown.

"No, *dolcezza*, I love it." He smiles, looking down at the collector's edition of *The Powerpuff Girls* series that I found online and ordered for him. It's a box set of the entire series, in a pretty foil hardcover.

"And I love you." I brighten, feeling on top of the world. I have my dream business ready to go, a man that I love, who loves me back, and I'm working toward a better relationship with my parents.

Instead of letting pride hide away who I wanted to be, I'm now proud of the person I've become. Of the life I'm building and creating with Elio, and our friends, who are like family.

"I love you more, trust me." He swoons, crashing his lips to mine.

And I do, with my heart leading the way for once.

Epilogue

Elio

5 MONTHS LATER

"Y ou know you're going to lose, right?" Jasmine hums playfully, her curls flowing in the wind as we sit on the terrace of a restaurant on the Amalfi coast, playing chess.

I paid for a private section, always wanting to have her to myself.

"Probably, but I enjoy losing to you," I tell her, loving how carefree she's been on this trip.

Her bakery opens in September, and she's been working like crazy to get everything set up. This trip came at the perfect time, giving her a chance to unwind before she has to start running her own business.

I know she's going to fucking crush it, and I can't wait to watch it happen.

I also happened to open a business down the street from her. My own mom-and-pop shop mentoring business. I also don't open until the fall, giving us time to get prepared before jumping into the world of being entrepreneurs.

The only thing left to do? Propose to the love of my life and make her mine forever, *officially*.

So far, we've been to France, The Netherlands, England, Spain, Portugal, Germany, and now, we're in Italy. There have been many moments where I nearly gave the photographer the signal that I was going to propose, but something in me said *not yet.*

I wanted us to enjoy our trip, without the excitement of the engagement taking away from it.

Jasmine knocks out my king, her squeal of joy overpowering the crash of the waves on the coast. It's then that it hits me. It wasn't under the glittering lights of the Eiffel Tower, nor on a gondola in Amsterdam or on the sandy beaches of Portugal.

It's now, with her infectious smile on her face, a chessboard between us and the water in the background, a light rain beginning to fall from the sky.

I flick my wrist twice to the left, then to the right, giving the signal.

I check my coat pocket, feel the square box there, and take a quiet, deep breath. I didn't anticipate how nervous I'd be, but dammit, I am.

There's a soft Italian tune playing on the speaker, floating in from the restaurant.

"Dance with me?" I ask her, standing from my chair.

Jasmine smiles, her eyes lighting up. "Of course."

I pull her up to me, cradling the back of her head as my other hand intertwines with hers in the air. The rain falls more rapidly now, but Jasmine's smile grows as laughter fills the space from both of us. I spin her around, watching her black dress twirl around her.

My wife, my mind screams. Even though it's not exactly true in this moment, it will be.

I let go of her hand and watch as she spins around once more with her eyes closed and head tilted up toward the sky. I take the time to get on one knee, with the box open and placed in front of me.

Jasmine stops dancing, opening her eyes. Her breath catches in her throat as she takes in the sight of me on one knee. She throws a hand over her mouth, tears mixing in with the raindrops on her cheeks.

"*Dolcezza*, come here," I say, needing her closer so I can slide the ring on her finger.

She walks toward me on wobbly legs, stopping right in front of the box. Her eyes fixed on me, not on the ring in the box. It makes me love her even more because she could've focused on the sparkly ring, but she's focused on me.

I take her hand in mine, the feel of her soft hand in mine giving me the contact I crave.

"I have always prided myself on being the smartest guy in the room. The best player on the ice. The guy who takes care of his family. And now, I want to pride myself on being the best husband." I chuckle, and she shakes with a sob.

"Loving you has been the greatest part in my life and the most important thing I've ever done. There's nothing else that compares in life to the joy I get from seeing you smile, hearing your laugh and watching you simply exist. You're the most breathtaking thing I've ever seen. Please do me the honor of being my wife and taking my breath away for the rest of our lives. Will you marry me?"

"Yes," she cries.

I slide the ring onto her finger, watching as her eyes fill with more tears now that she finally looks at the large oval diamond glistening under the rays of a summer sunset.

"It's beautiful, Elio. The whole thing was beautiful. Thank you. I love you." She flings her arms around my neck, crying happy tears into my neck as I lift her off the ground and spin her around.

"I love you, *dolcezza*," I murmur in her ear, tightening my hold on her with excitement brewing in my body for all that's to come for us.

Whatever comes our way, we'll be united.

Trust me.

THE END!

Want more of Jasmine and Elio?
Head to my website carliejean.ca to get a bonus epilogue.

What's next?
Camille and Ryker's story comes out summer of 2024.
You can expect a steamy, swoony romance between a runaway princess and RLU's grumpy baseball player.

Traditional Korean Recipe shared from Kylie's family
(@kyliesbooknook on IG). Thank you so much for
sharing this with me, and my readers.

Hotteok

Ingredients – Dough

1 cup warm water
2 tsp active dry yeast
1 tbsp sugar
½ tsp sea salt
1 tbsp neutral oil
1 ¾ cups all purpose flour
½ cup sweet rice flour aka glutinous rice flour
(If you cannot find sweet rice flour use 2 cups of all
purpose instead of 1 ¾ cup)

Filling

⅔ cup brown sugar
1 tsp cinnamon
⅓ cup hazelnuts (nuts of choice or exclude)
Can also use Nutella as a filling. It's so yummy!
This can be savory as well with kimchi.

Instructions

1. Mix the brown sugar, cinnamon, and hazelnuts together (or whatever
nuts/seeds you choose) and set aside.

2. Activate the yeast by combining with warm water & sugar. Let it
sit for a few minutes.

3. Add the sea salt & oil, mix, then add the ap flour and sweet rice
flour. The dough should stick to your fingers. Cover and let it ferment

for 1 hour. **Note:** If you don't have sweet rice flour, you can just omit it and use 2 cups total of all purpose flour.

4. After 1 hour, the dough will rise and double in size.

5. Knead the dough to release the air, then cover again for another 30 minutes. This time the dough should stick less to your fingers than the first time. After 30 minutes, the dough should will rise a little again.

6. Sprinkle a little flour on the surface then knead the dough once more and form a ball.

7. As evenly as possible, cut the dough into 8 or 10 pieces (depends on size you want). Flatten out the dough to about 5 inches in diameter.

8. Add filling in the middle. Anywhere between 1-2 tbs depending on your preference.

9. Gather the edges of the dough together, pinching to seal.

10. In a nonstick pan on medium low heat, add enough oil to shallow fry the pancakes. Place them seam side down and fry until golden.

11. Flip over, then flatten with a solid spatula. Continue frying until both sides are golden brown.

12. Remove from heat and let it cool for a couple minutes before serving.

Acknowledgments

Wow. To write this a third time in less than a year is insane. How lucky am I? And it's all because of YOU, my amazing readers.

All my love goes to anyone who has supported me and my books. Whether that be my readers, my loved ones, my agent Caitlin who is amazing, and anyone who has ever shown my books love in any way. I see you and I appreciate you more than you'll ever know.

To my editing team - Salma, Emily, Isabella - thank you for all your hard work and insights, you have helped shape this book into what it is today and I'm forever grateful.

To my beta and sensitivity readers, Kylie, Summer, Sabreena, Jordyn, Sandra and Patricia, thank you for all your love and excitement for Trust Me. You got to meet these characters before anyone else, and helped shape them into who they are now. Thank you for helping me create authentic characters that are relatable yet unique. Your comments and support were vital to the story, and I thank you for all you've helped me with.

To my cover designer Cat, for giving me and my readers the most beautiful cover ever to obsess over. The colour? The tiny details? All of it is SO perfect, much like she is. She's a dream to work with and deserves all the good things coming her way.

To Jen at Greys PR for being so helpful and quick to respond to my questions. Working with you and your team is always a pleasure.

To Nada at Qamber, you are amazing. Every book we produce turns out exactly better than I imagined due to your creative genius skills.

About the Author

Carlie is a romance author who loves all things swoon, sunshine, and spice. She lives in Canada. She has two brothers, and a dog named Milo. Some of her favourite things are sunsets, warm weather and iced matcha lattes. She loves to watch and play a variety of sports, which is where her obsession with sports romances originated. When she's not teaching, she loves reading, writing, going for walks, and traveling.

SOCIALS

Check out my website and socials for in-depth book information, what I'm currently writing, and bonus materials!
www.carliejean.ca

@carliejeanwrites on TikTok and Instagram.

Made in the USA
Las Vegas, NV
22 April 2024

89028313R00204